Her eyes glistened with tears, and he pulled her to him.

Kitty drew in a long, shuddering breath. He wasn't wrong about her. She cared deeply about her son and, he had to believe, about him. He could make her change her mind. "I wanted to talk to you. Come sit with me."

Kitty walked with him to the sofa. Campbell sat beside her and took her hands. The familiarity of the act made his heart ache with the pure satisfaction her nearness instilled in him. He rubbed the pads of his thumbs over the backs of her hands. "There's something going on between us. We've only known each other a few weeks, but don't you think we owe it to each other to see where this leads?"

Dear Reader,

If you're like me, you've probably heard that raising a child is the toughest job there is. I believe motherhood is the greatest responsibility we'll ever know and the job with the greatest reward.

I hope you enjoy the journey of Kitty and her troublesome twelve-year-old son, Adam. Both mother and son grow up in this novel, with the help of one American hero, an injured ex-pilot who flew in the Iraqi War. I don't know if it takes a village to raise one child, but it sure helps to have two good role models. One summer in the Blue Ridge Mountains proves to be a roller-coaster thrill for all three characters. I encourage you to come along for the ride.

I love to hear from readers. Please contact me at cynthoma@aol.com.

Cynthia

HEARTWARMING

Firefly Nights

—

Cynthia Thomason

H HARLEQUIN® HEARTWARMING™

Recycling programs
for this product may
not exist in your area.

ISBN-13: 978-0-373-36725-2

Firefly Nights

Copyright © 2015 by Cynthia Thomason

Printed in U.S.A.

www.Harlequin.com

Cynthia Thomason inherited her love of writing from her ancestors. Her father and grandmother both loved to write, and she aspired to continue the legacy. Cynthia studied English and journalism in college, and after a career as a high school English teacher, she began writing novels. She discovered ideas for stories while searching through antiques stores and flea markets and as an auctioneer and estate buyer. Cynthia says every cast-off item from someone's life can ignite the idea for a plot. She writes about small towns, big hearts and happy endings that are earned and not taken for granted. And as far as the legacy is concerned, just ask her son, the magazine journalist, if he believes.

Books by Cynthia Thomason

Harlequin Heartwarming

This Hero for Hire
A Soldier's Promise
Blue Ridge Autumn
Marriage for Keeps
Dilemma at Bayberry Cove

Harlequin Special Edition

His Most Important Win

Harlequin Superromance

The Men of Thorne Island
Your House or Mine?
An Unlikely Match
An Unlikely Father
An Unlikely Family
Deal Me In
Return of the Wild Son

Visit the Author Profile page
at Harlequin.com for more titles.

This book is dedicated to mothers and sons
everywhere, with a special shout-out to
John Patrick Thomason. You make me proud, son.

CHAPTER ONE

"OUCH!" THE SOUND of her own scratchy voice woke Kitty from a fitful sleep. The steering wheel of the old pickup she'd purchased yesterday was poking into her ribs through her Juicy Couture jacket. Her neck ached because her head had been jammed against the driver's-side window all night. Her right leg, draped awkwardly over the back of the front seat, was asleep.

She smoothed the wrinkles in her favorite eggplant-colored D&G sweatpants and was grateful she hadn't picked a pair of tight jeans for the drive. *Things could be worse.* She and her twelve-year-old son, Adam, had been warm enough all night, which was another plus. It could have been the dead of winter in... She struggled to remember the last road sign she'd seen. Oh yeah, they'd made it to North Carolina, the boonies somewhere in the Blue Ridge Mountains, and probably still a hundred and fifty miles from Charlotte. It might as well be a thousand miles if a person was trying to get there in a broken-down truck.

Kitty squinted through her windshield at the rising sun, sat up, stomped her foot on the floor to wake up her toes and then reached over the seat. She groped for the mop of blond hair that would identify her son. "Adam, you awake?"

A groggy voice answered her, "Yeah. But that doesn't mean I want to be."

"Me, either. But I suppose we have to start this day anyway."

Her son's droopy-eyed face appeared over the seat back. He wrinkled his nose. "This truck stinks."

Kitty sniffed and agreed. The truck did stink. It had that musty, road-weary smell of cracked vinyl and perspiration like most old vehicles.

"Why did you buy this piece of junk?" Adam asked. "Why didn't we just take the Beemer?"

"I told you why. It's the little matter of the title, which is in your grandfather's name. Legally I don't own the BMW."

Adam fell back against the seat. "You don't own anything important."

An image of the clothes and accessories in the massive walk-in closet she'd left behind flashed in Kitty's mind. She owned…or she *used to own* until this morning, dozens of pairs of shoes and too many designer blouses to count. She sighed at the image of her paychecks going to boutique stores. Many of the blouses she'd left behind still had the tags attached. A person couldn't bring everything in one vehicle.

Trying to assert herself to Adam, she said, "I own this pickup truck. And I paid cash for it. Besides, if we'd taken the BMW, Grandpa would have put out a trace on the car, and we'd be back in Florida by now."

"And that would be a bad thing?"

After last night, Kitty was still trying to convince herself that, yes, it would definitely be a bad thing. She had to stay focused on the bigger prize. She was removing her son from her father's all-powerful grip. And this time would be different from her last effort to leave Richland.

Adam stared at her with heart-stopping doe-brown eyes that always masked the devilish intent behind them. She reminded herself for the hundredth time that she was taking this drastic step for Adam.

He jerked his thumb toward the ignition. "Have you tried to start it this morning?"

"No, but with the smoke that was pouring from under the hood, I don't see much point." Nevertheless she turned the key and cringed at the grinding noise.

"Tell me again how you got us into this mess," Adam said.

Kitty dropped the worthless keys into her purse. "Which one?"

"Let's start with the one that put us on this road to nowhere."

"Give me a break. I wasn't responsible for that oil tanker overturning on 285. I didn't divert traffic off the Atlanta bypass."

"But it was your idea to leave the main road and drive past every cow pasture in Georgia."

Kitty was tired of defending herself, but she did it one more time. "I did that to get directions, remember? I thought we'd get good advice from a local business."

"How'd that work out for you, Mom?"

Count to ten, Kitty. "Adam, it was nearly midnight. I'd been driving for eleven hours without benefit of a GPS."

"You would have had a GPS if you'd driven the Beemer or turned on your cell phone," Adam pointed out.

Ignoring the same tired complaint, Kitty continued. "It's not easy to keep an eye on unending miles of blacktop while trying to read a map. Anyway, I thought we would get back to the highway eventually."

He stared out the window. "I wish I had my PlayStation. I wish I had all the stuff in my room."

Kitty couldn't blame him. His bedroom at her father's eleven-room Georgian mansion in central Florida was an adolescent boy's techno paradise. She twisted the rearview mirror so she could see her face, and immediately regretted it. "Why don't you wish for something we both can use?"

"Like what?"

"A bathroom."

He screwed up his face. "Or a million dollars."

She squinted hard to block the image of the bags under her eyes and the mental vision of Adam frantically shaking the contents of her purse onto the front seat a few hours ago and announcing that her wallet was not among them. Looking back, she wished she'd taken her purse into the convenience store instead of a couple of twenty-dollar bills to pay for gas. At least she would still have her wallet.

"If only you'd stayed in the truck like I told you or at least locked it when you came inside," she said, repeating herself.

"Yeah, and then those guys might have stolen me. Besides, we're not going to go through that one more time, are we?"

She sighed again, knowing the rehashing of events wouldn't ease her frustration. She'd paid for the gas, bought Adam a soda and they'd returned to the truck. She'd seen two men running down a narrow side road, but it wasn't until an hour later when Adam was looking for her wallet to pay for a motel room that she realized those guys had been making a getaway with her precious five hundred dollars. "No, we're not. It's history."

"So, are you gonna call Grandpa?" he asked. "No!"

"I wish I had my phone. I'd call him."

"I know, and that's why I made you leave it at home. And don't even think of borrowing someone else's or using a pay phone." Realizing Adam needed some assurances, she added, "We'll be fine. We're not totally broke."

"Right. We're only practically broke."

She glared at him.

"Well, how much have you got?"

She stretched her leg so she could get her hand into the pocket of her sweatpants and pulled out a wad of bills. She counted. "Thirty-seven dollars. There's money on the floor of the backseat, too. How much is it?"

She listened to her son scrape his hand over the rubber mat and then heard the jingle of coins. "Eighty cents."

"Great."

"You'd better call Grandpa."

"I am not calling him," she stated with greater emphasis. "I've still got my bank card. We can get more money as soon as I find an ATM." She quickly calculated what she had in the bank. Fifteen hundred for the truck, five hundred in cash. She had about twenty-seven hundred left in savings back in Richland. Plenty to get to Charlotte and enroll in school.

Adam set his chin on the back of the front seat and stared out the windshield at an unending panorama of pasture and trees. "Ought to be a lot of ATMs around here," he said.

Kitty ignored him. If only Adam had used some of that intelligence to succeed in his schoolwork instead of coming up with sarcastic comments. After finally taking this positive step, she was determined not to crawl home to Daddy like the first time, eleven years ago, when she'd called Owen Galloway and begged him to send money so she could leave Bobby Watley and bring her one-year-old son back home. Her father had spent the past eleven years reminding her of the mistake she'd made marrying the down-on-his-luck golf pro. Owen had consistently pointed an accusing finger with one hand while handing her cash with the other— and she'd let him.

Her friends might call her crazy for taking this step. After all, who had a better, more comfy life than Katherine Thelda Galloway? She lived in a fine house, drove a super car and had a cushy job in her father's corporate citrus groves offices. But Kitty, as she was called by those who knew her best, often thought about running away from home again. Only now her reason would be different from thirteen years ago when she was twenty years old, grieving over her mother's death and letting Bobby Watley fill her eyes with stars and her heart with promises. This time she needed to go for the sake of her twelve-year-old son.

Adam opened his fist and dropped coins onto the front seat. "I can't believe you cut up every single credit card."

His latest accusation brought her back to the present. "I couldn't use them anyway. The receipts would leave a paper trail for Grandpa to see where we're headed."

Adam rolled his eyes. "Grandpa knows a lot of people. I bet he can find anybody. Remember how he found us two summers ago when we barely made it into Georgia?"

She remembered. The failure still clawed at her insides.

"And I know he'll want to find me especially," Adam said.

Kitty had considered Owen's wide web of contacts, making her even more determined to fly under his radar. Yes, he would do almost anything to regain control of her son, the young heir to Galloway Groves that Owen had substituted for the worthless bundle of female his wife had handed him thirty-three years ago.

"And besides," Adam said, "why do you all the sudden hate him? He takes care of us. He buys us stuff…"

"I know that, and I don't hate him." That was basically true, but how did she tell Adam that she didn't admire his grandfather, either? Any more than she admired herself. She'd allowed her father to pull the strings of her life while she never tried to cut them—until two days ago when Owen had pulled those magic strings with the principal of the middle school to get Adam out of a theft charge.

"I'll handle this," her father had said. "Adam's just spirited. You know that."

Theft! She'd been completely shocked. Adam had everything, and yet he'd stolen an iPhone from a kid who'd just gotten it for his birthday and had justified his crime with a flippant remark about how the kid had irritated him by showing off the games he'd already downloaded. Since Friday had been the last day of school, and because he'd promised the principal he would punish Adam appropriately, Owen had once again avoided expulsion for his grandson. More strings and more lies. Ignoring Kitty's attempts to discipline her son with grounding, Owen had accused her of "sucking the spunk right out of the kid." And he'd even defied her by taking Adam to the racetrack in Tampa that very night.

Now, looking out the window of a rusty old truck, with thirty-seven dollars in her pocket, Kitty felt as if she'd finally severed those strings—with a chain saw.

"I thought you understood, Adam, that I think you and I need some time alone. Just the two of us." That was true. She hadn't shared nearly enough quality time with her son, and that was a major reason for his problems and attitude now. "Is that so bad?"

"No." He thought better of his answer and said, "It's just weird, that's all. Why now?"

Because now I need to seriously be your mother before it's too late. "Adam, don't worry," she said. "I'll think of something."

"Think of using your phone to call Grandpa."

She skewered him with a threatening glare before pointing to some bushes several yards from where the pickup had wheezed to a halt. "You gotta go?"

"Oh, right. Me, first. Then if anything bites me on the butt, I can warn you."

Kitty slid her feet into her chunky cork sandals, scooted to the passenger side and yanked on the door handle. "Forget it. I'll go first." She wiggled her fingers at the backseat. "Hand me that box of tissues."

When he did, she managed a smile. "See? Aren't you glad I thought to bring these?"

"I'm thrilled." He nodded at the window that separated the cab from the back of the truck. "We got a bunch of crappy material, a sewing machine and tissues. Fat City."

She got out of the truck, leaned inside and said, "While I'm gone, you get all that sarcastic trash talk out of your system, because when I get back I don't want to hear another word of it."

As she walked toward the bushes in her suddenly impractical designer slides, Adam hollered, "I'm hungry!"

Ten minutes later Kitty and Adam stood by the side of the road scoping out approaching traffic. When a van appeared, Adam stuck out his thumb. Kitty pulled his hand down.

"What'd you do that for?"

"We're not hitchhiking. It's dangerous."

"So is starving. We gotta get to a town somehow." Again Adam scrutinized the endless stretch of rolling hills and farmland. "If there even is a town in this state."

"I'm watching for just the right ride," Kitty said. "I'll know it when I see it." And she did—a farm truck loaded with watermelons. She waved at the driver, and the vehicle braked. Tugging

Adam behind her, Kitty ran to the passenger window and explained to a middle-aged woman in a cotton dress and straw hat about the truck breaking down.

"You wantin' a lift to town, then?" the woman asked.

"If you don't mind," Kitty said.

The woman looked to the driver, a man of her same approximate age. He nodded. "We're headin' to the grand opening of the twenty-four-hour Super Value-Rite," she said, "so we can get you that far."

A Value-Rite! Food. Bathrooms. An ATM. "That's perfect," Kitty said. "How far is it?"

"About two miles to Sorrel Gap," the man answered. "The Value-Rite's just on the outskirts. We're taking all the melons to set up a stand in the parking lot. You and the boy are welcome to climb in the back."

"Thank you."

Kitty and Adam climbed over a wooden gate at the rear of the truck and settled in among a mound of watermelons. When the truck lurched forward, Kitty patted Adam's hand. "There, see, it's better than walking, and the farmer and his wife were nice."

"You told me never to ride with a stranger."

"I told you never to get in a car with a stranger.

I never said anything about riding with watermelons. Anyway, this is a special case."

He leaned back on a large melon and lifted his face to the sun. "It's not so bad, I guess. But I'd sure like to know how you're going to get us out of this."

"I'm thinking. I told you I'd come up with a plan, and I will. We'll be back on the road to cousin Bette's house before you know it." Bette was Kitty's one true refuge. Her mother's cousin had been comforting and sympathetic when Kitty called her the day before.

"Of course I'll help you, Katherine," Bette had promised. "I'll find out about the fashion-design institute for you and lend you enough money to enroll. You and Adam can stay here as long as you need to."

"And if Daddy calls you," Kitty had said, "please don't tell him I contacted you." Bette had vowed secrecy.

"That's supposed to make me feel better?" Adam blurted out. "Going to some old lady's house I don't even remember? School just let out two days ago, and already it looks like this is going to be the worst summer I've ever had."

"You'll like Charlotte. They have museums and—"

"I hope I get my own room."

Kitty pictured Adam's bedroom in her father's house and even allowed herself an image of her lavender suite at the mansion. No doubt it was tough giving all that up. "You will have a room," she promised. "Just as soon as I can afford to leave Bette's and rent a place. And once my business takes off, I'll even replace some of the things you left at Grandpa's."

"Your business? You make it sound like we're never going back to Florida."

She hadn't meant to scare him with that conclusion. "Of course we'll go back. Sometime. But we'll definitely be away long enough for me to go to the design institute."

"You mean I might have to go to school in this Podunk state?"

"There's nothing Podunk about Charlotte," she said. "I'm sure there are very nice schools… if we need them."

"You think you can really design clothes that people will buy?"

Kitty had wanted to make clothes since she was a child. In the back of the truck, she even had a few original patterns she'd developed herself and fabrics she'd hired a graphic artist to draw in a modernist style.

Adam seemed to be staring at her nape-length, spiky blond hair. He scrunched up his nose. "Remember, I've seen some of the stuff you've made. It's kind of weird looking."

"That's why I'm going to school." She was used to hearing criticism of her fashions from the males in her family, and she hoped they were wrong. Except for the purchase of her new Singer, she'd always been too complacent to take the plunge and pursue her dream seriously. Or maybe she'd been too lazy. Or scared. But in the past twenty-four hours, she'd taken quite a few plunges into the unknown, so what was one more?

Kitty clutched her stomach as a familiar stab of pain took her breath. The doctors told her it was anxiety. She'd suffered from phantom bellyaches off and on most of her life, but they'd gotten much worse after her mother died. And now she was banking her and Adam's futures on her ability to succeed in a competitive business.

She kept telling herself that she had a plan, a good one. After a while, when Owen had calmed down, Kitty would call him and explain why she'd felt she had to leave, but right now he'd just have to be satisfied with the note she'd left telling him that she and Adam were taking a vacation. He wouldn't believe it. And even if he did, he was probably already raising holy heck to find them. Thank goodness he'd never think to look in the back of a watermelon truck.

Adam had settled into a sort of temporary acceptance of their situation and was watching the passing scenery. She hoped he hadn't picked up on her discomfort. She didn't want him to bear any responsibility for what the immediate future held. This was her decision, and she'd made it at a crucial time in her son's life. So she was the one who had to make it work.

The farm truck eased into a right turn off the highway and slowly crept along with the rest of the traffic entering the Value-Rite parking lot. It was eight-thirty on a Sunday morning, but already the lot was filling up, and people were heading toward the automatic doors.

The farmer drove to a large tent set up at one end of the asphalt where everything from corn on the cob to Georgia peaches was for sale. He chose a spot, and Kitty and Adam scrambled down.

"Thanks for the lift," Kitty said as Adam headed toward the store. "I need to get my son some breakfast, but after that we'll be glad to help you unload the melons."

"No need for that," the farmer's wife said. "You don't owe us for that ride."

Kitty thanked the couple again and caught up with Adam. "Can I have a couple of bucks, Mom?" he asked. "I'll bet they got doughnuts inside."

"No doughnuts. That tent is full of fruit and

healthy things. I'll buy you a banana and a muffin and orange juice."

He groaned his opinion of the breakfast menu. "At least let me go inside for a minute."

She studied his expression, trying to determine his motive for wanting to enter the Value-Rite. "What for? I thought you were starving."

"I am…or I was. But I have to use the bathroom."

"Okay. And while you're in there, find out where the pay phones are…so *I* can use one," she added.

"You calling Grandpa?"

Kitty ignored the glimmer of hope in his eyes. "No, I'm calling Bette to tell her we're going to be late."

"Then use your cell phone."

"I can't. Every call from the cell is listed on the company bill and will alert Grandpa to anyone I contacted."

"Then why did you bring the cell phone if you weren't going to use it?"

"I would use it if there were an emergency."

He gave her an incredulous look. "Mom, we have no car, no money and we're stuck in Nowheresville. What the heck do you call an emergency anyway?"

He had a point, and she was almost ready to admit it when she saw the answer to their problems. "Look there," she said, pointing to an ATM just to the right of the store entrance. "I can withdraw money from my account." She walked toward the machine and took her bank card from her purse. Thankfully she'd been smart enough to remove all plastic from her wallet, or the card would have been stolen, too. She slipped the plastic into the slot, started to punch in her PIN and then yanked the card out so quickly a bystander might have thought the machine had caught fire.

Adam stared at her. "What's wrong now?"

Kitty squeezed her eyes shut and took a deep breath, trying to quell the shock of what she'd almost done. She'd put this plan together in less than a day, but she'd forgotten one vital detail. "We can't get money this way," she said.

"Why not? You said you've got some in your account."

"I know, but…" She paused. Adam would never sympathize with the mistake she'd nearly made.

His eyes widened with impatience. "But what?"

But when I opened this account ten years ago, my father listed himself as a signer on the documents.

That move had been necessary at the time, since after she'd been with Bobby, Kitty's credit rating had been stuck somewhere in financial quicksand. Like it or not, Owen still had access to her accounts, and ATMs left paper trails. He'd know she'd used this machine and where it was located. Besides, Kitty wouldn't have been surprised if Owen had already closed the account, tightening the net that would force her and Adam back to Richland. She squeezed her eyes closed for a minute and drew a deep breath. She should have anticipated this problem.

Adam waited for an answer, so she repeated, "We can't get cash this way, but, Adam, don't worry…"

He shook his head. "I know. You'll think of something." He walked toward the store entrance. "I'm going inside."

Grateful he'd dropped the subject, Kitty watched him go. "I'll meet you here after I buy your breakfast." She dug a few precious dollar bills from her pocket. "Remember to locate the pay phones. But don't use one," she hollered after him. When she spoke to Bette, she'd have to ask her to wire money. She knew her mother's cousin had it to lend, but it wouldn't make asking any easier.

Kitty walked toward the outdoor market and considered the selections and how much each cost. She figured five hundred from Bette ought to cover the cost of truck repairs and gasoline. With any luck, she and Adam would be back on the highway and driving east to Charlotte by the afternoon.

She bought two blueberry muffins, a banana and orange juice for Adam, and a cup of coffee for herself. Then she stood in the parking lot, feeling the warmth of the morning sun, and the renewed confidence that comes from having a solution. She'd just swallowed a generous swig of coffee when a sudden commotion at the entrance to Value-Rite made the coffee percolate in her empty belly. It couldn't be.

It was. Adam was streaking across the parking lot, dodging cars, people and baby strollers. His arms were wrapped tightly around the elastic waist of his Tampa Bay Buccaneers jacket. And huffing and puffing, but steadily gaining on him, were two uniformed security guards.

Kitty dropped her paper cup, gripped the brown bag that held Adam's breakfast and ran toward the chase, which was now drawing a crowd. By the time she reached Adam, a security guard had his arm around her son's chest. He held Adam above the pavement while he attempted to dodge blows from Adam's wildly thrashing legs.

"Let me go, you big goon," Adam shouted. Sweat poured down his face. "You lay a hand on me and I'll sue."

The guard didn't loosen his grip. "Watch your mouth, kid. You're in enough trouble already."

A quick inspection of the parking lot confirmed what Kitty already suspected. At least a dozen electronic items lay scattered at the guard's feet. Digital cameras, MP3 players, video games… Kitty couldn't take it all in at once. "Oh, Adam, you didn't."

A man in a white shirt approached with the second security guard, who held a radio in his hand. "I've got Sheriff Oakes on the line," the guard said. "He's only a half mile away, so he should be here pretty—"

A siren cut him off as a patrol car careened into the lot and came to a lunging stop next to them. A large man in a uniform with a badge that proclaimed him Sheriff stepped out of the car and strolled around the hood. After appraising the situation, he removed his wide-brimmed hat and ran his hand through thick gray hair. Then he looked at Adam, whose face was the color of chalk. "Looks like you're in a heap of trouble, little buddy."

"What're you gonna do?" Adam squawked as the guard lowered him to the asphalt.

"Well, let's see here." He picked up the damaged remains of what was obviously an expensive camera. Adam didn't comment.

Next the sheriff examined the split blister

packaging that contained a handheld gaming system. The contents rattled in the throes of electronic death. The rest of the merchandise, which had obviously been stuffed into Adam's jacket, was in a similar state of ruin.

Kitty pinched the bridge of her nose to ward off a pain that had sliced between her eyes. She stepped between Adam and the sheriff. "Officer, I'm his mother, and…"

The sheriff touched the brim of his hat. "Sheriff Oakes," he said, and motioned to the man in the white shirt. "Quint, run a tab of what all this costs." He looked down at Adam and raised thick bushy eyebrows. "I hope you got a lot of money, son. It's not likely to get you out of this mess, but it's a start." He returned his attention to Kitty. "So you're the boy's mother?"

She nodded.

"Can't say as I envy you, Mrs.…"

"Watley. *Miss* Kitty Watley." She stared intently at her son, warning him not to reveal the truth about her name. "This is Adam."

"Where are you from?"

"Florida, most recently."

"You come all the way from Florida to attend the opening of our Value-Rite, Miss Watley?"

"No, of course not. My son and I were just passing through. We're on our way to Charlotte, but our truck broke down, and that's not all. We got lost. We've been robbed…"

"Sounds like a hard-luck case, all right," the sheriff said. "But how do you figure this justifies what your boy just did?"

Kitty felt her hopes for a sympathetic solution to this current disaster deflate like an old inner tube. "I'm not sure," she admitted, and looked at Adam.

He rubbed a dirty finger under his nose and stood ramrod straight. "You wouldn't let *your* mother starve, would you, Sheriff?" Poking the same finger in Kitty's direction, he added, "Look at how skinny she is. I was just trying to fetch a few dollars to keep her from fainting. You were close to fainting from hunger, weren't you, Mom?"

"Oh, Adam…"

The sheriff placed a hand on Adam's shoulder and nudged him toward the patrol car. "Let's go down to the station and see what charges will have to be filed."

Adam jerked away. "Charges! You got to be kidding." He gawked at Kitty. "Did you hear that, Mom? Are you happy now? He's gonna put me in jail for trying to save us from starvation." The look on his face was pure desperation when he said, "Cripes, Mom, it's time to use your cell phone and call Grandpa!"

Kitty looked away from the pleading in her

son's eyes and spoke to the sheriff. "He's not going to jail, is he? You wouldn't put a boy in jail."

"No, ma'am, but we do have the juvenile intervention center over at the Spooner County seat, and that's a strong possibility, especially with your boy's attitude."

"I have a right to a lawyer," Adam protested. "If you lock me up anywhere, my grandpa will sue you for every cent—"

"Adam, for heaven's sake, be quiet," Kitty said. "Even Grandpa can't sue somebody because *you* broke the law."

"I'd take your mama's advice, son," the sheriff said, leading them to his car. "I think now's the time to be quiet."

CHAPTER TWO

ADAM AND KITTY rode in the back of the patrol car to the downtown area of Sorrel Gap, North Carolina. The police station was a redbrick building on a shady two-lane street of similar structures designed to capture a historic feel.

Sheriff Oakes's office was sparsely furnished with three desks, a few filing cabinets and a gun rack. There was one other person in the office, a plump, fiftysomething woman. She stood up when they came in and appraised the prisoners with a disapproving eye. "These the folks who stole from the Value-Rite, Virgil?" she asked.

"Yep. This is Kitty Watley and her son, Adam. Folks, this is my wife, Wanda Oakes."

"How do you do," Kitty said, attempting a smile. Good manners couldn't hurt.

The woman nodded, disturbing tight gray curls in a nest on her head. "I knew something like this would happen," she said to her husband. "Once the Value-Rite opened, we'd have a crime wave, and you and I would end up working most Sundays." She handed a piece of paper to the sheriff. "Quint called from the store. He said the boy stole fifteen hundred and twenty dollars' worth of merchandise. Only a cordless mouse for $69.97 wasn't damaged."

Kitty stared at her son in disbelief. "A cordless mouse? We didn't even bring your computer."

"That's a serious crime, son," Sheriff Oakes said.

"Look, I can get the money," Adam said. "If you'd just let me make my one phone call..."

"No, Adam," Kitty said. "You're not calling anyone."

The office phone rang and Wanda picked it up. "It's Tommy," she said, handing the phone to her husband.

He listened, mumbled a brief response and hung up. "That was my deputy, Miss Watley, calling from where you left your truck. He traced the temporary tag to a dealer and says the vehicle is registered in your name. Your story checks out."

Thank goodness the car dealership had accepted her old driver's license as proof of identity. Of course when a person paid cash for a junker, not many questions were asked.

"Look, Sheriff," Adam said. "My mom and me—we're stinkin' ri—"

Kitty clamped a hand over his mouth. "Not now, Adam."

Sheriff Oakes asked for Kitty's driver's license. She could honestly say it was in her stolen wallet. "Run a check on her name anyway," Oakes said to his wife. "See if there are any warrants in Florida."

"There aren't," Kitty said.

Oakes did a quick head-to-toe appraisal of Adam. "And no rap sheet on the boy?"

"Of course not," Kitty said, though the words *not yet* came to her mind. "Adam was just trying to help me."

"Seems like he only made things worse," Oakes said.

"Sheriff, what can we do? What I told you about my money being stolen is true. I can't pay for that merchandise. But I'd be glad to work off the debt. I'll do anything you say that will make up for what my son did today."

The sheriff rubbed a thumb over his upper lip. "Well, Miss Watley, that's mighty generous of you, but you weren't the one who stole that stuff."

She felt color rise to her cheeks. She was doing exactly what her father had always done. She was making excuses and offering solutions for her son's behavior. Maybe now was the time to show Adam that he had to be responsible for his mistakes. They'd come to a symbolic cross-roads in the town of Sorrel Gap, and, as desperate as they were, Kitty decided it was time her son took the proper path.

"You're right, Sheriff," she said. "It was Adam who stole that merchandise. And I'll make sure he does whatever you think is appropriate punishment for his crime." She paused when another pain knotted her stomach. This time she analyzed it as a symptom of parental guilt. She wasn't blameless in all this. She was Adam's mother, and her complacent acceptance of Owen's dominance all these years made her responsible by default for what Adam did. She looked at Sheriff Oakes and said, "But I'm still his mother, and I'll do my part to make up for what happened."

Adam gulped. "What are you saying, Mom?"

"You're not going to get out of this so easily, Adam." She waited for Oakes's reaction. "What do you think, Sheriff? We'll do whatever you say."

"Kitty," he began with an almost fatherly patience, "I hate to see a boy head down a road of crime. I surely do, but this being Sunday, I suppose I'll have to remand him over to juvenile until tomorrow when he can appear before the county court judge…"

Kitty's empty stomach plunged, and she

fought a wave of nausea. She didn't know what she'd expected, but certainly not this. Not a detention facility. Maybe she could call Bette, ask her for more money. But fifteen hundred dollars plus the fine, and truck repairs…

And then Wanda Oakes called her husband over to speak privately. But in a compact office, privacy wasn't an option, and Kitty heard most of what she said.

"Virgil, Campbell comes home from the hospital today," Wanda whispered.

"I know."

"I've asked everyone in those hills to look after him. Even offered a small salary. Nobody has time what with planting going on now. Plus, it's not like your nephew's tried to fit in with us since coming home. Folks may admire what he did in Iraq, but he's changed."

"It's the accident, Wanda," the sheriff argued. "He's had a hard time."

"I think it's more than that. Every time I ask him what happened over there in Raleigh, he says he doesn't want to talk about it. If you ask me, he's been in the city too long."

"I know he's been secretive, but he served his country. He's due a little privacy."

Wanda sniffed. "Fine, but I'm just telling you. No one's going to put themselves out for him. And he flat out refused to come live with us till his leg and ribs are healed. Let's face it. I'm the one who'll be stuck going out to that place every day to see to his needs."

The sheriff scratched his neck. "Are you going somewhere with all this, Wanda?"

She passed a furtive look at Kitty before mumbling something about working off the theft, community service and totaling up the debt to Sorrel Gap.

"Do you think Quint will go for it?" the sheriff asked.

"I'll call him and ask, but I know he will. He'll want this incident to go away quietly so he doesn't get any bad press on the opening weekend of his store."

Virgil shrugged. "I suppose it could work. At least the bill will get paid. Plus, we'd be saving the county what it costs to keep the boy at the detention center." After a moment the sheriff returned to Kitty and Adam. "My wife and I are good judges of character," he said. "We can see that you two are good people deep down."

Kitty held her breath. This sounded like a snow job. Even so, she was willing to listen. Whatever Oakes was about to say might be their only hope of getting back on the road.

"Do you have time before you have to be in Charlotte?" Oakes asked.

"Yes, sir. Some."

"And you'll guarantee that your boy will take care of all debt to the village of Sorrel Gap and the Value-Rite?"

"Yes. Adam?"

"What?"

She pinched his arm.

"Okay, jeez!"

Sheriff Oakes grinned. "Then there might be a solution to this problem." He leaned against a desk and crossed his arms. "My nephew comes home from the hospital today. He had a little crash with his airplane and busted up his leg pretty good."

A little crash? Kitty pictured wrecked metal and broken limbs.

"He's a fine fella," the sheriff continued. "An Iraq war hero. Lives in a place down the road with lots of rooms. I don't guess he needs any serious nursing. Just general care. If you can see clear to staying out there and looking after him for a spell, and if your boy agrees to work with Quint over at the Value-Rite, I expect I can convince a judge and the citizens of Sorrel Gap to call your debt paid."

Was the sheriff acting a bit too casual? At this point, doubts flooded Kitty's mind. What exactly would their living arrangements be? How would she get along without her truck? And sure, the sheriff vouched for his nephew, but he was a complete stranger to her and Adam. He could be a jerk or worse.

As if sensing her reluctance, Sheriff Oakes stood straight and stared at her. "It's a fair solution, young lady," he said. "I guarantee you'll be treated right, and once this debt is paid, you'll be free to move on."

The sheriff waited for her answer, his features stern. Kitty knew she was out of options. It was this deal or detention and court for Adam—with all the evidence rightly stacked against him. She could put off her entrance to the design school if that meant Adam wouldn't be incarcerated. And since Oakes had said his nephew was in a plane crash, chances were his leg injury was severe. If she and Adam felt threatened by him, they could outrun him to the nearest neighbor's house to find help. And he was a veteran. That was a detail in his favor.

She took a deep breath, glanced at Adam, whose disbelief was etched in his features. The best part about Oakes's proposition was its benefit to her son. He'd finally learn that his actions had consequences. She put her hand on Adam's shoulder. "I'm ready to accept this deal, Sheriff," she said.

Adam gasped. She ignored him. "But I still have a problem with my truck. How will Adam and I get around?"

"My nephew has a Jeep," he said. "He might let you use it once you gain his trust. But your first obligation is to him. I don't want to hear that you're driving around Spooner County on joy rides."

Kitty almost smiled. As if she could do anything remotely joyful on thirty-seven dollars. In her old life, that didn't even cover a haircut. She nodded. "Agreed."

They could do this, look in on the sheriff's relative while Adam worked off his debt. Plus, there was an added bonus. They had a place to stay and Owen would never think to look for them in Sorrel Gap. "We'll do our best," she added.

"I know you will, Kitty, and to show my appreciation, I'll have your truck towed into town at our expense." He grinned. "But I'll keep the keys here in the office until this matter's settled."

"Mom!" Adam wailed.

Ignoring the sheriff's veiled warning, she said to Adam, "Would you rather go to the detention facility?"

He mumbled a brusque "No."

Kitty pressed her keys into the sheriff's outstretched hand. "Can I ask one question?"

"Now's the time."

"How long until I get those back?"

He gave the keys to Wanda. "A few weeks maybe. Give or take. Fifteen hundred dollars is a lot of money, especially when the boy can't work more than three or four hours a day. But it's pretty country here. Might be the best summer you folks ever had."

Adam grabbed her hand. "The whole summer?"

"No, surely not," Kitty whispered to him. "Not if you work real hard." But Kitty still had her doubts, both about her son and the man they were dedicating the next weeks to. But they were committed now. "We'll need our personal things from the truck," she said to Oakes.

"I'll have my deputy run them out to you later. But I'll take you to Campbell's place now so you can settle in."

Kitty walked to the door with Adam reluctantly beside her. When she looked over her shoulder to say goodbye to Mrs. Oakes, the woman appeared quite satisfied with the arrangements. Blissfully so.

AFTER A TWENTY-MINUTE ride in the patrol car down a narrow, two-lane road, Kitty was beginning to wonder if they were ever going to get to the home of Sheriff Oakes's nephew. But the scenery was beautiful—summertime green and lush—and she found herself relaxing despite her misgivings and listening to Sheriff Oakes's description of Sorrel Gap history.

The town had begun to thrive as a tourist destination once the four-lane road called the Spooner County Expressway opened in 1980. Before that, this narrow highway, which Oakes told her was called Old Sorrel Gap Road, was truly nestled in the elbow of two ridges of foothills rising from each side.

Kitty expected to see lavish homes bordering the country road, so she was surprised when they drove past an abandoned gas station and a couple of vacant clapboard buildings. "How much farther?" she asked the sheriff.

He pointed to a vague spot in the distance. "The Saddle Top Motel's just over that rise."

A motel? Good news. She and Adam wouldn't be alone with Oakes's nephew after all. There would be guests and employees around. When the car crested the hill, she spied a tall metal pole with a rusted oval sign on top. Then she saw the motel—a one-story brick building baking in the noon sun like a sedentary caterpillar. The sign on top of the pole proclaimed its identity.

Kitty made out the faded image of what might have been an engaging old cowpoke in chaps and stocking cap—years ago. His arm jerked crazily up and down in the wind, pointing first at the sky and then at the faded words, Saddle Top Mountain Motel. All of the letters except for the first ones in each word had paled to near obscurity. Three lightbulbs, out of an entire ring of empty sockets, clung stubbornly around the perimeter of the sign.

"Where the heck are we?" Adam asked. He'd sat up and had flattened both hands to the passenger window. His expression had transformed from disinterest to something resembling terror.

Sheriff Oakes veered left into a gravel parking lot riddled with potholes and ground to a stop. "We're at the Saddle Top Motel, son," he said. "This is where you and your mother will be staying."

Kitty shot a warning look over the front seat when Adam started to speak. Then she swallowed past a lump in her throat that accompanied the realization that vacationers hadn't stayed here in years. "Your nephew lives here?"

"Sure does. The place has been in Campbell's family for a long time. Camp's grandpa used to run it, but the business failed when the expressway diverted traffic. It's been closed now for nearly thirty years." Oakes stared out the windshield. "Doesn't look too bad, all things considered."

Right. If your current home was a park bench or the asphalt under a bridge. Kitty didn't see the point in expressing her own opinion, so she just said, "Why does your nephew live here instead of in town?"

The sheriff paused a moment before saying, "Free-and-clear housing, I would expect. Once Campbell's grandfather passed, he inherited the place."

So this man is an incompetent pilot with a busted-up leg, and no visible means of support. Great.

Oakes continued. "Campbell didn't need the motel until recently. Before coming home, he lived on the Matheson estate in Raleigh." Oakes's voice held a hint of pride. "Now, that's a name you've heard of, I'll wager."

"Matheson? No, sorry."

"Matheson Fine Furniture?"

Kitty shook her head.

"Well, I'll be. I thought everybody had heard of Leland Matheson. He's worth a few cool millions. Campbell lived on his estate and worked as his business adviser and personal pilot for the past three years since he got out of the Air Force."

Kitty felt as if she were on a roller coaster of good news–bad news. This last bit of information was encouraging. Apparently the nephew had recently held a decent job. But since she was here to take care of this pilot who had just crashed his plane, Kitty couldn't help wondering if his former employer, doubting his pilot's skills, had fired him. Figuring the best way to know was to ask, she said, "So, why did your nephew leave his job?"

Oakes frowned. "He said it had something to do with a personal matter. Plus, he wanted to start a business back here where he grew up. Bought his own two-seater aircraft for taking aerial photographs. Unfortunately the fuel line ruptured, so that plan's on hold."

A shiver ran down Kitty's spine. Her father often chartered personal aircraft in his capacity as owner of Galloway Groves. She always found an excuse not to accompany him on trips. The thought of being in a small plane was high on her list of least favorable ways to travel. And she figured that anybody who made a living flying one of those death traps ought to know he was only a loose screw away from disaster.

The sheriff opened his car door and stepped out. "Come on, folks. Campbell should be here in the hospital van any minute. Wanda says the motel key's under the potted plant by the office door."

Potted plant? Was he referring to that mildewed pickle crock with three spindly twigs sticking out the top? Kitty guessed he was because that's precisely where he headed.

She got out and opened Adam's door. When he remained in the car, she reminded him why they were here.

"Okay, already."

They stood side by side staring at ten worn-out, run-down, dismal units broken by a peaked-roof office in the center. If a building could droop, this one did. In fact, the entire structure looked as if it was just waiting for the mercy of a wrecking ball.

"How you doing back there, Captain Oakes?"

Campbell turned away from the familiar landscape flashing by the side window of the Spooner County medi-van. "I'm okay, Joe," he said to the young man in the front passenger seat. "And you don't have to call me captain. It's been plain old Campbell for quite a while now."

"Yeah, I know, but you're still a hero around here. Everybody knows what you did over in Iraq."

Campbell glanced down at the fiberglass splint that went from his ankle to his thigh and suppressed a grimace of disgust. *Everybody knows what I did four days ago, too*, he thought. A few years before, during Operation Iraqi Freedom, he had flown forty successful sorties over Baghdad in a Fighting Falcon. And then on Wednesday he crashed a single-engine

Cessna Cardinal into a cow pasture. "My status as a hero, if I ever had one, is over," he said.

Joe shrugged. "I still remember the stories about you. I think the town council should have had a parade or something when you came back home."

Campbell focused out the window again, mostly to hide the smirk he couldn't suppress. Joe didn't understand. Nobody in Sorrel Gap would have a celebration for a prodigal son who'd been living on Matheson property in Raleigh. A renovated six-room carriage house on the lavish twenty-acre estate was a cultural world away from this small North Carolina town.

And the truth was, Campbell wouldn't be here now except Diana Matheson had screwed him over one time too many. His future had come down to a choice between his pride and his cushy income, and Campbell had opted for pride. He'd left the estate just ahead of Diana, who caught a plane to Europe to get over her distress. Right. At least he'd been the one to say goodbye first.

The medi-van topped the hill and descended toward the Saddle Top Motel, a sad reminder of Campbell's childhood and the glory days when Old Sorrel Gap Road was known as the Gateway to the Blue Ridge. Campbell could have afforded better accommodations in town, but so what? The building, as pathetic as it was, was his.

Still, as the Saddle Top came into view, Campbell experienced the same melancholy that gripped him whenever he returned to the cheerless structure struggling to survive in the gap. Only this time it was worse. This time, instead of just feeling as hopeless as the old motel was, Campbell would have to suffer the indignity of being hoisted into his living quarters by the medivan driver and his helper.

And there would be no easy escape from the gap. Because of his leg, he wouldn't be able to walk or drive away for weeks. And even after five hours of surgery and a half dozen rods and pins, the doctors still couldn't tell Campbell for certain that he'd be able to walk without a limp, or ever pilot the Cardinal again. And that was assuming the plane's landing gear and right wing could be repaired.

Unfortunately this mishap had occurred just when things had started to turn around for him. He had a half dozen contracts for aerial photographs stacked up on his desk. Now he'd have to tell his customers to wait out his iffy recovery or hire somebody else.

Campbell pressed his lips together as a painful draw of air stretched the muscles in his chest. Hard to believe that the dependable Fighting Falcon hadn't suffered so much as a scratch on her steel-gray exterior during his entire deployment. Four months after he'd started Oakes Aerial Photographs, Campbell had watched the Cessna towed back to the airstrip in shambles.

The van pulled as close as possible to the covered walkway in front of the motel office. Even with two fellas supporting his weight, Campbell knew it wouldn't be easy to get his six-foot-two, hundred-and-eighty-pound deadweight inside the building.

Joe Becker jumped out of the vehicle and opened the wide side door, giving Campbell a clear view of his uncle Virgil's patrol car. Once he spotted Virgil at the breezeway where the washers and dryers were located, Campbell scanned the front of the motel for Virgil's wife, Wanda. He'd never hit it off with Wanda and dreaded the thought of having to endure her interference if she followed through on her threat to take care of him.

But it wasn't Wanda who appeared at Virgil's side. It was a skinny purple pole of a woman with electrified blond hair that stuck out every which way. And a gawking, curly-haired kid who looked as if he'd just lost his puppy.

"Oh, great," Campbell grumbled aloud. "You

don't think somebody actually wants to rent a room?"

Only one lone tourist, an old guy in a vintage Oldsmobile claiming he was experiencing America's back roads, had stopped at the Saddle Top Motel in the six months Campbell had occupied it. Campbell had sent the fella on his way with an unappealing but very accurate description of the lack of amenities to be found here. He hoped Virgil wasn't thinking he'd do him a favor by letting someone stay and contribute a bit of income. Campbell didn't need the money. He needed peace and quiet.

The van driver pressed a lever under Campbell's seat, and it swiveled smoothly toward the door. "I wouldn't know, Mr. Oakes," the man said to answer his question. "I can't see anybody wanting to stay here."

The two men each slipped one arm under Campbell's knees and another around his back. With perfect timing coordinated by a command from the driver, they lifted him from the van. Less humiliating, he supposed, than a ride in a wheelchair, but only slightly so.

The men supported Campbell as he hopped on one foot the short distance to the covered porch. Virgil met him and looped Campbell's arm over his shoulders to help him stand. The van attendants returned to the vehicle to get

Campbell's equipment, which included the detestable wheelchair, crutches, medical supplies and a bag of prescriptions. Campbell narrowed his eyes to get a look down the sidewalk at the couple standing in front of the breezeway. "Who are those people?" he asked.

"Oh, that's Miss Kitty Watley and her son, Adam," Virgil said. "They're going to stay here awhile."

Campbell wasn't certain of much in his life at this point, but he was darn sure of his response to Virgil. "No, they're not. Tell them to go into town to the Blue Ridge Lodge or the Sorrel Gap Chalet. Nobody's rented a room at this motel for years." He took a couple of quick hops toward his front door and regretted it immediately when his chest burned as if his broken ribs had erupted into flames. "There probably isn't a clean towel in the whole place," he said to Virgil after taking an agonizing gasp of air and letting his uncle support him.

"Well, there will be," Virgil announced. "That's what I'm trying to tell you. This lady and her kid are going to take care of you while you're laid up."

"Like heck they are…"

"Listen to me, Camp. You won't have to lift a finger. Just sit back and let these two wait on you until you heal."

Campbell's sharp gaze connected for a quick

heartbeat with the lady's remarkably round eyes. She attempted a smile and wiggled her fingers from the pocket of a pair of hip-hugging, baggy purple pants. The kid set his lips in a hard, tight line and scowled as if Campbell was his worst enemy. "No deal," Campbell said. "I don't want anybody taking care of me."

Virgil frowned. "You might want to reconsider, Camp. You need somebody and these two are willing."

Campbell's innate skepticism took over. "Oh yeah? And how much is this going to cost me? And why would anybody want to stay out here in the first place?"

"It's not going to cost you anything," Virgil said. "And they more or less got talked into volunteering as a legal penance."

Campbell almost laughed. "A legal penance? Come on, Virg."

"Sort of, yes. They've got a small debt to pay to society, and you're their means to that end."

Campbell shot his uncle a dubious look. He knew small-town justice worked in mysterious ways, but this was too quirky, even for Sorrel Gap. Was his uncle actually proposing that his incapacitated nephew harbor criminals desperate enough to agree to stay in what amounted to the Sorrel Gap Outback? "What'd they do? Murder somebody?"

Virgil chuckled, but the sound was forced. "Oh, nothing that bad."

Campbell returned his attention to the desperadoes. The woman, from this distance, at least, didn't look capable of tangling with a june bug. She worried a pile of dust with the toe of a sandal that had a heel high enough to make Campbell wonder how she didn't get nosebleeds. She wasn't looking at him anymore, and he took that as a sign that she was as uncomfortable with this situation as he was.

"Virgil, let's have it," he said. "The whole story. Where'd you find these two?"

The men from the van walked past them after bringing in the last of Campbell's gear and wished the patient good luck. Virgil hollered to Miss Kitty Watley to wait outside, and he helped Campbell hobble through the motel lobby to the former manager's quarters in back. "Let me get you settled," he said, "and then I'll tell you how all this came about."

He eased Campbell into a tan leather recliner, one of the newer pieces of furniture Campbell had brought with him from the carriage house to brighten up his living quarters. And, with his attention firmly fixed on his uncle's face, Campbell heard the tale of two Florida travelers down on their luck, a broken-down pickup on the side of the road and Adam Watley's involvement with the grand opening of Value-Rite.

Virgil proceeded as if the matter were settled. "So, can I go get Kitty and the boy and make the introductions?"

Campbell shook his head. "Not so fast. I don't like it, Virgil. I know you saw this as a temporary solution…"

"The only solution as I see it. I promised your dad I'd look after you, and you aren't making my job too easy."

Campbell held his temper. He'd told his father he'd deal with this on his own.

"You're not Superman, Camp," Virgil reminded him. "You need help."

"Okay, I guess I have to admit to that, but how much assistance am I going to get from a lady who looks like an underripe eggplant and her outlaw son?"

Virgil waved his hand, dismissing Campbell's concern. "You've got them all wrong. Kitty can do anything—cook, clean, do laundry. And her boy, why, he just stole that stuff to help out his mama. He's a good boy."

Campbell only believed about half of what Virgil was saying, since he'd seen the glower on the kid's face, and he'd already concluded that Miss Kitty looked as if she *needed* more help than she could give. A good stiff wind sweeping off Saddle Top Mountain could carry her all the way down the gap. But on the other hand, a woman without any means of support who was driving an old pickup could probably use the work. Of all the people Virgil might have brought to his door, she'd likely be so grateful for a place to stay that she'd just do her job and mind her own business as he'd tell her to.

Campbell chewed on his lower lip. He hated being dependent on anyone. But for now, like it or not, he was. Maybe it wouldn't hurt to give this living arrangement a chance—as long as the woman and her kid fed him and kept his clothes clean and otherwise left him alone. He thought of the alternative—Wanda Oakes force-feeding him collard greens and down-home advice—and decided that trying to make it work with the Watleys was a better solution.

"You win," he said. "At least I won't have to treat these strangers like family. But if it doesn't work, you're going to come get them."

Virgil nodded. "Oh, absolutely."

"Okay. Bring them in."

CHAPTER THREE

KITTY HURRIED FROM the breezeway to meet the sheriff when he came out of the motel lobby. "How'd he take the news?" she asked, shaking her fingers, which had become numb from clenching them so hard. "Is he okay with Adam and me staying?"

"He didn't like the idea at all, did he?" Adam said, his voice blatantly hopeful.

"He liked the idea all right—after I told him you could cook and clean, wash clothes and—"

"Okay, sure," Kitty said. "How hard can all that stuff be?"

Virgil's eyes rounded with shock. "What?"

"What I meant was that cooking and cleaning—it's all second nature to me. Not hard at all." Actually those tasks were second nature to Esmeralda, the housekeeper who'd been working for Owen Galloway for years.

"All right, then. Let's go inside."

Kitty and Adam walked ahead of the sheriff into the lobby. They passed a couple of tired old Danish chairs and a counter with a chipped

Formica finish. Adam's fingers wrapped around Kitty's arm like a claw. "Nice place you picked here, Mom," he whispered.

"*I* picked?" Kitty started to argue but realized the futility of bringing up Adam's mistake again.

"Do you know the difference between a washing machine and a stove?" Adam asked.

"Hey, I'm not the one who confused a jacket for a shopping cart."

They entered a living space just slightly larger than a typical studio apartment. Forcing her gaze to sweep quickly across the room, Kitty avoided for the moment the man whose presence was definitely the dominant feature. A queen-size bed covered with a colorful Navajo-print comforter sat next to an uncluttered desk. A knotty pine dresser held an assortment of men's toiletries on a wooden valet tray situated precisely in the middle of a pair of polished brass lamps. Brass drawer handles sparkled on each of the nine dresser drawers.

An immaculate kitchen occupied one corner. The gleaming white appliances appeared new. Two doors at the rear of the room were closed. Kitty assumed one was a closet and the other led to a bathroom.

And in the middle of this space, there was a distressed leather sofa and a pine coffee table with a notebook computer on top. And then, because she could no longer avoid acknowledging the man at the center of this meticulous display of orderly living, Kitty focused on a wide leather recliner, which was filled quite respectably by Campbell Oakes.

He wore a Charlotte Bobcats T-shirt and navy blue cargo shorts. A shock of dark brown hair fell onto his forehead and partially covered a fresh bandage. One long bare foot at the end of a well-muscled leg extended over the chair's footrest. Campbell's other leg, buried in at least a three-foot length of cotton batting and fiberglass splint was supported by a pillow.

He stared at her with an overtly appraising green-eyed gaze that made her feel like squirming. She tried to smile, but her lips refused to obey the command from her brain. She wondered how Campbell Oakes, even with damaged ribs and a broken leg, had the capacity to render a person speechless and smileless. Just imagining him standing fully upright, dominating everything around him, brought a strange quiver to her stomach. It wasn't like the trepidation she felt when she faced her father. It was strange in a different sort of way.

"All right, now," Sheriff Oakes said cheerfully. "I'll just make the introductions and be on my way. You young folks'll get along just

fine. Campbell, this is Kitty. Kitty, Campbell."
The sheriff reached over and tousled Adam's
hair. Adam flinched. Sheriff Oakes pretended
not to notice. "And this towheaded youngster
is Adam."

Campbell nodded, but his intense scrutiny
didn't ease up. In fact, his gaze settled above
Kitty's neck and refused to move.

Assuming something must be amiss, she ran a
hand through her hair, felt the blunt-cut strands
prickle her palm and spring back to attention
with what was left of yesterday's gel. She drew
her lips together. No lipstick, of course. What
little she'd applied before hitching a ride on
the watermelon truck had been chewed off in
the Value-Rite parking lot. She ran her tongue
over her teeth, searching for an embarrassing
food scrap, and then remembered that raspberry
lipstick and two swigs of coffee were the only
things she'd eaten all day.

Campbell's gaze wandered over her and ended
in a puzzling frown. "Kitty, is it?" he said, returning his attention to her face.

"Yes."

"You picked out a room to stay in?"

"No, not yet. Any one will do."

A low, rumbling sound that might have started
as a sarcastic laugh but ended as a stifled groan
came from his throat. Obviously something hurt,

bad. He pushed himself up in the chair. "Actually none of them will do, but it's take it or leave it."

"Don't worry about that," Virgil intervened. "I'll put Kitty and the boy in the first room past the breezeway. That way they'll be right next to the washing machines."

Adam cupped his hand over his mouth. "Lucky break, eh, Mom?"

"Is there a phone in there?" Virgil asked.

Campbell nodded. "Doesn't work, though. The only phone that's hooked up is this one." He pointed to a portable unit on the end table.

"No problem," Virgil said with a chirpiness that was beginning to get on Kitty's nerves. "I'll stop at the phone company and have Kitty's turned on. That way you can call her and Adam in their room anytime you need them."

"I won't need them much," Campbell answered.

"You could just keep us on a leash and yank," Adam said.

The sheriff laughed as if that was the funniest thing he'd ever heard and tried to tousle Adam's hair again. This time Adam was too fast for him.

"Wanda was here yesterday," Virgil said, sticking the hand that had swatted the air over Adam's head into his pocket. He walked to the kitchen. "She stocked the cupboard and icebox for you."

He opened the refrigerator door and stuck his head inside. "You've got milk, cola, orange drink, bologna, bread, bacon and eggs. You won't starve." He pointed to a broom closet. "I guess the cleaning supplies are in there, Kitty. Knowing my nephew, he'll have stocked up on everything you need to keep the place sparkling."

"Maybe he keeps the maid in there, too," Adam mumbled, and Kitty shushed him.

"Anyhow," the sheriff continued, "if you think of something else you want, just call the sheriff's office and either my deputy or I will bring it out to you."

Adam had moved to the cupboard, where he was investigating the food provided by Wanda Oakes. "Grape-Nuts and cornflakes? You got to be kidding! Where're the Pop-Tarts?"

Kitty rushed over and shut the cupboard doors. "Don't complain, Adam. Let's have Sheriff Oakes show us our room and then we'll come back and fix lunch for Mr. Oakes." She glanced back at Campbell. "Is that all right with you?"

He squeezed his eyes shut and laid a hand on his stomach. Kitty figured he was weighing the advantages of trying to eat through the pain versus starving to death. From the look on his face, it was a tough call.

"I guess I could eat," he said, opening his eyes again.

"Are you having pain?" she asked him.

"He sure is," Virgil said. "He's got, what is it, Camp? Three cracked ribs?"

"That's what they tell me."

"You've got pills for that pain, don't you?" Oakes asked.

"Yep."

"Make sure he gets those," Virgil said to Kitty. "But for now, follow me." He jangled the motel keys and nudged Adam to walk ahead of him. When they were in the lobby, Oakes leaned over to deliver a special message to Adam. "I'd advise you to rest up as much as you can today, Adam. Come Monday you'll be working for Mr. Quint Cheevers over at the Value-Rite."

Obviously the sheriff's cheerfulness in front of his nephew hadn't caused him to forget the real reason for this act of penance. And it was a stark reminder to Kitty that she and her son were definitely expected to fulfill their pledge as participants in this unique example of Sorrel Gap justice.

Kitty walked woodenly behind the sheriff and Adam. Maybe exhaustion and hunger were catching up with her. Maybe her commitment to a situation that could prove to be a disaster was making her stomach jump as if dozens of moths had been released inside. Or maybe it was Campbell Oakes himself. He hadn't done anything other than scope her out with those cool green eyes. But it was enough to make her feel as if her legs were made of matchsticks, and the lobby of the Saddle Top Motel was suddenly the size of a football field.

When they finally reached the porch, Adam held Kitty back. This time there was no joking in his voice when he said, "Mom, you've got to stop this. That guy's weird. You have to call Grandpa!"

She took a long, soothing breath of mountain air and straightened her spine. "No, Adam. We're going to do what's right even if we make a mess of it."

"You mean even if it kills us," he added.

She gave him what she hoped was a smile of encouragement. "Mr. Oakes is just unhappy because he's hurting. He'll warm up to us when we've been around for a while, you'll see."

It wasn't a lie, exactly, but it certainly was wishful thinking.

SHERIFF OAKES UNLOCKED the door to unit number six, slipped the key off the ring and handed it to Kitty. "Here you go. I hope you and the boy enjoy your stay in beautiful Spooner County."

"You won't forget about our things, will you, Sheriff?"

"Tommy will bring them out to you at the end of his shift, about five o'clock. In the meantime, I expect you'll find whatever you need in this room or in Campbell's place."

The sheriff stepped off the sidewalk and headed toward his patrol car. What remained of Kitty's confidence threatened to walk away with him. A wind had kicked up, sending a film of sand over the sidewalk. Loose gravel pinged across the porch shingles—the desolate, lonely sound of a place forgotten by the human race. Kitty shivered and fought an urge to rush to the car and beg Virgil Oakes for other options.

Maybe Campbell Oakes wasn't exactly weird as Adam said, and his injuries rendered him virtually harmless, but he seemed to have a chip on his shoulder large enough to fuel a bonfire. Plus, she feared that she would be a miserable failure at helping him. According to her ex-husband, Bobby, during the longest two years of her life—her marriage—she'd been a failure at nearly everything she tried. More recently, her father made her feel as if she wasn't even capable of taking care of herself and her son, an opinion that had been substantiated in the past twenty-four hours. How was she going to take care of an invalid?

The sheriff set his elbow on top of the car. "I'm counting on you to keep your word, Kitty, and to make Adam keep his. Don't make me regret giving you and the boy this chance."

His implied warning only added to her guilt and uncertainty.

"That fella in there is my brother's son. He's been through a lot over the years."

Right. Campbell was a war veteran. But he'd also worked for the wealthy Leland Matheson and made his home in Raleigh before coming to Sorrel Gap, so he hadn't bedded down with land mines without a break. "I'll look after him," she said, and sent a silent prayer skyward that she'd succeed. "You take care of my truck, all right?"

He smiled at her. "Yes, ma'am. I'll even have my mechanic look it over. That truck'll be all yours again about the same time my nephew can live out here on his own."

How long would that be? How long would she and Adam have to remain in this dusty, forsaken patch of North Carolina despair? "You won't forget to have the phone turned on in our room, will you?" she asked as a flood of panic returned.

Oakes indicated that he would remember. The promise of a connection to the outside world, the chance to call Bette and Esmeralda, erased some of Kitty's misgivings.

The sheriff climbed into the patrol car and backed out of the parking lot. Soon he was over the hill and returning to blessed civilization.

And Kitty and Adam went into their room.

Actually none of them will do.

The words Campbell Oakes had uttered a few minutes ago about the rooms at the Saddle Top Motel flashed in Kitty's mind. And now, standing just over the threshold of unit number six, Kitty understood what he'd meant. And she suddenly felt as tired as this abandoned old room looked.

Adam entered the room and covered his nose. "Phew. Now we have another gross smell."

Kitty yanked open the rubber-backed drapes covering the picture window. "That's neglect, Adam," she said. "Mildew. Stale air. Whatever you want to call it. Just please help me open the room up."

They each cranked handles on opposite sides of the glass until two large panes creaked open. A breeze swept inside, depositing dust from the sill on a round Formica table and two orange vinyl chairs.

The admittance of air helped eliminate the odor, but the accompanying sunlight emphasized the deplorable condition of the furnishings. There were two double beds, each covered with thin spreads in faded gold and avocado stripes. Kitty walked over flat shag carpet that might once have been a peachy color, but was now nondescript. She ran her hand over the top of a six-drawer brown dresser. Three of its pulls, which reminded her of the fins of a vintage automobile, dangled loose, hanging by only one screw. A television sat next to the dresser on a rusty metal stand.

Kitty went to the rear of the room where there was a gold vanity under a rectangular mirror held in place by a half dozen clear plastic mounts. She opened a door to reveal a bathroom decorated in small gold-and-white tiles. When she flushed the toilet, she was relieved to see the discolored water swirl over rust stains in the bottom of the bowl and disappear. It was replaced with a welcoming pool of clear water.

A sharp click followed by an electrical buzz sent Kitty rushing back to the sleeping area. "What's wrong?" she asked Adam, but immediately saw what had produced the strange noises. Her son sat on the end of a bed, his face cupped in his hands as he stared gloomily at a TV screen with more static than picture.

"It's not even color," he said. "I can't watch this."

She checked the back of the television. Its

bulbous shape convinced her the set was color even if the only remaining evidence of the NBC peacock was a sickly Martian green. "Probably just needs a new antenna," she said.

"This place sucks." Adam turned the channel wheel, which only had thirteen numbers. He was able to get minimal reception on four of them.

"We'll worry about that later," Kitty said. "For now, get off the bed."

"What?"

Seeing her son on the old linens had revitalized Kitty with the instinct to protect her young. "I don't want you sitting there."

He stared at her as if she'd lost her mind, but he stood. She ripped the linens from both beds and piled everything, sheets, spreads and two thin blankets, into Adam's arms. "Take these to the breezeway. I saw a decent washer and dryer and a bottle of detergent. Fill the washer with half the linens, dump in some soap and turn it on."

He grimaced at the load in his arms. "I don't know how to wash clothes."

"It's easy. Read the dials and choose whichever settings claim to have the most superpowers."

He trudged out of the room, sheets trailing behind him. Kitty followed him outside but stayed on the walkway. She leaned her elbows on a railing that ran the length of the covered walkway and took a deep breath. "Okay, Kitty," she said to herself. "You can do this. It won't be so bad."

The wind had calmed so that only a gentle breeze rustled the pitiful shrubs that stubbornly existed in nutrient-depleted beds in front of the motel. Kitty plucked a pale, drooping leaf from an evergreen plant and studied it. "All it would take is a little fertilizer and some serious weed removal, and this bed could be brought back to life," she said. "I'll bet these bushes could look as good as…"

She stopped, wondering where she had been going with that sentence. And then she looked across the two-lane road to hills that dipped and rose in elegant curves up from the gap and into the horizon. A wispy haze hovered over a cleft, a saddle-shaped indentation in the tallest peak, bathing the mountain top in a cool blue-gray mist.

It must have been a nurturing spring, she decided, because every tree in her view was dressed in the most remarkable shades of green, from deep emerald to pale olive. She twisted the leaf between her fingers. "Yep, you could look as good as what lives just across that road."

She blew the leaf into the breeze and glanced

over her shoulder into the bleakness of her room. What had seemed hopeless only moments ago now at least hinted of promise. "It's sure a long way from my father's house," she said, "but it's a heck of a lot better than Bobby's sixteen-foot travel trailer."

She'd been in her second year at the University of Florida when charming, sinfully handsome Bobby Watley played a golf tournament at a nearby resort. Kitty volunteered to be a scorekeeper. Her mother had died a few weeks before, and Kitty was desperately seeking any activity that would get her out of the classroom and the claustrophobic despair where her grief had taken her. Unfortunately it had been Bobby's dazzling smile that had taken her mind off her problems, not his less-than-stellar golf swing.

Two weeks later, she dropped out of school and married Bobby in the town where the next tournament had been held. Now she couldn't even remember the name of the place. Towns all ran together, and state lines became indistinct when you stayed in campgrounds that all looked alike.

She shivered now, thinking of that dismal time in her life when she was married to Bobby. They never had enough money. They never had enough room. When Adam came and he needed space, she'd been forced to toss out most of the possessions she'd brought with her. She fixed simple meals on a small, two-burner stove.

But of all the things she lacked with Bobby, the most glaring was encouragement. When she craved support, Bobby offered criticism. When she asked for help, Bobby demanded more than anyone could give. Had she known Bobby was so emotionally needy, she never would have married him. Had she realized the same of herself, she especially wouldn't have.

She'd been young when she married Bobby. But she'd felt old when she left him. After twenty-four months of watching her husband fail on the golf tour, Kitty called her father and begged for his forgiveness. A day later she walked away from a dry, dusty campsite in Arizona with nothing in her pocket but the credit card her father had overnighted, and her ten-month-old son in her arms. And because Bobby knew he didn't have a chance of seeing any of Owen's money, he signed the divorce papers sent by the Galloway attorney.

Even when she'd put those years behind her and moved back to Richland, she constantly struggled to move forward without being haunted by the past. It didn't help that Owen fanned the fires of her memories. Sometimes she thought the greatest satisfaction he had in life was reminding her of the foolish mistake that had cost her a college education, her independence and, most importantly, her self-esteem.

"Mom?"

Brought back to the present, she smiled at Adam. "How'd you do with the laundry?"

"I guess I did okay. I read the directions on the soap jug."

She drew him close to her side. He flinched at first and then stood quietly, as if he sensed that contact was what she needed. Stroking his hair, Kitty admitted that this child of hers was a handful, but he was all she had of Bobby Watley and all she wanted from him. At least Bobby had given her Adam.

During Adam's twelve years of life, Bobby had been little more to him than a crinkled copy of an internet article about the players in some insignificant tournament. Adam read that story over and over, connecting with his father the only way he knew how. Kitty had made sure the article was among their belongings in the broken-down truck. Adam wouldn't have wanted to leave that piece of his history behind.

"We'll get washed up," she said to Adam, "and then look in on Mr. Oakes."

The mention of Campbell's name brought a strange image to Kitty's mind, as if the Adonis beauty of Bobby's face had mutated like a Hollywood camera trick into the imperfectly rugged features of Campbell Oakes. She hardly knew anything about Campbell, but she sensed that he wasn't a bit like Bobby. Not that she should be thinking of Campbell as anything other than an obligation, but some things were just obvious. Bobby was sand, shifting with the tides, pretty to look at, but you couldn't build a house on it. Campbell, despite being bested by a busted fuel line, was definitely rock.

"We got some money left, don't we?" Adam said as they walked back into unit number six.

"*I* have a little. Why?"

He nodded at the television. "Maybe we can buy an antenna for that old piece of junk."

"I'll think about it."

He grinned at her. "Give me back my Tampa Bay jacket, and I'll pick one up at the Value-Rite when I go into work."

CHAPTER FOUR

THE RINGING PHONE irritated Campbell, but not just because he didn't want to talk to anyone. He couldn't reach the dang receiver. The phone mocked him from an end table at the far end of the couch, ten feet at least from where he had parked himself in the recliner.

He gripped the arms of the chair and pushed himself up. Swearing under his breath seemed to give him enough strength to hobble to the sofa and sprawl across the three cushions. He'd answer the darn thing now, but he reminded himself to keep the receiver nearby from now on. And then he reminded himself never to crash his plane again. He read the caller ID, *Travis Oakes*, and punched the connect button. "Dad?"

"Oh, good," came the calm, authoritative voice of the decorated Army Lieutenant Colonel. "You're out of the hospital."

Campbell painfully hoisted himself into a sitting position. "Yeah. They released me about an hour ago. I've only been at the motel a few minutes."

"I'm not happy with your decision, Campbell. I had it all set up with Virgil for you to stay with him and Wanda."

"Much as that idea warms the cockles of my heart, Dad, I chose this option."

His father chuckled. "I know Wanda can be difficult…"

"She's a self-righteous harpy," Campbell said.

"But she knows how to make chicken soup," his father pointed out.

"I don't like chicken soup."

There was a pause during which Campbell figured his dad was preparing a lecture about common sense in times of adversity.

Thankfully Travis surprised him. "So, what arrangements have you made?" he asked. "Who's looking in on you?"

"Virgil found someone. I'll be fine."

"Someone with medical experience?"

Kitty Watley? Campbell wasn't one to draw upon stereotypes when evaluating an individual, but in this case he would bet money on the fact that he knew more about nursing than this quirky, out-of-luck, out-of-options lady did. And his expertise was limited to the variety pack of bandages in the tin under his sink.

"I assume so," he said. "Virgil thinks she

can handle the job. And besides, I have a home health person coming twice a week to clean the surgery incisions."

"That's good. Can the woman Virgil hired fix your meals?"

"He claims she's a great cook."

"Okay, I guess that will suffice. How are you feeling?"

Campbell pressed his hand over his chest. "Pretty good." *Lousy. Like I could spit hot nails.* "Still some pain, but it's not too bad."

"This is a mess, son. I can't locate your mother in South America or I'd demand that she come to Sorrel Gap and take care of you."

Playing host to his mother had all the makings of a nightmare. Campbell knew Vivian Parnell Oakes didn't respond well to demands. She and Travis had been forced to accept that fact three years after they married, and Vivian had run for the hills. At that time, the hills had been the Pyrenees, not the gentle rises of Sorrel Gap, North Carolina. It seemed Campbell and his father had both chose women who hated having their wings clipped.

"Don't worry about it, Dad," Campbell said. "Mom'll probably call me in the next few days, and I'll tell her what happened. But I don't need to ask for her help."

His father sighed. "You're better off not to

expect it, Camp. I wish I could have stayed longer."

"Hey, you were here after the accident. That's enough. I'm a big boy. I can take care of myself."

"I know you can, most of the time. Just keep this woman Virgil found on her toes. I know how you like things around your place—neat and orderly. Don't let her slack off and take advantage of you."

Campbell smiled to himself. He'd grown up under the strict but fair supervision of Travis Oakes. Now they both believed in the same motto. No slackers allowed. "Would I do that?"

"No, you wouldn't. I've got to run. I'll call you again in a couple of days. You know where you can reach me."

"I do, Dad." The last thing on Campbell's agenda was whining to his father. Besides, Fort Irwin, California, was a long way from the Saddle Top Motel. Campbell was on his own. And as bad as his situation was, he thought of Wanda and knew things could be worse.

He set the phone back on its cradle and reached across the sofa for his book. He'd just found his place and resumed reading when he heard a tap at his door.

"Hey, you in there?"

He laid the book on the coffee table and stared

at fingers wrapped around the partially open door. "I am," he said. "Where else would I be?"

The door swung open the rest of the way and banged against the wall, leaving a permanent mark on the new paint job. Adam Watley, his shorts reaching below his knees, sauntered inside. "Oh yeah, I guess you're stuck here even more than we are. At least we can walk away."

Campbell acknowledged the obvious conclusion with a frown.

"My mom sent me over to see if you have any soap larger than a bottle cap and maybe made in this century." To illustrate, he unwrapped a pint-size bar of motel soap, held the paper by a corner and let the crumbling contents of Cashmere Bouquet fall to the floor.

Campbell stared at the polished honey maple planks he'd recently refinished and imagined the kid pulverizing soap shavings into a gummy mess with his bulky sneakers. "In the bathroom," he said, pointing over his shoulder to the door to his right. "Under the sink. And clean up the mess you just made before you walk in it."

Satisfied for the moment when Adam sidestepped the soap, Campbell picked up his book and tried to reacquaint himself with the hero's dilemma. Trapped in a dank basement, his wrists handcuffed to a steam pipe and the bad guys just upstairs, the fictional cop's problems were worse than his own, but only barely.

The kid returned with a regular-sized bar of Dial and stood directly in front of the couch. Without waiting to be acknowledged, he blurted out, "Are you a neat freak?"

Campbell dropped the book to his lap. "What?"

"That cabinet in the bathroom. All the bottles are in a line, shortest to tallest. The towels are in rolls, for Pete's sake. It's like you're expecting the queen of England to stop by."

Campbell reminded himself to give the kid the benefit of the doubt for now. Maybe nobody had ever taught him basic manners. "No. I'm not expecting *anyone* in here for any reason. Got the message?"

Adam snorted through his nose. "Yeah, but it won't work. Mom's coming over to fix your lunch." He bounced the bar of Dial in his palm. "She just wanted to wash her hands first. Our room is disgusting."

"I'll tell housekeeping."

"Huh? We've actually got a maid?"

Campbell rolled his eyes.

"Oh. Funny." When Campbell started reading again, Adam turned toward the door, but stopped when he spied the fifty-two-inch TV in the middle of an oak entertainment center.

A baseball game was on the screen, the volume turned low. Adam squawked. Campbell looked up to see the kid's jaw drop. He backed up a couple of steps and plopped onto the sofa. "You've got cable!"

"No, I don't," Campbell said, wincing at the pain the kid's uninvited and inconsiderate movement had caused in his chest. "There's no cable out here. I've got a satellite dish."

"Even better!" His eyes lit up when he spotted the remote control on the table. "I want to be connected in our room!"

Campbell scowled at him. "They don't let juvenile offenders have luxuries like three hundred TV channels."

"Heck, if I was in prison I'd have a better TV in my cell than that crappy ol'—"

"Adam!" Kitty Watley burst into the room like an avenging angel and swooped over her son. "I just told you not ten minutes ago to stop complaining."

He shrugged. "I forgot."

"Apologize to Mr. Oakes."

"For what?"

"For expressing your opinions in such a vulgar way."

Campbell raised his eyebrows. "Actually I've been known to use worse language than that."

Like when I'm in a plane heading nose-down with fuel spraying in all directions.

A full thirty seconds passed before Adam responded to a nudge by his mother and mumbled, "Sorry."

"While you're being so humble," Campbell said, "get the dustpan and a whisk broom out of the closet and sweep up those soap crumbs. Maybe the next time you want to make a point you won't use visual effects."

Adam shuffled to the closet, and his mother took his place on the sofa. At least when she sat, she didn't send shock waves into Campbell's cracked ribs. But she did wiggle, and for some reason, that bothered Campbell more than the kid's unceremonious plopping. She placed her hand flat against her bare chest above the top of a tank-type shirt. "I'm so sorry, Mr. Oakes. Adam is high-spirited. He doesn't mean any harm, but…"

"Do you always apologize for your son?" Campbell said. "If so, it must take up a lot of your time."

"Well, there are days. Unfortunately Adam has had some bad influences on his life."

Typical cop-out for lack of discipline. "So you're using the wrong-crowd theory as a defense for the boy's behavior?"

Kitty's clear, disturbingly blue eyes locked

on to his. "It's more the wrong role model. But Adam won't cause you any trouble, I promise." She stood up and headed toward the kitchen. "I'll get your lunch now."

"You don't have to. I'm not hungry after all."

She stopped, turned and placed her hands on the waistband of her low-slung pants. "You've got to eat. Otherwise you won't get your strength back."

He turned a page in his book. "That, Miss Kitty, is up to a power much greater than the meager benefits of a bologna sandwich."

Confusion veiled her eyes for an instant. But then her foot started tapping in its ridiculously impractical sandal. "I told your uncle I would take care of you, and I intend to keep my word."

"Yeah, you've got to keep the hoodlum out of jail…"

Her eyes narrowed. She took in a sharp breath that seemed to raise her up a couple of inches. "However…" She drew the word out for several seconds. "I can only put food in front of you. I can't give you the good sense to eat it." She lifted her chin in a defiant gesture. "I guess either you were born with that or you weren't."

He stared at her, waiting for her to look away. She didn't, so he hitched one shoulder in what he knew was childish insolence. "Suit yourself."

As he watched her walk to the refrigerator, he

pondered the information she'd given him. What role model had the kid had in his life? Was Kitty talking about the boy's father? Was she married? If so, where was the man who should be taking care of this desperate pair? Was he going to show up at the Saddle Top Motel someday?

That was all he'd need. Campbell felt the first manifestation of unease coil like a spring in his gut. He didn't want to be in the middle of a domestic dispute, forced to defend this duo, not in the condition he was in. Then he remembered Virgil had referred to Kitty as "*Miss* Watley." That eliminated the husband possibility, if Virgil was right. But it didn't eliminate an ex-boyfriend one.

After she took a can from the cupboard and a package of lunch meat from the refrigerator, Kitty looked over her shoulder at him. It was the first time he realized he was still staring at her and that he probably shouldn't be.

"Is something wrong, Mr. Oakes?" she asked.

Truly he was gawking at her as if he'd been trapped in a mine shaft for a week and she was the sun. "Nothing's wrong," he barked at her. She lifted her eyebrows, waiting for a logical explanation. He certainly couldn't tell her that he'd been memorizing every curve under that shirt, so he improvised. "It's those clothes you're wearing. They're, uh, interesting to say the least."

That was a stupid thing to say. What did he know about women's clothes? Only that the hip-hugging pants and top that Kitty wore had to be the most unforgiving garments he'd ever seen on a female. If she'd had a blemish anywhere on her torso, he'd have seen the outline through that fabric. But the more he looked, the more he concluded that she was awfully pretty.

She grinned bashfully and turned her attention to heating something on the stove. "Thanks, Mr. Oakes. These clothes certainly aren't fashion statements, but they're comfortable."

Kitty Watley was strange. He'd expected her to blast him for what some women would have interpreted as a snide comment about her appearance. That's exactly what Diana would have done if, heaven forbid, there had ever been a reason for him to question her impeccable taste. And yet Kitty had taken it like a compliment.

Once again he found himself searching for the right words. "I wish you'd stop calling me 'Mr. Oakes,'" he finally said. "It makes me feel old, as well as lame."

She slathered something on two pieces of bread. "Okay. You're certainly not old, Campbell. And once your leg heals, you won't be lame, either."

If only the doctors were as confident, he

thought. "When you've got that food ready, you can leave it on the end table. Then you and the kid can take yours and go."

A few minutes later Kitty quietly set a tray on the table without disturbing his reading as her oblivious son had done. But this time it wouldn't have mattered, since Campbell hadn't done anything but stare at the pages as if they were blank. She brought him a glass of water and his pain pills and then took her own food and left with Adam, who had spent the past minutes zipping through the channels on his remote.

Almost as if he owed Kitty some consideration, Campbell forced himself to eat the cheese and bologna sandwich and, of all things, chicken soup.

When he finished eating, Campbell took his pills and watched a few minutes of the baseball game before shutting off the TV. He picked up his book, slammed it closed and set it down again. He glared at the useless leg, which prevented him from going outside in the cleansing mountain air and walking off the restlessness.

And then he opened the end table drawer and took out the half dozen postcards from Diana that for some stupid reason he'd saved over the past few months. He flipped through them, staring at the typical tourist photos again. The Piazza San Marco in Venice. The Place Royale in Bordeaux. The Grote Markt in Antwerp. Beautiful places that, at one time, he could have imagined visiting with Diana.

Once he finished reading, Campbell ripped the cards into shreds before realizing he'd have to pick up all the pieces from the floor.

He blamed Kitty Watley for this infuriating and completely uncharacteristic emotional outburst. Before this darn accident, when work occupied his days, he'd convinced himself that he was finally over Diana Matheson. Cool, sophisticated, boarding school–bred Diana, who'd knocked him for a loop the first time he saw her. He had adored her since the night she showed up at her father's estate, home from her European trip.

The day she agreed to become his wife had been the happiest of his life. He'd given her a ring and urged her to set a date. He was anxious to settle down with her, have a family. She kept putting him off, and she did it so cleverly he hardly noticed. Or maybe he just wasn't smart enough to read the signs.

Eventually Campbell realized that Diana would never be his. She'd never commit to a simple ex-military type like him, who worked for her father. To preserve what was left of his dignity, he told Diana goodbye. And then, weeks later, the postcards started to arrive, and

Campbell resented the heck out of the fact that Diana didn't want him but wouldn't let him go.

It wasn't Kitty's fault that her very female-ness sent Campbell spiraling down to that dark period after he'd packed his bags and left the Matheson estate. When he settled back in Sorrel Gap, he gave himself time and permission to think of Diana. He missed what he'd hoped they would have together with a deep ache that stole peace from his daylight hours and sleep from his nights. But he didn't regret his decision, any more than he regretted tearing up those postcards today. In Sorrel Gap he'd hoped to start over. But he wasn't doing such a bang-up job of it so far.

Kitty and Diana were nothing alike except that they were both women. Diana had everything she'd ever wanted. Kitty obviously survived on the barest essentials. Campbell had sworn off all women for now, but especially rich, spoiled ones who would choose money and possessions over everything else.

The phone rang again, jolting Campbell from his pathetic self-pity. He picked it up. "Hello."

"It's Virgil. Just wanted you to know I got the phone turned on in unit six so you can reach Kitty when you need her. Here's the number…"

Campbell scribbled it down on a pad, though he wasn't likely to use it. He was a long way from admitting that he needed anyone.

CHAPTER FIVE

"I DON'T LIKE HIM," Adam called from the shower where he was supposed to be scrubbing the tiles with the contents of an old can of Comet.

Kitty fluttered a clean sheet over a newly laundered mattress pad. She breathed deeply, grateful the linens smelled as promised on the bottle—*mountain fresh*. "Why don't you like him?"

"He's grouchy."

"A little, maybe." She tucked the ends of the sheet between the mattress and box spring. "But mostly I think he's sad."

Adam's disparaging snort was amplified by the tile walls. "What's he got to be sad about? He's got a satellite dish."

"I don't know, but I think it's something more than the plane crash. Although that would be enough."

Adam popped out of the bathroom. "He should have our problems. Then he'd have a reason to mope."

"Be patient. We should all try to get along for the time we have to be here."

Adam frowned at his mildew-stained sponge. "Yeah. I guess there's no escape from Motel Psycho, is there?" He gave Kitty a ghoulish look and made stabbing gestures with his free hand. "Just be careful when you take a shower, Mom."

"Never mind," she said, genuinely smiling for the first time that day. "If you're done in there, come help make the beds."

When they were finished, Adam left for Campbell's place to see if Wanda had stocked potato chips. Kitty sat on the worn but fresh spread and picked up the telephone. A dial tone! Things were definitely looking up even if her contact with the outside world was an antiquated gold princess phone. She punched in Bette's number and nearly cried with relief when her mother's cousin answered.

"You're going to need some money," Bette said after hearing about Kitty's plight. "I can send you a check."

Kitty had known she could count on her relative, but it was reassuring to hear that trust in Bette's words.

"If you could spare a hundred dollars I would appreciate it," Kitty said. "And I'll pay you back. I promise I will."

"I know you will, Kitty. I'm not worried. You've

got to have some cash. But is that enough? What if Adam or you get sick? You need money for emergencies."

Kitty had thought of that herself and knew that her dwindling stash of money wouldn't go far.

"Give me an address," Bette said. "I'll put a check for double that amount in today's mail."

Kitty opened a desk drawer, pushed a few yellowed papers around and searched for something that had the motel's contact information on it. "Thank goodness," she said when she uncovered a notepad with the logo of the man-on-the-moon sign on top. She gave Bette the address, hoping a letter would reach her despite the remote location of the motel. "Thanks, Bette," she said. "I won't use the money if I don't have to. Our expenses will be paid while we live here..."

"That's another thing, Kitty," Bette said. "What kind of place is this? What is that wounded man like? If you have any reservations about this arrangement, I can drive down and get you. Together maybe we can persuade the sheriff to let Adam off the hook."

Kitty gripped the telephone and resisted the urge to accept Bette's offer. It would be so much easier for her if she just said yes and let Bette come to their aid. But she drew a deep breath and responded the way she knew she should, the way a responsible parent would. "The place is okay," she said, looking around at the dingy walls. "And Mr. Oakes has been decent to us. Plus, Adam needs to make amends for what he did. We'll be fine," she added. "I'll call you once a week to let you know how we're doing. This is just a delay, not a change in plans. And please, Bette, if Daddy calls you…"

"He already has called, Kitty, and I told him I haven't heard from you."

"Did he believe you?"

"I think so. But you really must call Esmeralda occasionally to tell her you're all right. Despite the way you feel about your father, it would be cruel not to let someone in the household know that you and Adam are well."

"I'll call her," Kitty said. "Thanks for everything."

"Stay well, dear, and please remember to call. I'll be worried if you don't."

Kitty hung up the phone. After talking to Bette she was even more determined to follow through on her pledge to Sheriff Oakes for Adam's sake. But it was nice to know she had a backup plan.

THE SECURITY DEVICE at the entrance to Galloway property sent a warning to the house that

someone had come in the drive. At the sound
of the buzzer, Owen got up from the recliner
where he'd been vacantly watching a golf match
on television for the past fifteen minutes. He
wasn't expecting anyone. His aide, Terry, was
thirty feet away in the home office still making
calls from the list of friends, relatives and employees of Galloway Groves the two men had
comprised earlier in the day. And Esmeralda
was off to church for the second time to pray
for the family.

Hopeful that Kitty had returned with his
grandson, while at the same time struggling to
tamp the anger building inside him at his daughter's utter lack of concern, Owen hurried to the
kitchen window that looked out on the driveway. Recognizing the car, he prepared himself
for Billie's entrance. He'd left her a message
earlier about Kitty's latest escapade, but with
Billie, a man never knew what to expect.

Terry appeared in the doorway. "Who is it,
boss?"

"Only Billie."

Terry disappeared back to the office as Billie Bonneville, wearing a colorful long skirt
and peasant top swept in the back door. His
longtime "dance partner," as he euphemisti-
cally called her, walked by him and deposited
a take-out carton on the kitchen table.

He eyed the box while she returned to kiss him on the cheek. "What's in there?" he asked.

"Pulled pork barbecue and coleslaw," she said in the honey-toned drawl of a woman born to Southern aristocracy and raised in mint-julep comfort.

Normally just the sound of that voice whispering in his ear could incite Owen to acts other men his age only dreamed of. Right now he didn't know if Billie's interference in his misery would be helpful or more stressful. She had an uncanny way of finding him to blame for some of the fixes he got into, and he didn't want to hear those theories today. "I'm not hungry," he said.

She tucked a strand of platinum hair behind an ear decorated with a spangled hoop and smiled. "It's nearly five o'clock, darlin'. I'll bet you haven't eaten a thing all day."

He walked out of the kitchen and through the dining room. She followed him to the living room, where he'd left a glass filled with three fingers of bourbon. He lifted the glass from an end table in a mock toast. "I'm getting my nutrients." In defiance of the look of exasperation on her face, he took a long swallow, just one of many he'd taken this Sunday.

She settled into a chair and fluffed the folds of her skirt around her hips. Owen had to admire her style, even today. Some women who carried a little extra weight tried to hide it. Not Billie. She flaunted every gram.

There had been a time when Owen believed if Billie didn't accept his proposal of marriage, he would die an incomplete man. She'd told him too many times that she never once regretted her decision to remain single for her entire life. She'd turned down the first suitor who asked her daddy for her hand when she was only seventeen. Since then, for the next forty years, she'd rejected countless others, including Owen Galloway. Now he accepted her as he had to, no strings but with her gift of absolute loyalty, though he'd still marry her in a heartbeat.

"I take it you haven't heard from Kitty," she said when he'd finally taken the chair across from her.

"No. And Terry and I have called nearly everyone we can think of. Plus the airlines and rental car agencies."

"What about Greyhound? Maybe she and Adam took a bus."

Owen almost laughed out loud. "Katherine Galloway on a bus? Come on, Billie, you can do better than that."

She shrugged. "It's something I might do if I wanted to fly under the radar."

Owen thought a moment and then hollered

toward the office door, "Terry, check the bus lines!"

"Yes, sir."

Billie went to the bar and fixed herself a gin and tonic. When she returned she said, "Owen, you're going to worry yourself sick."

"What else would you have me do? Kit's taken the boy and left me with only a ridiculous note about her and Adam going on a vacation. No mention of where they've gone. The BMW's in the garage. Her cell phone's been turned off." He sighed heavily. "She didn't even tell Esmeralda where she was heading."

"Still, maybe you're getting excited over nothing. Maybe she is on a vacation, and she'll be back in a couple of days."

"Hogwash," Owen said. "Kit's run away before. She's always been unstable."

"I don't agree," Billie said. "In my opinion Kitty is uninspired."

Owen set his glass down so hard that liquid sloshed over the side. "What kind of new age mumbo jumbo is that, Billie? Since she came back from that disastrous marriage, Kit has had enough vacations and lavish shopping trips to inspire herself for the rest of her life." He looked down at the floor. "No. Kit's doing this to punish me, and meanwhile, I've given her everything…"

"But maybe not what she needs," Billie said softly.

Owen half stood, ready to pace off his anger, and Billie motioned him back into the chair with a delicate wave of her hand. "You act as if Kitty is purposely trying to ruin your time on earth," she said.

"That's exactly what she's doing," Owen said. "Only she isn't content to ruin my life and her own life—again! This time she's taking Adam down with her, and I can't let that happen. I have resources and I intend to use them."

Billie leaned forward. "Darlin', why don't you eat your dinner and give this situation a couple of days before you sic the hounds on Kitty? Let her think this out…"

"Darn it, Billie, if you're not on my side, you can leave this house. I don't need your advice on how to run my family."

She stood and glared down at him, and for a moment he considered that he'd gone too far. No one bullied Billie Bonneville, the only child of circuit court judge Royal Bonneville, who'd died and left her that fine brick house in the center of town and all the money she'd ever need. But too bad, Owen thought. She didn't understand what he was going through.

"Fine," she said, heading for the back entrance. "I'm going. You can rot in your self-pity and your obsession over Adam for all I care."

He rose from the chair. "Obsession? I'm all the stability that boy has in his life."

Owen didn't know if she heard him. Without another word she left the house with only the slamming of the back door to mark her exit.

Owen sat in his chair and drained the last of the bourbon from his glass. The liquor mellowed him, made him think about what he'd just done.

After a few minutes Terry came in the living room. "Nothing from the bus lines," he said. "What happened? Where's Billie?"

"She had to leave."

"Oh. I'm going to run out for supper. You want anything?"

"No. There's barbecue on the table. You're welcome to it."

"Thanks." Terry went into the kitchen. A few seconds later he called out, "Boss, you probably should see this."

Owen walked to the door and looked down. Pulled pork and barbecue sauce swirled together with a sloppy mess of pungent coleslaw in the center of the kitchen floor. He exhaled a deep breath. "Darn that woman."

Terry yanked about a hundred sheets of paper towels from the roll as Owen went to the wall phone. He dialed a familiar number. "Paulette? Owen Galloway. I know it's Sunday, but I need a rush order." He paused while the town florist questioned him.

"Yes, today," he said. "And when I want your opinion, I'll ask for it. Just send two dozen roses over to the Bonneville house right away."

SHORTLY AFTER FIVE, just when Sheriff Oakes had promised, an official SUV pulled into the Saddle Top Motel. "I think our things are here," Kitty said to Adam, who had reluctantly settled down to watch the green television after returning from Campbell's with a soda and potato chips.

He punched the power switch, leaving a gold bead of light in the center of the picture tube. "At least now I can read my comic books instead of watching this stupid TV," he said. "If we're going to be here awhile, we should get a new one. Why don't you tell Campbell to pony up for it?"

"Right. Like I have bargaining power with Campbell." Kitty nudged him outside. "Forget about the television. You can help unload our stuff."

A tall man with a fair complexion who was wearing a uniform similar to Virgil Oakes's got out of the SUV and touched the brim of his hat as a greeting. "You must be Kitty," he said.

"That's right. You're Sheriff Oakes's deputy?"

"Tommy Gibbs." He walked around to the back of the vehicle and opened the cargo door. "I'll bet you're anxious to get your hands on what's in here."

Kitty and Adam stepped off the porch and looked inside the SUV. When she saw her belongings, clean clothes, makeup and the sewing machine, Kitty released a sigh of relief. "You have no idea, Deputy."

Adam started to slide the trunk to the rear of the cargo area. "All my comic books had better be in here, Mom. You said you packed them."

"I didn't pack *all* of them, Adam. I only brought one trunk."

"Did you look inside?" he asked Deputy Gibbs.

"Are you afraid somebody took your comics?" The deputy gave him a tilted grin that showed a line of crooked teeth. "There's practically no crime in Sorrel Gap." Then, smiling at Kitty, he added, "Until today, that is." He handed Adam a suitcase. "Here, kid, take this. You'll need help with the trunk."

Adam lugged the bag across the gravel lot to their room.

Gibbs carried the sewing machine to the door, and Kitty felt as if she'd been reunited with an old friend. Her future might well depend on the elaborate Singer. It was equipped with all the bells and whistles she'd used to create many of her own clothes and the features she planned to use to sew masterpieces of design. The model had cost her nearly two weeks' pay when she'd purchased it last year. But now she knew every dial and lever and could operate it in the dark if she had to.

"Hey, Mom," Adam called from inside. "We need to go to a comics store. I've got to get the next issue of Wolverine. You promised, remember?"

"That was before you left the truck unlocked in Georgia," Kitty said. She gave Tommy Gibbs a withering look. "I wish he'd stolen a dollar-and-ninety-five-cent comic book instead of fifteen hundred dollars' worth of electronics. I'm sure they had Wolverine at the Value-Rite and I could have covered that debt."

The deputy hitched one shoulder and said, "That's kids for you." He gave her another grin. "Seems like your boy could use a strong male role model in his life. I might be persuaded to volunteer."

Just as Kitty was deciding whether the deputy was flirting with her, she glanced toward the office where Campbell was swaying on his crutches at the entrance. She shielded her eyes against the late-afternoon sun and peered at him. His face was flushed, indicating he'd experienced a slow and painful journey across the lobby to the door. "Should you be up walking around?" she called to him.

"According to the doctors I shouldn't be, but anybody'd be curious about all the racket out here."

Tommy put down one of the boxes of fabric he'd been carrying and strode toward the porch. "Hey, how ya doin', Camp? That was some kind of bad luck with the plane." He stared at Kitty as she walked up behind him. "But you got some good help out here, I see." He removed his hat, wiped his shirtsleeve over his brow and gave her one more boyish grin. "If you need anything, just give me a call…"

"We won't," Campbell said.

Kitty skirted around Tommy to reach Campbell and offer her assistance, but stepped back when he scowled. "For heaven's sake," she said. "You're obviously in pain. The deputy and I can help you back inside."

"I don't need any help," Campbell said in that bristly tone Kitty was getting used to. "Besides, I wouldn't want to keep the deputy from performing his duty."

Refusing to react to Campbell's sarcasm, Kitty managed a tight smile. "You probably want some dinner. Just let me get my things inside. As soon as I have a shower, I'll be right over."

A burst of laughter from Tommy Gibbs drew Kitty's attention to the SUV. Tommy pointed at Adam. "Take a look at the superhero over there. Looks like your son is showing off his muscles."

Lines of exertion pinched Adam's face. He had somehow dragged Kitty's antique trunk full of their possessions to the very edge of the vehicle, and now her second-most valued possession was teetering dangerously. She looked at Campbell and back at Adam trying to decide which situation needed her most. The endangered antique won.

"Don't drop it, Adam," she hollered, flashing Campbell a grimace of apology as she ran to save the trunk. He'd gotten himself out here, so he'd just have to manage to get back inside the same way.

INEXPLICABLE FRUSTRATION SIMMERED inside Campbell. Heck, he'd known the Gibbs family forever, had gone to high school with Tommy's older brother, and the two athletes had been rivals. And now here was little Tommy, watching Kitty as if she was the newest addition to the Sorrel Gap Diner's menu. Tommy had to be ten years younger than Kitty, but that didn't seem to stop him from staring at her. "Seems to me you'd be more help to the lady if you'd actually move your butt off the porch," Campbell said in the same sarcastic tone that had become second nature lately.

Gibbs moved toward Kitty. "You know something, you're right, Camp. I'm more than willing to help her out, today or any day."

Campbell frowned. "Wouldn't you score more points with someone nearer your own age, kid?"

Gibbs grinned. "I don't let age limit my opportunities, Camp. You have to admit, she's a nice-looking lady." Campbell hobbled a couple of steps back toward the door. He wasn't about to agree with Tommy, but neither was he willing to flee the scene.

The deputy shook his head slowly and began enumerating on his fingers. "I know the stories about you, Campbell. You're one lucky guy."

Campbell looked down at his splint. "Yeah, Gibbs. Lucky."

"Let's check out the facts which everybody in this town seems to talk about," Gibbs said. "You get mononucleosis in high school and have to drop out of football. Everyone thinks, 'Poor Campbell. Won't get no scholarship now.' And then the miracle boy takes the basketball team to the state finals and the Air Force Academy is suddenly knocking on your door."

Campbell scowled but couldn't think of a comeback. So far Tommy had his facts straight.

The deputy continued. "You go off to the Iraq war where they assign you a cushy flyboy detail and you come home to a job piloting the Learjet of one of the richest men in North Carolina."

Campbell opened his mouth to remind Tommy that during the conflict he'd also shared space with scorpions while every day he wondered if he was going to be shot down over scorching desert sand.

Unfortunately Tommy wasn't finished. "And then…and this is the best one of all. You crash your own plane, the one you paid for with Matheson money, and I start to think maybe your bubble might have finally burst." He pinched his lower lip with his thumb and forefinger as he returned his full attention to Kitty. "But I was wrong. You end up with a sweet nurse, with an even sweeter smile."

Anger clawed inside Campbell and struggled with a taped chest and a three-foot splint to find an outlet. Part of that anger came from the fact that he'd been telling himself all afternoon that he would never be attracted to Kitty. She was too scrawny. Her eyes, though big and blue as the sky, lacked the hint of a sparkle. And her hair defied description. Women's hair ought to be soft and silky, not a nest of spikes that looked like a haystack after a windstorm.

So it irked him that he resented Tommy Gibbs showing appreciation for a woman's attributes that Campbell refused to acknowledge in the first place. He didn't need to be thinking of Kitty as anything other than a temporary annoyance he had to put up with to avoid an even bigger annoyance, Wanda Oakes. So he said something purely irrational and purely primitive male. "Just finish your job, Tommy."

Tommy tugged on his hat and sauntered away from Campbell with the confidence of a boxer who'd just found out his opponent had ten broken fingers. "Thanks for the advice, Camp. I will do just that. And do me a favor, okay? Let me know if she mentions me."

Campbell exhaled a long breath. "You know why she's here, Tommy. I don't think she came to Sorrel Gap looking for romance."

"A guy can hope," Tommy said.

Campbell stayed on the porch, determined to wait until Tommy was back in his SUV and headed toward town.

"My makeup case!"

Both men instantly focused on Kitty. She'd grabbed a bag Tommy had pulled from his vehicle and clutched it to her chest. "Shampoo. Hair gel. Body splash."

She waved at Campbell before she went in the door of her room. "I'll be over in about an hour to fix your dinner," she called, apparently oblivious to Tommy's attentions.

Campbell groaned. Dinner. And another lecture most likely. He only hoped that once Deputy Gibbs left the Saddle Top, he'd calm down enough to face another one of Kitty's meals. But the way he was feeling now, all he could look forward to was a raging case of indigestion.

CHAPTER SIX

"You want me to put my clothes in that creepy old dresser?"

"Of course," Kitty said. "You take the drawers on the left. I lined each one with clean fabric."

From the bathroom, she heard a drawer slide open and Adam speaking, "Oh, great. I got the flowered stuff."

She emerged from the bathroom and ran her hands down the hip-hugging pants printed with quirky tiki huts. "Fuji Funk" she'd planned to call the original line when she revealed it to the public.

She stood quietly, watching her son put his clothes in the drawers. He didn't look at her, his concentration intent on his task. After a few minutes during which he rearranged the same bunch of shorts several times, she became suspicious and walked toward him. "Why are you making such a big deal of putting clothes away?" she asked him.

He stared at her, his eyes narrowing. "I'm not.

I'm finally doing what you ask, and you jump all over me."

"I didn't jump on you." She sat on the edge of the bed. "What's going on?"

He slammed the drawer shut and walked to the window. "What's with this radar you've got all of a sudden? I feel like I'm under a microscope."

"I'm sorry. It's just not like you to be so meticulous with a chore. You want to talk about it?"

"Sure. You've brought me to Podunk and it sucks. You happy?"

She smiled. "Yeah, I'm delighted with how this whole day has gone. It's exactly what I wanted to happen to us."

He let out a long breath and then turned around to face her. "While you were in the shower, I called Grandpa."

"What?" She stood up, her heart racing. "Oh, Adam. I asked you not to."

"Don't have a cow. I disconnected before it rang."

"You did?"

"I couldn't do it. Yet," he added. "You actually did come up with a plan like you said earlier. The plan basically stinks, but I guess I can give you more time, especially since I'm partly responsible for how things turned out."

She could have argued the obvious differences in their interpretation of events, but didn't. "Thanks."

"But you know I can call him any time I want. From here or Value-Rite. Any number of places."

"Yes, I know you can."

"But I'll wait awhile, see what happens."

"I appreciate that." She stood and went to the full-length mirror on the door, pretending to examine her outfit. Inside, her stomach was turning over. "We'll be fine, you know, if we stick together."

Adam stuffed the last of his T-shirts into a drawer. "You ready to feed the beast?"

He hadn't argued with her last statement, so at least she felt she could trust him not to call home, for now anyway. "In a minute." She grabbed a towel and buff-dried her short hair. Then she upended a bottle of gel, squeezed a small amount of the contents into her palms and spread the cool, slick substance through her hair. She plucked damp strands into a haphazard arrangement.

"Grandpa says you look like a punk rocker with your hair that way," Adam commented.

"Shows you what Grandpa knows. This happens to be a very trendy style."

"Whatever. But you did look punky that one time, when your hair was pink on the ends."

"Well, maybe a little, back then." Her life had been on a serious downward spiral six years ago. But she'd learned that she couldn't gain Owen's respect by trying to scare him to death with hair paint and body piercing. All she accomplished was getting his attention in a negative way. At the time, that seemed better than nothing.

"Grandpa told me he didn't know how he was going to get anybody to marry you with that ugly ol' pink hair."

Owen had at least narrowed his matrimonial hopes to just one guy, the incomparable Terry Spenser. Now Kitty only had one potential groom bullet to dodge. "I guarantee you, Adam," she said, "I'd never have married anyone associated with Grandpa's good-ol'-boy buddies. I'm glad my hair was pink. And if Grandpa doesn't quit trying to marry me off to Terry, I may dye it blue."

Adam shrugged. "Terry's not so bad. Grandpa says you need a man like him, one who is responsible. And he's got a way cool wave runner."

"I don't need a man to teach me responsibility," she said.

"Well, you gotta get married sometime," Adam said. "I can't take care of you the rest of my life. I've got my own romantic future to think of."

Kitty turned away from the mirror. "You? What sort of woman are you considering?"

Adam plumped a pillow and sat back against the headboard. "I don't know. Maybe one of the waitresses at the drive-in where Grandpa takes me."

Kitty's jaw dropped. "You mean one of those girls in the short skirts and halter tops?"

"Yeah, and roller skates. What's wrong with that?"

Calm down, Kitty. Adam is twelve years old. He stopped eating Happy Meals a long time ago. Realizing her son was growing up made Kitty sad and angry at the same time, especially since Owen was educating her son into manhood in his own image. Until yesterday, Kitty hadn't been able to defend every sneaky trick her father pulled in his efforts to "make a Galloway man" of her child.

She picked up a pile of Adam's socks and put them in a drawer. "In the first place, neither Grandpa nor anyone else can pick out a woman for you. When you find a nice girl you're interested in, you date her, show her respect and then perhaps the two of you choose each other."

Adam stared at her. "Fine. But I'm going to choose a waitress on roller skates."

Kitty smiled to herself and looked at her

watch. "Let's go over to Campbell's. You must be starving and I know he must be."

Adam dropped his portable game system into the pocket of his baggy shorts. "Yeah. The only thing left in his snack cupboard is a bag of pork rinds. I'll puke if I eat those."

They walked down to the lobby and went to the door of Campbell's apartment. "We're here," Kitty announced cheerfully as she tapped on the door.

The brief response lacked cordiality. "Funny thing, so am I."

"He still sounds grouchy," Adam commented.

Kitty slowly pushed the door open. "Of course he is," she whispered. "You don't think his injuries have healed in a few hours, do you?"

Campbell was stretched out on the sofa with one pillow under his shoulders and another supporting his injured leg. His other leg was bent at the knee so his foot reached the floor. Goodness, he was an impressive man, Kitty observed once again. When she'd been in the apartment earlier, she'd thought the sofa was oversize. Now, with Campbell's large frame sprawled over the three cushions, it almost seemed minuscule.

He still wore the Charlotte basketball team T-shirt, and Kitty tried not to stare. But she couldn't help admiring the way the jersey stretched over his solid upper body. Campbell didn't have the sculpted muscular physique of the overbuffed men in Richland who worked out so they could boast at the pool hall about how many pounds they could bench-press. Campbell's priorities were obviously different. He probably exercised for good health and cardio fitness. His wasn't a perfect body, but it was a good one. Kitty felt a sudden burst of heat in her face when she realized she was analyzing Campbell as if he were an art project.

A TV reporter droned softly in the background. Campbell picked up the remote and looked at Adam, who was staring down at him with a crestfallen expression. "What's the matter with you?"

"You're watching the news again. Can't I turn on something good? You get the TV all the time."

"Probably because it's *my* TV," Campbell said, but he tossed the remote to Adam anyway. "If it'll stop you from pouting, change the channel, but keep the volume low."

"Cool." Adam sat cross-legged on the floor and began channel surfing. "After supper can I go on your computer?"

Kitty stopped on her way to the kitchen area. "No, Adam. I don't want you on the computer."

He gave her his most exasperated frown. "Just to play games, Mom. Don't get all excited."

She continued to the kitchen. "Oh. Well, then, it's up to Campbell."

"I don't have any games downloaded," Campbell said.

Adam leaned back against the sofa. "Figures. I can download some."

Campbell shrugged. "I suppose you could if you know what you're doing."

"Your friend is really nice," Kitty said as she poked around the freezer.

Campbell twisted so he could see her. "What friend?"

"The deputy. He said you've been friends with his family for years."

"Don't believe everything you hear." He narrowed his eyes and stared at her pants. "Are we having a pig roast for supper?"

"What do you mean?" She followed his gaze in an effort to interpret his question. She tried not to react to what seemed an obvious insult. "These are tiki huts." She walked over to him and set her chunky-looking sandal on the sofa next to his waist. "My own design."

He half grinned. "Pig roast it is, then."

"You don't have to be rude. If you don't like the material, it hardly matters to me. But I'll have you know this is polyester silk. That's why it shimmers. It cost me almost a half week's salary to have a screen-print guy make a sample."

"Yeah? What kind of work did you do?"

She took a few seconds to think of an evasive answer. "Clerical stuff mostly."

"Oh." He scowled. "Maybe you should have used your paycheck to get a better truck."

"Look…"

He immediately raised his hands. "Hey, forget it, okay? What do I know about ladies' pants anyway?"

She forced a smile, knowing he was humoring her. "I have a half bolt left. I'll make you a shirt out of it."

"I'll let you know." He crossed his arms on his chest and turned his attention to the TV, where a *Simpsons* episode was playing. "So, what are we really having for supper?"

KITTY WARMED UP a stew Wanda had left in the refrigerator and cut up some tomatoes and cucumbers for a salad. Campbell didn't ask her and Adam to leave when the food was ready as he'd done earlier. The hoodlum was enjoying the heck out of a *Simpsons* marathon, and was behaving himself. Halfway through a heaping bowl of Wanda's acceptable stew, however, Campbell decided it would have been wiser if he had asked them to go. He hadn't been able to concentrate on anything but Kitty, especially since she was decked out in that iridescent fabric that stretched perfectly over her hips and a T-shirt that fit her much too well.

He'd never been a guy to notice what a woman wore. Even with Diana, who always looked as if she'd stepped out of a fashion magazine, he was only aware of whether she had on pants or a skirt, or a drop-dead dress. He did notice certain factors about women's outfits, though, like how the clothes fit and what attributes they showed off, but he figured all guys had radar about the interesting stuff.

Later, while Adam fought computer-generated villains, Kitty washed the dishes and stacked them in a creative mountain of china, sort of as if she was playing pickup sticks with his dishes. If Campbell had done the chore, he would have dried them all and put them away in the cupboard where they belonged, not left them to air-dry. On second thought, he would have made a perfectly capable twelve-year-old boy handle the job.

She hung the damp dishrag over the sink divider. "Can I do anything else for you, Campbell?" she asked. "Bring you your medications?"

"Never mind. They're on the nightstand. I'll take them later."

"I'll just turn down your bed, then."

"You can leave a chocolate on the pillow while you're at it." He regretted the sarcasm the minute he said it and avoided looking at her. It wasn't like Campbell to act this way. He had been raised in Travis Oakes's atmosphere of military correctness, which, where women were concerned, approached an almost courtly reverence. So he didn't understand why Kitty's fawning over him made him behave like such a lout. She was only fulfilling her forced labor agreement. Maybe it was because Campbell couldn't get past the realization that he actually needed someone to wait on him—even someone like this scrawny, spiky-headed woman. Or maybe it was because he hadn't been around a woman in months, and he'd had his heart shredded by the last one.

"I can see there's nothing else you need," she said. "I'll be back first thing in the morning."

"There is one thing…"

"What?" She almost sounded hopeful.

He looked at Adam who was staring at the computer monitor as if he were trying to burn the pure, undiluted colors on his retinas.

Finally becoming aware that he was the object of Campbell's regard, Adam said, "You want something from me?"

Campbell nodded toward the plastic shower chair near the bathroom door—one of the medical necessities the hospital had sent home with him. "You can set that thing in the bathtub."

Kitty scurried to the chair. "I'll get it."

Campbell held up his hand. "Let your son do it. I asked him."

Adam shuffled to the chair with the enthusiasm of a kid being led empty-handed from a candy store. He carried the appliance into the bathroom.

"Anything else?" Kitty asked. "Do you need help…" She stopped the flow of words, but not the blush that crested her cheekbones.

"Do I need help with my shower?" Campbell finished for her.

"No. Well, if you need…"

"I don't need a nursemaid, Kitty. I can take my medicine and my shower."

She looked relieved, and for some inexplicable reason, he felt a bit disappointed.

"Well, good," she said. "I'll see you in the morning." She went toward the lobby but turned around before going out. "Do you want me to lock the door?"

Campbell darted a glance at Adam. "I don't see the point. The only outlaw in Sorrel Gap is right here under my nose. And I don't think he can carry that television by himself."

Adam's face tightened into a pucker. "You're funny as a crutch, you know that, Campbell?"

"Yeah, I know it." He nodded at his own crutch leaning against the sofa. "And I'm just the guy who can see the fun in one of these. But get used to my sense of humor, Adam, because as I understand it, my only function around here for the next few weeks is to watch that you don't get into any more trouble. If part of your rehabilitation is having to endure my jokes, that's a bonus for me."

He glanced at Kitty who was waiting by the door. A subtle smile curved her lips, and for some reason, that pleased him. Kitty Watley's smile was kind of nice.

ADAM LEAPED DOWN to the parking lot when they left the lobby and scooped up a handful of gravel. With each plodding step he took toward unit number six, he hurled a few pebbles into the night. "I've changed my mind," he said to Kitty when they were near their own door. "That guy's not just grouchy. He's nuts."

Kitty stopped and rested her forearms on the porch rail. "I don't think so. He's independent and wants to stay that way despite a really tough break. I like that about him." *Maybe because I'm finally trying to be that way, too.*

"Great," Adam said. "So I say we leave him alone and get the heck out of here."

She smiled at her son before turning her attention to tiny lights that blinked over the parking lot, some far away, some close enough to touch. "Look, Adam," she said. "Fireflies. Dozens of them."

He actually came up beside her and watched the show. "They're cool, I guess. You don't see very many in Florida."

"There are probably lots of creatures in these mountains that you and I don't know about—animals that love being closer to the sky than the sea." She looked down the walkway to where Campbell lived. Tiny insects circled the yellow glow of a bare overhead bulb in the breezeway. "I wonder if Campbell likes living in the mountains," she said mostly to herself.

Adam grunted. "I don't think he likes anything."

She thought of Campbell's military background, his job as a pilot and most recently his accident. "He must like challenging the sky," she said. Considering her own fear of flying, she found something to admire about a man who should have been born with wings.

CHAPTER SEVEN

CAMPBELL CRUSHED HIS PILLOW over his face to
block the sound coming from outside his apartment. Still the gentle tapping continued. He
tried to roll over, but his efforts were thwarted
by the cumbersome weight on his leg, which he
forgot about only during a few precious hours
of drug-induced sleep each night.

"Campbell? Are you awake?"

How could anyone manage such a cheerful
voice this early in the morning?

He lifted the end of the pillow so one eye
could venture a peek into the room. There was
sunlight, all right. It had slipped through the
curtains he'd neglected to close all the way the
night before.

"I really need to come in, Campbell," came
the persistent voice of Kitty Watley. "I have to
make sure you're okay."

"I'm fine," he hollered, figuring the announce-
ment wouldn't stop her. *Truly I may never be
fine again*, he thought, *and certainly not if well-*

meaning people don't let me deal with the after-math of my screwed-up life on my own terms.

Yet this was the third morning that Kitty had wakened him with a disposition she pretended was as sunny as the light in the morning sky. He suspected her good humor at 7:00 a.m. was as artificial as her professed concern for his welfare, which he knew was the result of being trapped in Virgil Oakes's web of judicial bargaining power.

He didn't say any of that, however. What good would it do? Kitty and the outlaw weren't going to leave. She'd stuck this out for three whole days, enduring his dour outlook and even a visit from an overbearing Wanda when she restocked the pantry. Resigned to his caretaker's infernal optimism, he tossed the pillow onto the floor beside the bed, covered his eyes with his arm and said, "Yeah, I'm awake. Come on in."

A breeze swept from the lobby when she opened the door. "Adam's still sleeping," she said, as if he would need to know that. "It's a beautiful morning." She walked to his window, and with a grinding swish of hardware that told him she hadn't bothered to use the proper draw cords, she pushed the drapes all the way open.

"I know you don't lock your door," she said, "but I hate to come in without knocking."

He was tempted to peek over his arm to see

what she was doing, and wearing, but he didn't want to appear overly interested. Fortunately, or unfortunately for his meticulous living space, he didn't have to look. Kitty made enough noise in the kitchen to identify her every move. *Thud.* She shut the cupboard door. *Bang.* She slammed a drawer closed. *Clunk, clunk.* She put two mugs on the tiled countertop. Then he was stumped. He couldn't identify a sound like finely sifted gravel hitting a hard surface, followed by Kitty's mild oath, "Oh, shoot."

Succumbing to curiosity, Campbell raised his head. His bag of coffee lay sideways on the counter. Half the dark-roasted contents were scattered across his immaculate floor in front of the sink. Kitty stared at it. "Sorry. The bag slipped out of my hand."

She soaked a dish towel under the faucet and then swiped the sodden lump over the spill. "There. All cleaned up."

Right. Thank goodness he didn't have mice in his apartment or they would be climbing the walls on a caffeine buzz by noon.

"You could have waited until I called you," Campbell said.

She absently passed her hand over that indefinable hair and said, "What?"

"I'm just saying that you know I have the phone number to unit six. From now on, why don't I just call you when I need you? That way you don't have to inconvenience yourself by coming over here at the crack of dawn." He emphasized the last three words.

"It's not an inconvenience. I have to come over this early. You need your medications on time, and this is where the coffee is." She shot him a satisfied grin. "I'm an early riser."

The rest of the coffee procedure went fairly well, and soon the rich scent of Columbian brew permeated the apartment. And made Campbell acutely aware of personal needs that hadn't been tended to. He sat up and lowered his healthy leg to the floor. Pain shot through his chest as it always did until he'd had his medicine. He stayed still for a moment, exhaling a long breath while the pain subsided. Then using his hands, he moved the leg in the splint to the edge of the mattress.

Kitty was at his side immediately, bending over him. "Here, let me help."

Suddenly it wasn't coffee he smelled. It was something lighter, sweeter, flowery. And it came from Kitty's neck, or perhaps from behind her ears, or maybe from between... He shut his eyes and tried not to concentrate on the scent, or the spot where it originated. No use. Mountain laurel, or something close. What little he knew about flowers was lost somewhere in a vague memory from his childhood and the very real image of the present.

A cool hand curled over the strap of his undershirt. Fingertips pressed against the bare flesh of his shoulder. His eyes snapped open, and he drew in an audible gasp of air. "I don't need any help," he ground out. "I can make it to the bathroom."

She removed her hand and stood straight but stayed close, as if she didn't believe him. His eyes connected with hers and what he noticed in them trapped his next breath in his chest. He saw unexpected concern, not grudging servitude, not even legal obligation.

Could he be wrong about her? Was the artificiality he'd attributed to her only the outlandish attire and the crazy hair? The possibility almost knocked the wind out of him—as did her continued close proximity.

He forced his gaze downward, breaking the sudden and inexplicable connection he felt to her. She wore an aqua T-shirt decorated with two heavily lined cartoonish eyes. In multicolored sparkly letters stretched over the midriff was the simple statement, "Fashionistas are fun." He stared at the words as if he were suddenly face-to-face with one of Bartlett's great quotations.

How many women dressed in glitter anyway?

Diana never had. She'd always presented herself as if she were going to a boardroom. He forced himself to stop concentrating on Kitty. Too much staring could knock a man right off his center of gravity. And for a guy with only one functioning leg, the results could be disastrous.

Kitty and Diana were about as different as two women could be. Every time he'd thought his position was secure with Diana, when he'd believed he knew where he stood, she'd up and leave for some new, exciting corner of the world that beckoned her. He doubted Kitty had been farther from Florida than Sorrel Gap.

During Diana's unpredictable absences, he'd tell himself, among other platitudes men use when their pride has been shattered, that he was better off without her. But Diana always drew him back. He'd adored her beyond what was rational. Now, at least before this darn plane crash, he'd begun to rebuild his life on the foundations left from the lessons he'd learned from Diana.

And he'd tried hard to become at least content with his life in the gap and now this new woman who seemed determined to be in his life every waking moment. He'd almost convinced himself that he'd acquired a practiced immunity from female temptations. If the new Campbell

Oakes became involved with a woman again, he would have the upper hand.

But then Kitty Watley came to the Saddle Top Motel—down on her luck, homeless and destitute with a kid she couldn't control. The opposite of Diana in every way, but every bit as big a threat to a man's stability for her lack of worldly possessions as Diana had been for her abundance of them. Kitty brought with her a bundle of responsibility, and no doubt she was looking for a man's shoulder to hang it on. And so this morning he shrugged away from her touch, knowing if she put her hand on him again, he'd like the feel of it way too much.

"You don't have to be so stubborn all the time," she said, placing her palm at the small of his back and urging him to rise. "It's not a sign of weakness to admit you need help."

He wanted to shout at her to back off, but instead he gave in to her gentle prodding and inched toward the edge of the mattress. Accepting her assistance, he slowly stood.

She looped his arm over her shoulder and clutched him tightly around the waist of his flannel pants. Then, acting as the crutches that lay against his nightstand, she maneuvered him toward the bathroom. He imagined they made a ridiculous sight. Tall, cumbersome man hanging on to a fragile stick of a woman. The image vanished as quickly as it had come. Mountain laurel, violets, lilacs—he didn't know what that flowery smell was, but it was making him dizzy. Mercifully he reached the bathroom, hobbled in and slammed the door.

This strange attraction to her didn't make any sense. Kitty wasn't his type. She did weird things to draw attention to herself without seeming to realize she was doing anything at all. Another way she was different from Diana. Diana chose every article of clothing and every accessory to complement her looks. Kitty, despite her professed interest in clothes, looked as though she haphazardly pulled outfits from drawers while blindfolded. Looking at her in all her unconventional getups was like risking his eyes staring at a solar eclipse. And yet he did look at her. Too long and too often.

FORTY-FIVE MINUTES LATER, Kitty left Campbell's apartment with a tray of food for Adam. "What is wrong with that man?" she ranted to herself. "Nothing pleases him."

She mentally cataloged her attempts to elicit some sort of genial response from Campbell. All her efforts had been fruitless. She'd helped him to the bathroom. Then she'd brought his pain pills and antibiotics to the recliner where he'd plopped himself after finally emerging and grudgingly accepting his coffee.

She'd made his breakfast, which, as instructed, had to include bacon and eggs. Granted she'd broken the yolks, but what was the big deal about having to eat scrambled? And she'd never seen bacon strips that thick before, so how was she to know they couldn't be nuked into crispiness in the microwave?

Try as she might, Kitty couldn't figure out what the man had to be so miserable about. Yes, he had a busted-up leg and a couple of cracked ribs, but he'd actually survived a plane crash, and to someone like Kitty who thought any two-seater flying machine was the Wright brothers' joke on mankind, that was tantamount to a miracle. Campbell Oakes should be counting his blessings, not cursing his fate.

And didn't the man ever look in a mirror and see beyond his perpetual frown? Couldn't he appreciate the gifts he'd been born with? Maybe his face wasn't perfect, but the fine lines around his eyes only reflected his experience and said that he'd lived in the sun far more than he'd avoided it. A little scar that zigzagged through one eyebrow gave him an interesting past with a hint of mystery. Just looking at Campbell made a person want to trust him—until he opened his mouth.

In fact, staring at Campbell when he wasn't scowling was like snuggling into a slightly worn blanket—comfortable and inviting. All Campbell's face needed was a smile once in a while to soften his rugged features with laugh lines. A real smile, that is, if Campbell even knew what that was.

And his hair. Women would kill for such a rich, nutty-brown color and thickness. Kitty figured that when the military-bred Campbell ran his hands through such lushness, he only fretted over missing a trip to a barbershop. And, of course, he'd be totally unaware of the effect on the opposite sex of those strands falling onto his forehead. Or the way they pointed toward green eyes that would be memorable if they snapped with humor and not peevishness.

Kitty sighed when she reached her door and admitted that she wasn't quite ready to accept that Campbell was hopeless—*yet*.

She went inside unit number six and slammed the door with the heel of her sandal. She'd just leave Mr. Campbell Oakes alone as he'd asked her to. She would do her duty, fix his meals, see that his immediate needs were met and then let him stew in his desolation for the rest of his miserable hours. And she'd find productive diversions to occupy herself while she was stuck doing penance.

Adam woke, sat up, and stared at her. "Jeez, Mom, why'd you slam the door? I was sleeping!"

She set Adam's food on the Formica table. "I'm not apologizing," she said. "I've had enough of men complaining at me for one day."

"I haven't complained since last night when I had to try and sleep on this lumpy mattress again, so don't take it out on me."

"Why not? You're the reason we're here." She waved a fork at him. "Now get up and eat."

He threw back the covers and stomped to the bathroom. When he came out, he sat at the table and lifted the aluminum foil on his plate. He frowned, started to speak, but stopped when Kitty nailed him with a warning look. Wisely, he took a few bites of overdone egg in silence. "So, what did the beast do?" he asked.

"It's not so much what he did," she said. "It's his attitude. He's got so much and yet he doesn't seem to appreciate any of it."

Adam took a swallow of milk. "Mom, until you yanked me out of bed in Richland a few days ago, I could have said the same thing about you. Remember the BMW? Your closet full of shoes?"

"Never mind. Our situation is totally different from Campbell's."

"Yeah, and I'm different from Campbell. I appreciated all the stuff I had."

"Campbell owns this motel, you know," she said.

Adam wrapped his hand around his throat and pretended to choke on his eggs. "Wow. He truly is nuts not to appreciate all this."

"He has his own business…"

"Which right now is a busted plane."

"He has friends and family."

"You mean Sheriff Smokey the Bear and his goofy deputy?"

"Adam…"

"We have family, too, Mom, and ours can do a whole lot more for us than Smokey can do for the beast."

"Don't start up about Grandpa again."

"Okay. I wouldn't want to point out that a simple phone call could be our ticket to civilization."

When she didn't relent, he shoved his plate to the edge of the table and went to his dresser for a pair of shorts. "I've got a while before Virgil picks me up to go to Value-Rite. I'm going over to watch the beast's TV."

"No, you're not."

He gawked at her. "Why not? In a while Quint might have me scrubbing toilets."

Kitty rolled her eyes. "How many times have you scrubbed toilets so far?"

Adam yanked a T-shirt over his head. "Okay, none, but I figure Quint's just waiting for the right moment to give me the really dirty jobs."

She smiled. So far Adam had worked in the supply room and helped customers carry packages to their cars. "You never know," she said, "but just in case, you should practice your cleaning skills right here."

He scratched his scalp under his mop of hair and stared.

"Go over to Campbell's and borrow some disinfectant, cleansers and a vacuum. Let's make this place sparkle."

Adam's chin jutted out in pure defiance. "What's got into you? You put all that fancy material in the bottoms of the dresser drawers. Isn't that enough?"

"We've got to make this place livable whether we like it or not. And no TV while you're over there."

The echo of the slamming door only made Kitty's smile broader. She'd feel better once this drab old room gleamed with polish and smelled of lemons. Not as good as she'd feel if she saw a gleam of good spirit in Campbell's eyes, but it was a start. Some transformations took longer than others.

CHAPTER EIGHT

Kitty greeted Virgil when he arrived thirty minutes later. "Nice morning, Sheriff," she said.

"Most are here in the Blue Ridge." He opened the car door for Adam. "You ready to go, son?"

Kitty handed Adam the lunch she'd hastily packed, and then went back in to finish cleaning their room. A fresh scent greeted her, and she inhaled deeply. Her germ-busting campaign was working, both on the old Formica and her spirits.

She opened the curtains and grabbed a rag and some Pledge and attacked the old nightstands. When she opened a drawer, a clean aroma, smelling faintly of lavender, wafted into the air.

Looking inside, Kitty discovered several articles of clothing and a sprig of the dried herb. The second nightstand contained more garments and more lavender. She shook out each one and laid the pieces on the bed. There were three blouses and two ankle-length skirts, each made of pale hues of a thin, gauzy material that would permit freedom of movement and allow the pieces to hang loosely on a woman's frame. The sleeves were long and gathered at the elbows with elastic.

Each stitch was fine and precise. Two of the blouses had been hand-embroidered with small butterflies and flowers. Kitty checked the pieces for a label and, finding none, determined that the clothes had been handmade, which explained why the work was as exquisite as the finest couture garments. She had no idea how long the clothing had been in the drawers, but only a slight yellowing had discolored the soft cream-colored tones, a defect Kitty decided might be eliminated after a gentle washing.

Holding a skirt to her waist, Kitty looked in the mirror and felt transformed. The clothes were not her style, but the fabric flowed smoothly, conformed to her shape and made her feel feminine down to her toes.

She rolled up the waistband and let her imagination soar. "If I shortened this hemline, gave it a ragged scarf effect…"

She tossed the skirt to the bed, held up a blouse and ran her fingers under the ruffle at the scooped neckline. "I could exchange this ruffle for a drawstring, add a bit of elastic under the bodice for a gathered look."

Suddenly all Kitty wanted to do was ask

Campbell about the clothes, and she would do so when she went to fix his lunch. She refolded each piece of clothing carefully and put the entire stack on the top shelf of the closet next to the bathroom. Then she continued her cleaning until noon when she went to Campbell's apartment. He looked up from a stack of mail on his lap when she came in.

"There's some ham in the refrigerator," she said. "Can I fix you a sandwich?"

"Sure."

She spread the ingredients on the countertop and opened a jar of mayonnaise. "We're cleaning our room," she said after a moment.

He remained absorbed in his mail. "I suppose it could use it."

"It's a big job."

"Imagine so." He pulled an envelope from the stack and held it up. "This is for you. Might have been here a couple of days. I don't look at the mail regularly."

The check from Bette! Kitty rushed over to retrieve the letter.

Campbell lowered it teasingly to his chest and studied the impersonal typed address. "Hope this isn't from an ex-boyfriend, a prowrestler type who's coming to find you."

She stuck out her hand. "It isn't."

He hesitated, still holding the envelope in his grasp.

"It isn't!" she said again, snatching the letter. She folded it and tucked it in the waistband of her shorts.

"You don't have to bite my head off," Campbell said.

"Yeah, well, you don't have to know my business."

He returned his attention to his mail. "Okay."

Walking back to the counter, she decided to ask him about the clothes since he seemed to be in a rare, teasing mood. "I found some clothing in the nightstand drawers in our room," she said. "Ladies' blouses and skirts."

He mumbled an expression of surprise, waited a moment and said, "They must have been left there by Mrs. Avery's daughter."

"Mrs. Avery?"

"She was the last manager of the Saddle Top before the new highway opened. She lived here in my apartment, and, as I remember, her daughter lived in your unit for a while. I think the daughter's name was Patsy."

"And you think these clothes were Patsy's?"

He shrugged. "Maybe. I was just a kid, but I remember her sewing in that room."

"What happened to these women?" Kitty asked.

"Both of them took off years ago when my grandfather closed the place. I heard Mrs. Avery died just recently."

"And her daughter?"

"She was killed in a car accident out in California."

"Oh, what a shame. Did she leave any heirs? I'd be happy to package the things and send them."

"I never heard that Patsy even married," he said. "You might as well just throw them out."

She slapped a slice of ham over the mayonnaise, inexplicably irked at Campbell's response. The garments had been lovingly created, perhaps by Patsy's own hand. Of course Campbell, or most any man really, wouldn't appreciate that fact. "I can't do that," she said.

"Why not?"

"They're perfectly good clothes. Someone would like them." *And I would like to add my own touches to what Patsy started.* "Maybe I'll put them in the washer and see how they come out," she said.

Obviously uninterested in laundry talk, he opened an envelope and read.

"Clothing is important to me," she said. "It tells a lot about a person."

The corner of his mouth hitched up in a curious way. "You don't say? What do your clothes say about you? Are you fun like the T-shirt says?"

She plucked the sparkling letters away from her chest. "Some people might think so." She thought of Owen. He'd be likely to add *irresponsible* and *frivolous*, as well. But Kitty knew she hadn't been fun lately.

Not since Adam stole from another student and opened her eyes to her shortcomings.

"About the things in the nightstands," she said, bringing Campbell back to the topic. "They're not really what I wear, but if you're suggesting that I can keep them, I'm happy to."

"I couldn't care less." He turned away but did not resume reading his mail. Instead he moved in the chair, raising himself up as if trying to find a comfortable position.

"Can I help you?" she asked, expecting his usual curt reaction. She wasn't disappointed.

"No. Just finish what you're doing."

She sliced a knife through Campbell's sandwich as resentment started to build inside her once more. There wasn't a soft spot or an ounce of gratitude anywhere in this man. She set a tray with his sandwich and a soft drink on the table beside the recliner and stood by the arm of the chair. "Look, Campbell, I know you don't want me here, but the fact is, while you're healing, you need me. And I need to stay here until my debt to Sorrel Gap is paid."

He reached out and grabbed her wrist. She let out a squeal of surprise and locked her gaze on to his. For the first time she saw something other than indifference and self-pity. Anger flared in the deep green of his eyes.

"Wake up, Kitty," he snapped at her. "It's not *your* debt. You didn't run out of Value-Rite with half the electronics department in your jacket."

"But Adam is my responsibility. His mistakes are my mistakes."

"Your only mistake as I see it is failing to discipline him, probably from the time the kid took his first step."

Campbell's comment was like salt flowing into the wound of her seriously damaged self-esteem. Anger and guilt boiled up inside her. "You don't know what you're talking about. I'm his mother…"

"Then act like it," Campbell's eyes narrowed. His glare became even more disapproving. "Quit squabbling with him like you were a couple of kids on a playground."

She wrenched her hand free. A whisper of heat spread up her arm that she realized had nothing to do with her anger. She tried to rub it away with her other hand. "What do you know about raising a child?" she shot back. "For that matter, what do you know about anything other than being miserable and feeling sorry for yourself? At least I've got someone to care about. You don't seem to care about anyone but yourself."

She regretted the words as soon as they were out of her mouth. She regretted them even more when Campbell's features registered shock and something else that she couldn't identify, a sort of undefined longing.

She stepped back, suddenly frightened that he would send her away for one emotional outburst. She didn't treat people this way. She cared about people's feelings. Yet not only had she insulted Campbell, she might have condemned Adam to the juvenile detention facility after all. Or worse. She might have to call Owen and beg for leniency.

"I'm sorry," she said, hating the pleading tone in her voice even though Campbell deserved every harsh word. But she had to think about the immediate future. "I had no right…"

He looked away. "You did. You had every right. I was out of line. You're the lawbreaker's mother, and for the first time, you actually convinced me of that."

His response, so unexpected and uncharacteristic, rendered her speechless. After what seemed an interminable silence while she groped for words, she said, "Still, I never should have spoken to you like that. It was disrespectful after you've been generous enough to take us in."

He regarded her with a baffling expression, making her think that her apology would be rejected as pitifully inadequate. "From now on I'll just do my job and leave you alone," she said. "I'll even call Virgil to see if he has a spare coffeemaker at the sheriff's office so I can put it in our room, and I won't have to bother you so early in the mornings."

He picked up the ham sandwich and lifted the bread to see what was underneath. Then he did the strangest thing. He smiled before removing a piece of butcher paper she'd left stuck to a slice of cheese. "Forget about the coffeemaker," he said. "You can use the one in here whenever you want. In spite of everything, Kitty, you've got a heck of a way of jump-starting a guy's day."

LATER THAT NIGHT, after Kitty recognized the soft, rhythmic sounds of her son's deep sleep, she dialed the phone number to a neat, small house on the outskirts of Richland. Esmeralda answered on the second ring.

"It's me," Kitty whispered.

The housekeeper's voice rose to an excited pitch. "Kitty, where are you? What have you done?" She paused a few seconds before admonishing her husband. "Go away, Hector. I'll tell you when I'm finished." Then, her voice finally calm, she spoke into the phone. "Your father has been calling everyone to find you. He called the police," she added with increased urgency.

After first shutting down my checking account, I'll bet, Kitty thought, realizing again that her father's efforts to find her had very little to do with concern for her welfare.

Esmeralda sighed. "Are you all right? Is Adam?"

"Yes, we're fine. I just needed to get away for a while."

"Mr. Owen is like a raging bull," Esmeralda said. "He asks me a hundred times a day if you've called."

"I left him a note."

"Yes, but Mr. Owen doesn't believe what you said about a vacation."

"I didn't think he would," Kitty said. She looked at the drab furnishings around her, cleaner now and slightly more acceptable in the low light from the bedside table. "This isn't exactly a fun trip," she added. "But I sent him a letter. It was mailed from a location near Baltimore. He should get it tomorrow."

Esmeralda sighed. "Kitty, why do my instincts tell me that you are nowhere near that city?"

"I have a friend there who agreed to send the letter."

"So, where are you, and when are you coming back?"

"I don't know for sure. And I can't tell you where we are. I wouldn't want you to have to lie for me."

"I am against lying," Esmeralda stated emphatically. "But maybe for you…"

"I won't ask you to," Kitty said quickly. "Other than to avoid telling Daddy that you spoke to me tonight. Knowing my father, he could arrange to have your phone line tapped."

"No one will tap this phone, *cariño*," Esmeralda said. "You call anytime. I'll tell Mr. Owen that I know in my heart that you and Adam are well. Our Blessed Mother is watching over you."

Kitty smiled. A bit of faith-based assurance couldn't hurt. "That's a good idea. Even Daddy can't argue with the Blessed Mother. And don't worry, Esmeralda. I'll write him every week."

"That's good, but it won't keep Mr. Owen from fretting and looking for you. He's plenty mad and wants you back home."

You mean he wants his grandson, Kitty thought. She closed her eyes, blew out a long breath. Owen Galloway was a powerful man. Could his feelers reach even this remote corner of North Carolina? "I'll call you again in a few days, Esmeralda."

"You take care of yourself, *cariño*."

Tears burned the backs of Kitty's eyes as she depressed the button that would disconnect her from Esmeralda. She pictured the housekeeper in the colorful living room of the home where she and Hector had raised three fine sons.

As she dialed the number to cousin Bette, Kitty realized that there were two people in her life who really cared for her. And she said a special thank-you for Esmeralda, because in all of Richland, she was the only one praying for Kitty Galloway.

AFTER ASSURING BETTE that she and Adam were fine, Kitty walked out of her room to breathe in the fresh mountain breeze. She was beginning to think that this cool, clean air was as important as water to the people who lived in these hills. She took a deep draw and let the breath settle in her lungs.

"So, what are you doing?" came a voice from down the walkway. "Can't sleep?"

Campbell stood with one crutch under his arm and his other hand on the porch railing supporting some of his weight. He looked tall and fit, and if it hadn't been for the crutch, every bit like the hero the people in the gap believed him to be. Suddenly Kitty had no doubt that he would recover fully, probably sooner than either of them anticipated. The thought made her a bit sad.

"I haven't been to bed yet," she said. "Do you need something? Are you in pain?"

He hobbled a few steps closer to her but still maintained a respectable distance. "No, I'm all right except for a severe case of cabin fever. At least I can come out here and see the expanse of mountains across the road and know there's a never-ending sky up there." He smiled under the light by the breezeway. "Beats the heck out of staring at my ceiling."

"I know it's hard," she said to him. "But you're doing very well. You'll be walking and flying again before you know it."

He stared over the parking lot at dozens of glowing lights. "Just like those guys, eh?"

Kitty stretched her hand over the railing, and a firefly settled on her finger. It blinked several times almost as if he were telling his companions that he was safe on this human's hand. As safe as she hoped Campbell would soon feel with her.

The insect took off and became indistinguishable with the many. "They are unique," she said. "They have everything they need to exist on these dark nights. The ability to fly and to light their way. I've come outside every night to watch them."

Campbell sighed. "As soon as I'm able, we'll catch a few of them. I think I still have a glass jar with holes in the lid."

"And then we'll let them go?"

"Absolutely. That's mostly how I fish and how I catch fireflies." He turned to go back inside. "Seems only fair. Sleep well, Kitty."

She smiled to herself and thought that perhaps at last she would.

NOT WANTING TO read too much into the discussion about fireflies, Kitty kept to herself as much as possible, only preparing Campbell's meals and doing those chores he specifically asked her to do. These included phoning in their grocery orders to Virgil, housecleaning and washing his clothes and putting them away according to his strict preferences.

Since the morning when Kitty had helped him to the bathroom, Campbell was always up and dressed when she arrived. He never said much as she prepared his breakfast, but he seemed to be acutely aware of everything that went on around him. She sensed his alert green eyes following her as she moved around the apartment.

In her spare time, she made unit six as homey

as she could before attempting alterations to Patsy's clothes and experimenting with new designs she hoped to sell to a clothing manufacturer when she finished her training in Charlotte. Often she explored the area at the back of the motel, beginning with the sadly neglected patches of grass, remnants of what must have once been a lush green lawn. Now mostly dirt and rocks stretched a hundred yards to the hills that marked the beginning of the majestic rise of the Blue Ridge Mountains.

One day she ventured up a path that led into the foothills of the mountain behind the motel. She stopped periodically and gazed down narrow, shady roads. Occasionally a car or seasoned truck would navigate a sharp turn and disappear into the thick cover of trees. Without fail the driver would wave at her, usually a two-fingered salute she'd begun to recognize as a country hello.

She decided she would ask Campbell where the secondary roads led and who lived in the forest. But for now she was content to enjoy the wildflowers that bloomed in abundance by the side of the main road. She didn't know the names of the flowers, but she soon developed a fondness for certain ones. She picked spikes of fluffy pink blossoms, clusters of petals as blue as the sky and floral bursts of yellow and coral that looked like miniature lilies. Borrowing a glass from Campbell's kitchen, she made a fresh bouquet of flowers every afternoon and set it on a colorful scarf over the faded old Formica table in unit six.

And then, one day more than a week after her truck had broken down on the Spooner County highway, Kitty decided to take a bouquet to Campbell. It was time to let more than sunshine into his dreary existence. She would breathe the color and life of the mountains into his apartment whether he appreciated it or not. Returning from a walk, she arranged fresh flowers in a glass and took them to Campbell's quarters. When she went outside, she saw Tommy Gibbs's official SUV heading over the hill away from the motel.

"I see you've had company," she said when she entered Campbell's apartment and placed the flower arrangement on his coffee table. "That's nice."

He glanced at the bouquet, narrowed his eyes, and mumbled something about them being pretty. Kitty accepted his statement as practically an explosion of appreciation.

Campbell nodded toward the kitchen counter where several sacks of groceries had been left. "I don't think he came to see me," Campbell said. "He brought the stuff you wanted. And by the way, that's the third time Gibbs has been here in a week. In case you haven't noticed, the boy has developed a crush on you."

Kitty had suspected this was true. "He's just a young man. He must know that I'm quite a bit older than he is."

"That fact doesn't appear to bother him."

"He's a nice kid," she said. "He'll be over his crush soon enough."

At one time, Kitty had reasoned that Gibbs's visits had something to do with her father's search, but thankfully that hadn't turned out to be the case.

"I don't think Tommy will get over you that easily," Campbell said. "Today he showed up in a spanking-clean uniform, his hat in hand and his deputy badge polished to a shine. He was real disappointed you weren't here."

Kitty tried to ignore the sharp tone in Campbell's voice. Surely he wasn't jealous—not of a man who was more than a decade younger than she was. Just when she was convincing herself that such a scenario was impossible, she saw Campbell pick up an amber-colored bottle from the end table and take a swig of liquid. Forgetting Gibbs for the moment, she marched over to the chair and sniffed the air. She leaned closer to Campbell and sniffed again. "You're drinking!"

"It's just one beer, Kitty. Don't get so excited."

"Where did you get it?"

"I purchased a six-pack before my crash and this is the lone survivor."

Kitty took the bottle from his hand. "Your visiting nurse left specific instructions about alcohol. You're on antibiotics. Liquor dilutes the effect of the drugs." She walked to the sink and poured the rest of the beer into the drain. Campbell groaned.

When she returned to the recliner, she brought him a glass of lemonade.

He grimaced. "Wow. Thank you."

She couldn't help smiling. "You're welcome."

He took a sip of lemonade and looked up at her. "You know, Kitty, despite your vigilante tactics, you might actually convince me you care about me."

She paused before answering. Of course she cared about him, but to admit it was to admit too much. "I care about doing a good job for your uncle."

He patted the sofa cushion next to him. "Sit down a minute, okay?"

She debated. He looked calm if she didn't concentrate on the light coming from behind those green eyes. She sat. "What?"

"I'm going to choose to believe that you care as much about making me well as you do about pleasing my uncle Virgil."

She hitched one shoulder. "Think whatever you like. I can dispose of your beer, but I can't get into your brain."

He chuckled. "You're wrong. You already have. In fact, I'm getting a clear message from you that you're wondering if a few swallows of beer can affect a man's judgment."

"Not a man your size," she said, feeling heat in her cheeks.

"Then why do I suddenly want to kiss you right now?"

The flush deepened until she thought she might combust. "I can't imagine. Of course you can't be serious. We don't have that kind of relationship. We don't have any kind of relationship aside from caretaker and patient."

"That's kind of a shame, isn't it?"

"No. It's appropriate..."

He slipped his hand around the nape of her neck and pulled her to him. "Kitty, you've scolded me. You've thrown away my beer, and to be perfectly frank, you've come close to poisoning me a couple of times. Can't you please be quiet and let this happen, just this once?"

Her lips parted but no words came out. In one startling moment she realized she definitely was going to let this happen.

She stared at his face which was so close to hers that she could see the subtle flare of his nostrils, feel his labored breathing as warm bursts of air on her cheek.

She swallowed, put her free hand over the crazy tap dance her heart was performing in her chest.

He bit his lower lip. His gaze moved over her features with a slow, sober perusal that made her feel special, as if it were the two of them together against the world.

The hand she'd intended to use to push him away dropped to her lap, the fingers slightly bent and trembling. With his fingertips he traced the skin on the underside of her arm from her wrist to her elbow, and Kitty realized she could no more stop that concentrated exploration than she could have stopped breathing.

"Kitty, you capture a man's imagination in a way that's hard to explain," Campbell said.

He slipped his hand around to her back and lifted her chin to bring her lips to his. His kiss was soft and scented with a tanginess. His mouth moved over hers, tasting, teasing.

Kitty's scruples, those nagging reminders that she'd promised herself she was never again going to succumb to the Bobby Watleys and Terry Spensers of the world, vanished for the duration of that long, incredible kiss.

And then his tongue made insistent probing stabs at her lips, and the scruples came crashing back. Kitty jumped up from the sofa as if she'd been sitting in smoldering ashes. She stood in front of him, her eyes blinking, her lips quivering. "I don't know what's gotten into you," she said.

He ran his tongue over his upper lip. "I'm not sure I do, either."

"I have things to do."

"Okay."

She took a deep calming breath and pointed to the glass of flowers. "I brought you these. You didn't even say thank-you."

He looked at the flowers, smiled. "Thanks. Though I'm not sure they make up for what you just did to my nice cold beer."

"I did that for your own good. I'm going now."

"You probably should."

She whirled around and marched toward the door. "See you for supper," she said over her shoulder. "And if you have any more alcohol hidden in this apartment, you'd better hope I don't find it. You have six more days on your prescription."

She was halfway through the lobby when she heard him call out, "Thanks for stopping by. It was a genuine pleasure."

So much for that calming breath. Right now she could only agree.

CAMPBELL STARED INTO space long after the screen door slammed. He picked up the simple kitchen glass that held the flowers. Campbell Oakes with a bunch of posies in his hand wasn't an image he would have picked for himself. Flowers had no place in the apartment of a man who had bombed the Iraqi Ministry of Defense.

He sniffed the tallest blossom and vividly recalled Kitty, the kiss, the burst of bravado that had preceded her exit. He smiled in spite of his conflicting emotions.

He'd given in to a growing impulse to taste those lips and touch her. He laid his head against the back of the sofa and closed his eyes, careful to keep the flowers upright in his lap.

He had to admit that he hadn't acted strictly on impulse a few minutes ago. He'd been imagining Kitty's kiss since…well, maybe since he'd first seen her on the porch of the Saddle Top.

The kiss had stirred something deep inside him that touched more than just the past few months of monastic living. The truth was, he never should have kissed her for the simple reason that it only made him want to do it again.

He sat straight, opened his eyes and plucked one delicate flower from the glass. Water dripped from the stem onto his shirt. He stared at fragile yellow petals around a milky-white center—a miniature sunburst he could hold in his hand. It made sense for Kitty to give him this flower. Kitty, who waltzed into his apartment every morning and stripped open the drapes and yanked up the blinds to make him aware of the sun.

It was just a kiss, he said to himself. *That's all*. It meant nothing. And it probably shouldn't have happened. It wouldn't happen again.

After Diana, Campbell had vowed never to get involved with a rich, spoiled woman. But Kitty, who appeared to have nothing but a run-down truck and a sewing machine, made him realize that a poor, desperate woman could be just as big a threat to a man's peace of mind as a rich one was. Kitty was as poor as Diana was rich, as needy as Diana was independent. But both of them demanded more than most men could give.

So he'd be careful not to give too much. He'd endure this situation until his leg was healed and Adam Watley had paid his debt. Then he'd maybe kiss Kitty one more time. He'd kiss her goodbye.

CHAPTER NINE

KITTY STARED AT the flushed face in the mirror. Her eyes, ordinarily a placid gray-blue, shone like polished quartz and seemed to belong to someone else's face. Would Adam be able to tell what she'd done simply by looking at her? Would Virgil? She finger-combed her hair, splashed water on her face. She had been trying to deny her feelings for Campbell since she arrived at the Saddle Top, successfully she'd believed, but now… Falling for Virgil's nephew hadn't been part of the deal.

She patted her skin dry and tried to convince herself she looked almost normal. But she didn't *feel* normal. Campbell's impulsive kiss had shaken her even more than a stolen wallet and a broken-down truck had, especially since she hadn't done anything to stop it. In fact, she'd encouraged the kiss to continue well after her initial shock. And as long as she was admitting the truth, she had to confess that something inside her wanted that kiss to be a beginning.

"You can't allow this to happen," she said.

"This is only a temporary stopping point on the road to your new life with Adam. And this man's life is on hold just as yours is. He will soon have no need of you and will probably watch you drive away without a moment's regret."

A blast of guilt, cold and sudden, washed over Kitty. She'd always been stupid with men. Yes, this one, Campbell, seemed much more decent than the others, but there was still no way to know how this would turn out, or if he cared about her beyond one simple kiss. She heard Virgil's car pull into the lot, so she took a deep breath and went outside. Adam climbed out, ran across the parking lot and bounded up the stairs, a can of soda in his hand. "Hi, Mom."

Thank goodness her inner chaos had completely escaped her son's attention. Would Virgil be oblivious, as well?

The sheriff got out of the car and gave her a lazy grin. "Afternoon, Kitty. How's my nephew doing? He's not giving you any trouble, is he?"

None I can tell you about. "No. Everything's fine."

He waited as if he expected her to say something else. She struggled to come up with a topic that would steer the conversation away from Campbell. When an old Ford convertible turned up the road that ran next to the motel, she said,

"Sheriff, I've been wondering about the roads that lead into the hills. Who lives up there?"

"A whole community," Virgil said. "The first place you come to belongs to Ginny and Cliff Lowe. Then there's old Jack Ashton, and Suzie and Luke Crum and their brood of kids. Good bunch of folks."

"Are they farmers?"

"Mostly. And they're a pretty self-sufficient group. Some of the men raise a few crops, come into town to sell them and pick up odd jobs now and again. The women come once or twice a month to stock up on supplies. You don't have to worry about trouble from the hill folks."

"Oh no, I wasn't thinking that. Actually I'd like to go up there one day and see who I could meet. It gets lonely in the motel, especially with Adam gone."

"You go on if you have a mind to. They'll welcome you. I have a hunch they all know you're here taking care of Campbell anyway. They got their own gossip trail working, so you might as well go introduce yourself."

The sheriff drummed his fingers on top of his cruiser. "In fact, Kitty, you mentioning wanting to go up in the hills reminds me of a subject I wanted to discuss with you."

"What's that?"

"You're doing a fine job here. My nephew's got no complaints."

"Thanks. I'm trying."

"I was thinking that maybe it's time to give you more responsibility."

"What are you talking about, Sheriff?"

"The truth is, these trips from town are interfering with my work," he said. "And I can't keep sending my deputy out here every time you decide you need a quart of milk."

Kitty didn't allow her mind to jump to a conclusion that might be totally false. "I can see that would be a problem," she acknowledged.

"Campbell's got that Jeep out back in the shed. As long as he doesn't have any objections, I'm thinking you can drive to town to get supplies. Maybe even drop the boy off at Value-Rite in the mornings. It would take some of the burden off me."

Yes. A car, a chance to drive. Kitty felt dizzy with pure joy until she recalled one significant hitch to this arrangement. "But what about my driver's license? It was stolen, remember?" She didn't want to apply for a license and have to use her real name.

Virgil waved off her concern. "I'll give you a temporary permit. You're just driving locally. But you should go ahead and request a replacement. You'll need it when you leave."

"I'll get right on it," she lied. "And I'll talk to Campbell today about the Jeep."

"I think it'd be better if I talk to him. Besides, there's one more favor I have to ask of you."

"Oh?"

"I'd appreciate it if you'd take Campbell to his doctor's appointments and his physical therapy sessions, which will be scheduled pretty often now that his ribs are nearly healed." Virgil blew out a long breath before adding, "That won't be easy. I have a hunch Campbell won't like admitting he's going to need a lot of rehabilitation. But he might listen to you." Virgil leaned against the car. "So, what do you say?"

"I'll be happy to take Campbell to his appointments, Sheriff."

"Okay, then. I've got to get back to town, but I'll give Campbell a call this afternoon, and if he agrees to this arrangement, you're free to drive."

Watching Virgil leave, Kitty felt like hooting with sheer exhilaration. To actually go into that charming little town, shop in a store, even if it was just to buy food with Campbell's money. This was certainly a day of surprises, even if some required more careful reflection than others.

WHEN THE PATROL car had crested the hill, Kitty went into her room and walked over to Adam's bed. She ruffled his hair. "How was your day?"

"It sucked."

His typical answer. "Did it really?"

He hitched a shoulder with macho indifference. "Could have been worse, I guess. Mostly I filled shelves in the health and beauty section."

"That doesn't sound bad."

"Maybe not to you. Did you know it takes an entire aisle to stock shampoo at Value-Rite? And I heard on TV once that dish detergent has the same ingredients and would do the same thing for a lot less money. They ought to just put bottles of dish soap on every shelf in that department."

"When you get promoted to manager, you can suggest it."

"Yeah, like that'll happen." He took a squished bag out of his back jeans pocket and tossed it to the end of the bed.

Recognizing the food she'd packed earlier, Kitty picked it up between her thumb and finger and dropped it in the garbage can. "You didn't eat your lunch?"

"Quint said you can quit packing it. He gave me a five-dollar credit to eat in the store cafeteria."

"That was nice of him."

Adam rolled his eyes. "Don't get all soft on Quint. He's a professional do-gooder and a nutrition nut. He says a growing boy ought to eat a healthy lunch every day, not that junk you pack for me."

"He said that?" Kitty didn't care much for the manager's opinion of her lovingly prepared bologna sandwiches, especially since her ingredient choices were limited. "So, what healthy food did you eat today?"

"A double order of fries and a bowl of chocolate ice cream." He patted his belly. "What Quint doesn't know won't hurt him."

"No more of that," she said. "From now on, order something that's good for you." She sat on the bed next to him and placed her hand on his knee. "Anyway, it sounds like you and Quint are getting along okay."

"I suppose. He did take a giant step toward being an okay guy today."

"What did he do?"

"He said he'd lend me this television he's got in his office. It's not much, only a thirteen-incher, but it's cable-ready. He looked so proud of himself when he made the offer, I didn't even try to bargain with him to get a brand-new set still in the carton."

"That was probably smart."

"Anyhow, he said I can use it while we're here at the motel." Adam set the soda can on the nightstand and jumped up from the bed. "So I gotta talk to the beast and convince him to get his cable run into this room."

Kitty stood. "You want to talk to Campbell now?"

"Sure, now. What good's a cable TV if he doesn't get us cable? I figure I'll ask him now, which will give him an hour or two to get over the shock of maybe doing something nice for somebody. He can give me his answer at supper."

Her last encounter with Campbell came flooding back to Kitty's mind—the kiss. If Campbell had been half as rattled as she had been—and still was—over what they'd done not even an hour ago, then now wasn't a good time for Adam to barge in demanding a favor. "He's sleeping," she said.

"What? In the middle of the day? I thought he only hibernated at night."

"He's recovering from a plane crash, Adam. He sleeps when his body tells him to so he can heal. You want him to be rested and in a good mood when you ask him, don't you?"

"Well, yeah, I guess."

"Then talk to him at supper."

Adam stood with his hand on the doorknob while he debated his chances of winning Campbell over. Apparently deciding that his mother might be right, he dropped his hand to his side.

"Okay. But if I can't go over there to even watch the beast's TV, what *can* I do?"

Kitty took a pair of jeans from her dresser drawer and headed toward the bathroom. "It's a beautiful Friday afternoon. I have the perfect solution to your boredom."

He looked hopeful.

"We're going for a walk."

He flopped back onto the bed. "A walk! As if the aisles at Value-Rite aren't enough exercise!"

She stopped to pick up her sneakers from under the bed. "This walk involves fresh air and meeting our neighbors." Room number six was suddenly small and cramped and no place for a woman whose nerves were stretched to their limit.

Adam reluctantly reached for his ball cap. "Are you talking about human neighbors? The only creatures I've seen around here have more than two legs."

She herded him to the door.

"And most of them are bigger than me and make milk."

KITTY HUGGED THE EDGE of the road while Adam darted back and forth from one side of the narrow road to the other. He gathered rocks and flung them into the brush. When spooked animals ran from the ground cover, he laughed and boasted, "I guess I showed them."

Kitty frowned at him. "Yeah. Big man scaring defenseless little critters. Can't you think of something else to do?"

He juggled a pebble from one hand to the other, his eyes scoping out his next target. "Why should I? This is fun."

"No, it isn't. It's mean. How would you like it if somebody fifty times bigger than you threw rocks at your home?"

"You mean my *real* house, the one at Grandpa's? Even a giant couldn't destroy that place. If you mean the dump I live in now, I'd be grateful."

Kitty gave him a threatening look. Adam waited a moment before dropping the remainder of his rocks to the ground. "Okay. The varmints are saved. But what else is there to do?"

"Enjoy nature." She peered up into the deep green leaves hanging over the road. "It's lovely here."

Kitty recognized most of the trees from her high school botany book. Tall stately oaks, shady maples and wide-crowned elms. And of course the spruces and pines whose leaves she could imagine heavy with snow in winter.

She rubbed her arms briskly as they continued climbing. The mountain seemed to be working its magic. Almost a full minute had lapsed since she'd last thought about Campbell. "See how the temperature drops as the trees get thicker and we go higher? You won't experience a change like this in Florida where the land is mostly flat."

"Yes, you can," Adam said. "Haven't you heard of air-conditioning?"

She shook her head with exasperation. "You're impossible, you know that?"

After a minute he pointed to a break in the trees. "That's kind of cool, I guess."

She shielded her eyes from a spear of sunlight that pierced overhanging limbs and followed his gaze. A clear creek tumbled over boulders and meandered gracefully for a distance before disappearing around a bend that led farther into the forest. "It's definitely cool," Kitty agreed. "I'll bet it flows into that creek back near the highway where the motel is. There's probably some good fishing there."

Adam gawked at her. "So now you want to fish? Who are you and what have you done with my mother?"

She gave him a playful shove, but he came right back and fell into step beside her. When they rounded the next curve in the road, Kitty heard the tinkling notes of wind chimes. She studied a pair of worn tire tracks and looked down a pathway a couple hundred feet to where a log house sat nestled in tall trees. She read the name on a mailbox perched on top of a thick wooden pole. "Clifford Lowe. Sheriff Oakes mentioned this family when I asked him who lived up here."

Adam groaned. "You're not thinking what I think you're thinking?"

She passed the mailbox and headed toward the cabin. "We should introduce ourselves."

He stopped her by grabbing on to the waistband of her jeans and digging his heels into the dirt. "Haven't you seen *Deliverance*?"

She spun around, forcing him to release his grip. "*You've* seen *Deliverance*?"

"Remember when I was at Larry's house a few weeks ago? It was guys' movie night. We watched that and *Texas Chainsaw Massacre*."

Kitty shook her head, once again convinced that she hadn't paid enough attention to her son's social activities. "I think I got you out of Richland in the nick of time."

Adam stared at the cabin and cupped his hand around his ear. "I'm not going up there. I hear banjos."

"Don't be ridiculous. I told you Sheriff Oakes said—"

"Who's there?"

An authoritative female voice seemed to emerge from the roots of the ancient trees. Kitty squinted into the oaks as a tiny old woman dressed in denim overalls and a flowered blouse came down the path. Wispy gray hair framed her face like worn violin strings. Snapping gray eyes locked on to Kitty as if they'd spotted prey in the crosshairs of a rifle.

She held a leggy, snarling black-and-white terrier that churned its legs in an attempt to escape the crook of her elbow.

When the woman made a noise like the clucking of a hen, the dog resigned itself to emitting a rolling growl. "Did we scare you?" she asked.

Kitty swallowed and lied. "No, of course not."

"Lady, you and that mutt are *still* scaring me," Adam said.

"Adam!" Kitty scowled and resumed speaking to the woman. "My name is Kitty. This is my son. We…"

The woman set the dog on the ground and kept him from charging forward with the toe of a scuffed black boot. "Git back, Lucifer." The terrier ran a few feet toward the cabin, stopped and barked, and repeated the game several times. "I know who you are," the woman said. "You're the folks taking care of Camp down at the Saddle Top Motel."

"That's right."

She patted the side of her overalls, and the dog scuttled back to her. "'Bout time you came up this way. I don't drive too well anymore or I'd have come down to the motel to welcome you." She stuck out her hand and Kitty grasped it. "I'm Ginny Lowe."

"Nice to meet you." Kitty nudged Adam forward and he shook Ginny's hand.

"I've got tea brewing if you have time to come inside. And lemonade for the boy."

"We'd like that," Kitty said.

Ginny turned and headed to her cabin with Kitty and Adam following. Adam grabbed Kitty's arm and whispered, "That old lady's gonna shoot us if we go up there. And that crazy dog will gnaw on our bones for his supper."

Kitty pushed him forward. "You've definitely seen too many horror flicks."

He stopped complaining when they entered Ginny Lowe's front yard and encountered an entire city of birdhouses. Every shape, size and color. There were houses on posts, on the ground, hanging from porch eaves and tree limbs. The feeders were miniature replicas of mountain buildings, cabins, stores, churches, along with gazebos, barns and even lighthouses.

Kitty stared in awe at the aviary community and said, "Where did you get them all?"

"Clifford makes 'em," Ginny said. She opened the screen door to her cabin and motioned Kitty and Adam inside.

"Clifford's your husband?" Kitty said as she crossed the threshold.

"For the last fifty-two years." Ginny led the way through a parlor filled with sturdy pine furniture. When they entered a large kitchen in the rear of the cabin, she nodded to the back door. "He's out there now in the shed, probably putting the finishing touches on another birdhouse. Toby Crum's out there with him." She spoke to Adam. "Toby's about your age. Why don't you go out and see what they're up to?"

Adam pressed his face against the screen to get a better look at a slat-side shed with a metal chimney peeking out from its tin roof. "I don't think so," he said. "I'm not very good at building birdhouses."

"Go on," Kitty coaxed. "You might enjoy meeting someone your age."

He gave her a look that suggested plans of revenge were already forming in his mind. Nevertheless he stepped outside and, with Lucifer jumping and yelping at his heels, headed for the shed.

Ginny stepped up to a porcelain stove and sniffed the steam coming from a cast-iron kettle. "Hope you like burnet tea with a touch of mint."

"That will be fine," Kitty said, though she had no idea what she'd agreed to drink.

Ginny took two crockery mugs from an open

hutch next to the stove and poured light golden liquid into each one. "I grow the leaves myself," she said, "so when I tell you it's fresh, you can believe it."

Kitty accepted a mug, held it up to her nose and inhaled deeply. Definitely mint. She took a sip. The brew was warm and sweet. "You grow your own tea leaves?" she asked.

Ginny gestured at a big window with at least a dozen clay pots lined up on the sill. "That's just a few," she said. "The rest are on the porch."

Each pot overflowed with green, leafy plants. Ginny's kitchen garden spilled over the window onto tables and shelves on the porch. Easily a hundred pots in all, each filled with vegetation in different stages of growth. "These all make tea?" Kitty asked.

"Gracious no. But all these herbs are good for something."

Kitty carried her mug to the back porch to get a closer look and wandered among the pots. "This herb garden is fascinating."

"Glad you think so. I have about thirty varieties growing right now." Ginny fingered the bisected leaves on one plant. "This is burnet, the one you're drinking."

Kitty stopped at a pot that held long, pointy leaves with explosions of red, pink and blue blossoms. "What's this one?"

"Ah...you like the pretty ones. This is bee balm. If you put the leaves in boiling water for an hour and drink it down fast, it'll cure a stuffy nose. I set these pots outside in the mornings because they attract butterflies."

Kitty smiled. "I didn't know butterflies had sinus problems."

Ginny chuckled. "That's a good one. I'll have to remember to tell Cliff." As they made the circuit around the porch, Ginny explained that lemongrass was used in cider, and ginger root, dried and put in capsules, cured morning sickness. She plucked several arrow-shaped leaves from a plant, crushed them in her hand and held them up for Kitty to smell.

Kitty breathed in the citrus scent. "Nice and fresh."

"Put these in your shoe. They make your feet smell good. 'Nature's lemonade,' it's called, but its true name is sorrel."

"Like the town," Kitty said.

"Right. And the gap. The mountains are wild with this herb. A lot of the farmers still pick the leaves in the heat of summer and nibble on them through the day. They're good for digestion, especially when it's hot."

"What do you do with all these herbs?" Kitty asked.

"Mostly just give them to my neighbors. I'm

sending Toby home with ginger-root capsules this afternoon. His aunt Lyssa is in her second month and can't keep anything down."

"Couldn't you sell the herbs?" Kitty asked. "And what about the birdhouses? Does your husband sell those?"

"Sometimes. Just recently we set up in the parking lot of the new Value-Rite. Did okay." She gave Kitty a sly smile. "I hear you were there, too."

Kitty sighed. "Oh yes, we were there."

"And then at the autumn festival, once a year, when the tourists come to see the leaves turn, Cliff and me, and some of the other folk-craft people, bring our goods to show. I put my herbs in small pouches with a recipe on each one." She took a sip of tea. "We all do fine for a long weekend."

"What do some of the other artists make?"

Ginny smiled. "Artists you call us? I suppose that's true of some. Herb McElroy makes wind chimes from stained glass. Lyssa's handy with a needle and thread."

"Really? I am, too," Kitty said.

"Most of us ladies are experienced sewers, but Lyssa's the best. I'll introduce you to her. She's got lots of sewing supplies she's gathered over the years. Anyway, you'd be amazed what those sunbirds will buy."

"Sunbirds?"

"What we call folks from Florida." Ginny

walked back into the kitchen and pulled out a bentwood chair at a scarred farm table. "Enough about plants and things. I want to know how you and the boy are getting on with Camp. I've known him all his life, and he can be contrary."

Kitty sat and waited for Ginny to take a seat across the table. "It seems to be the general consensus of opinion around here that Campbell is hard to get along with," she said.

"Well, isn't he?"

Kitty smiled. "No. He's…well, yes, I guess he could be called difficult."

"I know Camp better than I do most of the ones raised in town," Ginny said. "He spent more time in the hills than the boys his age. He used to come up and hang out with Lucas Crum, Toby's daddy. The Crums go way back. Their ancestors have lived in the hills since before the Civil War. Campbell and Luke were thick as thieves. Camp seemed like one of us from the first day he showed up here."

Giving in to an intense thirst for any information, Kitty said, "Tell me about his family."

Ginny pushed a strand of wiry hair off her forehead. "It was just him and his mama and daddy. His daddy came from Sorrel Gap. His mama was from the city—Atlanta, I think. Travis was military and he met Vivian Parnell when he was stationed in Georgia. After they married, he moved her up here to the gap. Then he was gone a lot—sent to the four corners of the world. Vivian didn't like it in the mountains. She left as soon as she could. None of us was surprised when Camp followed in his daddy's footsteps and went to the Air Force Academy. We were real proud of him back then."

"And you're not proud of him now?"

"Now I suppose we just don't understand him."

"What do you mean?"

"Camp's been gone a long time, and it was pretty obvious that he didn't want to come back here last fall. Folks don't take to anyone being standoffish, even if that person used to be like family. We figured he'd stay a short while, get his business going and then head out again when opportunity presented itself. Now he's had that crash, and that might change everything." With a sad shake of her head, Ginny added, "It's hard, I guess, to settle in at the Saddle Top after you've lived with the cream of Raleigh society."

Remembering Virgil's reference to Leland Matheson, the furniture tycoon, Kitty simply said, "Campbell's injuries are pretty serious. He's hurting right now."

"From deeper wounds than he got from that plane plunging to earth, if you ask me," Ginny said. She took the empty tea mugs to the sink, leaned against the counter and smiled at Kitty.

"You're good-hearted to look after him, even if Virgil Oakes did more or less hog-tie you to his nephew's bedpost. But to my way of thinking, you're the one needs looking after. Skinny little thing."

Kitty smiled to herself. She guessed she had at least twenty pounds on Ginny Lowe.

"Anyhow, if Campbell gives you any trouble, you tell me, and I'll come down there and set him straight."

An old man slammed the screen door. "Who you gonna set straight this time, woman? Not me, I hope."

Kitty stared into the man's clear eyes. He had thick brows the same pure white as the thatch of hair on his head.

"Clifford Lowe, it's not polite to eavesdrop," Ginny chastised, and then introduced Kitty to her husband.

"I hope my son's not giving you any trouble," Kitty said.

"Don't worry about your boy." Cliff ambled across the room. "He and Toby are shooting pebbles at cans."

"Shooting? Like with a rifle?"

Cliff chuckled. "Nope. Not like that. With a slingshot. Toby's an expert." He chugged a glass of water. "I heard what you women were talking

about, and it won't do you any good to specu-
late about Camp."

"And why's that, you old know-it-all?" Ginny
asked with an easy familiarity Kitty had never
experienced in her own family.

"Because I don't expect Camp will be around
these parts long."

"And I suppose you know where he'll be
going?" Ginny said.

"I don't have the faintest idea, but I'll tell
you this much. Camp's wings may be clipped
for the time being, but he's likely sittin' down
there at the Saddle Top watching for a break in
the clouds. And when he sees it, he might swoop
on out of the gap quicker'n a jaybird after the
first snowfall."

"I don't know," Ginny said. "I think Camp
just needs a reason to stay."

Cliff wiped his hand across his mouth and
shrugged. "Could be. I can't say as I've ever
heard of the mountains going completely out
of a man."

Kitty nodded. She could already feel a part of
the mountains inside her, and she'd only been
here a short time.

"BOY, WHAT A WASTE of time," Adam said later
as he and Kitty headed back toward the motel.

"The old man had me peeling off pieces of tree bark to use as shingles on a birdhouse."

Kitty smiled at Adam. "I don't think it's a waste of time to create beautiful treasures like those birdhouses."

Adam thought a moment. "You should have seen ol' Cliff soak hickory twigs in water so he can bend 'em to make tiny bird swings. He taught me to make wide circles and be real gentle or the twigs'll snap." Adam snorted. "You'd think that geezer would find something better to do with his time. And the same with Toby. Shooting cans with a slingshot. There's nothing to that. I hit a can on my third try."

Adam kicked a stone down the road. "Wait'll you hear this, Mom. Toby and his brother got a PlayStation for Christmas, but they hardly ever turn it on. I'll bet they don't even know how to use it right."

When she didn't respond, Adam clapped his hands. "Mom? Are you listening?"

"Of course I am." It wasn't a lie really, but she knew better than to overreact to what she realized was carefully concealed enthusiasm coming from her son.

Adam ran ahead when they reached the boundary of the motel property. Kitty slowed, giving herself a few extra minutes to wonder if the Lowes could be right about Campbell.

Did his wounds go deeper than the ones he received in the crash? Was he just biding his time in Sorrel Gap? Would he leave when his injuries healed? And if he did, why did the prospect weigh so heavily on Kitty's thoughts? She planned to be in Charlotte once this penance ended, so why should she care what Campbell did weeks from now?

Adam stood up from the rickety lawn chair where he'd been waiting for her. She picked up a handful of loose, rich soil near the old barbecue grill and let it sift through her fingers. She imagined sprouts of cool, soft grass peeking through again. "I'll bet this is good soil," she said. "It could be the bed for a beautiful lawn."

He stared at her. "Why do you care, Mom? Planting a lawn back here is just dumb."

"About as dumb as good mountain dirt, Adam," she said.

CHAPTER TEN

THE ORNATELY CARVED wall clock chimed six times. Owen Galloway glanced through the heavy brocade draperies in his office, poured another two inches of bourbon into his tumbler and frowned. "Fine thing," he said aloud. "A Friday night, and nothing to look forward to but more of the same." By that he meant hours of wondering, speculating and getting nowhere in his search to find his grandson.

He took a sip of his drink and swallowed.

"Mr. Owen?" Esmeralda opened the door and stuck her head inside. "I'm going home now. I left your supper in the oven."

"Have you heard anything since I last talked to you?" he asked.

"Do you mean has Kitty called in the last two hours? Or are you asking if Miss Billie called?"

He frowned. "Either one."

"You must have heard the phone ring a few minutes ago."

He had, but refrained from picking up in the

office. He'd experienced enough disappointment for one day.

"It was Miss Billie," Esmeralda said.

Ah, a ray of hope at last. Owen settled back in his chair and cupped his tumbler between his hands. "What did she want?"

"She wanted me to tell you to stop sending her flowers. Her house smells like a funeral parlor."

He smiled in spite of his misery. Billie Bonneville didn't make his life easy. "I'm assuming that was the only call."

"Don't you think I would tell you if Kitty tried to reach you?" Esmeralda said.

He pondered her question, and then answered honestly, "I don't know. Maybe."

"She hasn't." Esmeralda pointed to a postcard lying in front of him on his desk. "I see you received another message from her."

He picked it up. "Right." He'd read it a half dozen times without finding a clue to his grandson's whereabouts.

"Oh, by the way," Esmeralda said, "Mr. Spenser was pulling into the driveway as I was coming to tell you I was leaving."

"It's about time." Owen knew Terry was just stopping by to check in. Then he'd head out to wherever single guys went on Friday nights, and Owen would be alone. "You can go," he said to Esmeralda. "Send Terry back here to the office."

Less than a minute later, Terry Spenser came into the room. He removed his sport coat, flung it onto the leather sofa and loosened his tie. "Any news since this afternoon?" he asked as he lowered his well-muscled form into a plush leather wing chair on the other side of the desk.

Owen tapped the postcard on his desk blotter before handing it over. "This came today."

"A second one," Terry said.

"Doesn't tell me squat. Just that both of them are okay. But it's mailed from the same Baltimore location."

"That may not mean much," Terry said. "Kitty could have a contact in Baltimore who's mailing the notes for her."

"Still, it's all we've got. I want you to double-check with Bill Ramsey over at the sheriff's office. See that he's sent bulletins to every police station on any route from here to Baltimore. Make sure pictures of Kitty and Adam have been included."

"I already did and he has." Terry leaned forward. "But I think it's time you considered my suggestion."

"About the private investigator?"

Terry nodded. "The guy I found is good."

"And expensive."

"You don't get good without paying a price."

Owen thought a moment. He had no reason to

believe that Kitty and Adam were in any danger. He was still convinced that their disappearance was the result of some feminine whim his daughter had concocted to make him suffer. He wasn't having any luck on his own, so maybe he should invest in the services of a PI. "Call him. Let me know what you work out."

Terry retrieved his jacket and headed for the door. Before leaving, he turned back to Owen. "I want them found, too, you know."

"Not as much as I do. That boy means everything to me."

Owen blinked hard, astounded at the sting of tears in the backs of his eyes. "Why'd she do it, Terry? Does she hate me that much?"

"She's willful, sir."

"She's a damn fool. I gave her everything."

"Unfortunately the only thing she gave you is the very thing she can take back. Her son."

Owen took another swallow and felt his throat muscles relax at the sweet, slow burn. "You tell that PI to find them, Terry."

"I will, sir."

WANDA OAKES GLOSSED over the latest digest of routine announcements to come across the internet. She hadn't checked the messages in a few days, and her computer screen was burdened with dozens of unread emails.

Virgil came in the door to the station, took off his hat and put it on the nearest desk. "I'm bushed," he said. "Let's grab a bite to eat and call it a day."

"Fine with me," she said. "You don't have to ask me twice not to cook."

He sat on the edge of his desk. "Anything interesting come in on those digests?"

"Just the usual. A few lost dogs, a couple of stolen cars, some truancies…" She stopped when a pair of images scrolled onto her screen. A thin woman with short blond hair and a towheaded kid. Silently she read the item's subject line: Whereabouts Unknown.

"Close that thing down and let's go," Virgil said.

She raised one finger, her eyes skimming the details. "Just a sec."

Any persons having information on the following individuals, Katherine "Kitty" Galloway, age 33, and Adam Galloway, age 12, are to contact the Richland, Florida, Sheriff's office.

She stared at the photos, her initial skepticism replaced with a certainty that the Watleys were the couple in question. What had they done? Why were they wanted? She continued reading.

Foul play is not suspected. Persons are not sought in connection with a crime. Need information of whereabouts only.

Wanda drew an immediate conclusion. The woman using an alias and currently caring for her husband's uncooperative and unappreciative nephew wasn't a criminal, but she was hiding out from somebody. An abusive relative, perhaps? This wasn't the first time Wanda had been sent information on a runaway.

"What are you reading there?" Virgil asked.

"Nothing important." She scrolled past the item. "By the way, I've been meaning to ask you, how are Kitty and Adam working out at the motel these days? Still no complaints from Campbell?"

"Nope. Things seem peachy out that way."

And I don't have to trek out there and take care of him. "That's great," she said.

"You had a good idea there."

"I guess so." She then did what her instincts told her. She deleted the file, stood up and pulled her sweater off the back of her chair. "I'm ready. They're having the country-fried steak at the Sorrel Gap Diner."

Satisfied that she'd done the right thing, Wanda set her sights on thick gravy and fresh-baked biscuits.

KITTY TOOK A SHOWER and put on a Vivienne Westwood sleeveless blouse with a splashy grape design that she'd bought on eBay. She paired the blouse with the same skinny, acid-washed jeans she'd worn on her walk into the hills. All the practical things she'd packed in Florida were now dirty, and the laundry soap she'd asked Virgil to send hadn't arrived yet. No problem really. Now that Virgil had suggested she might use Campbell's Jeep, she could drive into town and get supplies herself. As long as Campbell hadn't vetoed the idea.

She and Adam went to Campbell's apartment to fix dinner. He sat on the sofa, his attention glued to the television. She didn't know what she'd expected. Maybe that his eyes would still reflect the impulsiveness of that kiss. Or maybe he'd see that hers did. But tonight Campbell seemed relaxed, in control again.

He glanced her way, sat a little straighter. "You okay?" he asked.

She walked by the sofa without stopping. "Why wouldn't I be?"

"No reason."

"I'll get supper."

"Fine."

Adam dropped down beside him. "What are you watching?"

"Discovery Channel. They're showing a doc-

umentary about these guys who are weather an-
alysts. They're chasing storms across the—"

Adam held out his hand toward the remote.
"Can I change it?"

"No."

"Why not?"

"Two reasons. One, it's my TV, a fact that I've
pointed out to you on more than one occasion.
And two, you're rude."

"Oh."

Kitty opened the freezer and took out a package of chicken tenders. The two males sat glumly,
both with their arms crossed over their chests in
macho posturing.

"How long till it's over?" Adam finally asked.

Campbell looked at his wristwatch. "At seven.
Five minutes."

"Good. I've got something I have to talk to
you about later."

Campbell stared at him, his eyes narrowed
with what could have been genuine interest.
"Okay."

Kitty shredded lettuce for a salad. Though
she tried to concentrate on preparing a meal,
just hearing Campbell's voice put her nerves on
edge. He was acting perfectly normal, but the
air in the small apartment seemed to crackle
with the leftover energy of unfinished business.

As the minutes ticked by, she became acutely

aware of a strange smile that played around Campbell's lips. She noticed drops of water glistening on his recently shampooed hair. A subtle scent of pine wafted toward her from the sofa, crisp, clean and very masculine. She caught a sigh in her throat.

His program over, Campbell turned off the TV and shifted toward Adam. "So, what'd you do today, outlaw?"

"Just dumb things. My mom made me go with her up that mountain behind the motel. We met a couple of old people. The man makes these birdhouses. He works so hard at it you'd think he was planning to shrink down and live in one of them."

Kitty slid a sheet of chicken tenders into the preheated oven and took a package of macaroni from the cupboard. She listened to the conversation while she worked.

Campbell propped himself against the arm of the sofa. "You met the Lowes, right?"

"Yeah."

"Let me tell you something, Adam. Hooking up with those two wasn't dumb at all. In fact, it might turn out to be one of the smartest things you've ever done. A fella can get quite an education if he only remembers a tenth of what comes out of Ginny's mouth."

Kitty smiled to herself, thinking how Ginny

might be surprised and flattered to learn that Campbell had such a high opinion of her. It must be true that you can't take all the country out of the man.

"The Lowes are okay, I guess," Adam conceded. "I met this kid, too. His name's Toby."

"That's Toby Crum," Campbell said. "I used to hang out with his father."

"But you don't anymore?"

Campbell simply replied, "No."

Adam sat taller on the sofa. "Remember I said I have to talk to you about something?"

"I remember. So talk."

"I want to make a deal with you."

"What kind of deal?"

Adam explained about his day at Value-Rite and Quint's offer to give him the color television. "So you see, me and Mom could have a television in our room that was actually made in this century, one that's cable-ready."

"That Quint is a stand-up guy, all right," Campbell said. He looked over his shoulder at Kitty. "You excited about this, too, Mom?"

"I'm all tingly," she said.

Campbell chuckled. "Okay, so what does this have to do with me?"

Adam leaned close, his eyes wide with impatience, and said, "Jeez, I just told you, cable-ready. Get it?"

Campbell nodded slowly. "I think I do now. You want me to foot the bill to have cable run from my satellite dish to unit six."

Adam rolled his eyes. "Well, yeah. That's pretty much it."

"So what's the deal?"

"Huh?"

"You said you were striking a deal with me. When one person makes all the arrangements and invests all the money, that's a favor, not a deal. What do I get out of this?"

Adam focused a startled gaze on Campbell's placid face and groaned. "Isn't it obvious?" he finally said. "You get rid of me and keep sole rights to your remote again."

"That might have been a deal maker last week," Campbell said, "but now I'm getting kind of used to you."

"You mean you like having me around?"

"I wouldn't go that far. You're like the kid brother I'm glad I never had. You make me thankful my parents stopped with one."

Adam set his closed fists on his knees. "Aw, come on. This town is bleeding me dry. I'm working my butt off. No decent TV to come home to. What more do you want from me? It's just a dumb cable connection."

Kitty smiled as she placed a pot of water on

to boil. She had to admire Adam's gift for dramatic flair.

Campbell cleared his throat. "Tell you what. I'll make a deal with *you*."

Adam slouched into the sofa. "Oh yeah? What?"

"I'll call the satellite company tomorrow and have them come out and run a line into your room..."

A grin lurked at Adam's mouth. He wanted to be happy, but the internal warning mechanism that manifested itself in his furrowed brow kept him from rejoicing in his good fortune. "Okay, then what?"

"And then you help your mother with supper and do the dishes afterward for two weeks."

Adam released an indignant squawk. "Two weeks? How much does a stupid cable line cost?"

"How much have you got?"

"Nothing."

"Well, more than that, but that's the deal. Take it or leave it."

Adam stood up and walked around the sofa to give Kitty a pleading look. "Mom, isn't this extortion or blackmail or something illegal?"

Kitty picked up the box of macaroni and placed it in Adam's hands. "I wouldn't know, but I did read the directions on the back of this box. It says you should boil the noodles for eight minutes or until tender."

Her son stared at the box while mumbling words like *conspirators* and *traitors*. He ripped the tab on the top of the carton and poured half the contents into the pot. "Is this enough?" he asked.

"Should be."

He scowled at the back of Campbell's head. "I guess you'd better put cooking lessons on my list of things to do every day, Mom."

"My pleasure." Campbell turned and winked at her and she smiled. Oh yeah, she was definitely tingly.

AFTER FORCING DOWN overdone chicken fingers and lukewarm macaroni, Campbell concluded that he was going to suffer more as a result of his brilliant deal-making than the outlaw would. But it was worth some indigestion to see the pride in Kitty's eyes. She praised Adam's efforts as if he'd suddenly become Wolfgang Puck. Campbell considered that it might be the only time the kid had ever helped her out.

Once the dinnerware was dried and stowed in the cupboard, Campbell asked Adam to go outside so he could speak privately with his mother.

"What about?" Adam asked.

"This concerns a deal I have to make with

your mother this time," Campbell said, unable to ignore the look of obstinate curiosity in Adam's face. "Look, don't worry about it. If this works out, you could be watching TV in vivid color as soon as tomorrow."

Adam relaxed his prowrestler stance and headed for the door. "Whatever it is, Mom, agree to it."

Kitty waited until Adam had left the lobby before saying to Campbell, "You've got his hopes up now. Can you deliver on that promise?"

"I'm going to try." He gestured at the recliner. "Sit down, Kitty." When she didn't, he leaned against the sofa cushion and spread his arm across the back. She'd been as skittish as a jackrabbit all evening, stealing peeks at him while maintaining a safe distance. And why not? He hadn't been able to put the earlier incident out of his mind, and he figured she hadn't, either. What Campbell didn't know was if Kitty, despite her protests, wanted it to happen again. Drawing on the reserves he'd perfected during years of military training, he took a deep breath and focused on anything but his lips against hers.

She sat in the chair as if it were upholstered in eggshells.

He cleared his throat and reminded himself

that Kitty and the kid were the sort of major headaches he didn't need. With her hands clasped primly in her lap, Kitty seemed small and vulnerable in the oversize recliner. And still much too appealing in a pair of tight jeans and a blouse with bunches of juicy-looking grapes all over it.

She sat still as a statue, her spine at least a foot from the back of the chair. "Okay, Campbell," she said after a moment. "We're alone. What did you want to say?"

"Virgil called before you came over. He said he'd given his permission for you to drive my Jeep if I didn't have any objections."

Her facial features tensed in preparation for the ultimate letdown. "So now I suppose you're going to tell me you have a list of objections a mile long."

Did she really think he was that unreasonable? Well, maybe he had given her that impression. "It just so happens that I agree with Virgil," he said. "I think it's stupid for him to drive out here to get Adam and pick up grocery lists. And even more ridiculous for Gibbs to show up when Virgil can't."

He gave his forehead a mental slap. The last thing he'd intended was to bring Tommy into any conversation with Kitty again. "I have a perfectly good running vehicle out back," he said. He glared down the length of his splint. "And as long as I'm not going to be driving it for a while, you might as well."

"I appreciate your letting me drive the Jeep," she said. "I really do…"

She trailed off and he waited. "But?"

"But you told Adam you were going to make a *deal* with me. So what do I have to do to get those keys?"

Unlike her son, Kitty knew she wasn't likely to get something for nothing. "It's very simple," he said. "I agree to let you drive my Jeep, and you agree not to wreck it."

If possible, her spine straightened even more. "That's really funny, Campbell. And more than a little insulting…"

"Not quite. You have to promise not to nag me about my physical therapy. I'll do my exercises. I know I need to, but on my schedule, not yours."

She stood up, shaking her head before he'd finished speaking. "Sorry, but I already promised Virgil, and I called your home health nurse today, and—"

She stopped what he already interpreted as preliminary nagging when the phone rang, interrupting her. She stared at the receiver and waited for him to pick it up. "Aren't you going to answer that?"

Three rings. He glanced at the caller ID. "Nope."

Four rings. "It could be important."

"I doubt it, but if you think it is, you answer it."

Five rings. She blew out a long breath and snatched up the receiver. "Hello. Yes, this is Kitty. How do you know my name?"

Campbell snickered. This was Sorrel Gap. By now, everyone knew who she was and why she was here, especially Greg.

"Well, yes, it would be nice to meet you, too." She nodded. "Yes, he's here. Just a minute."

She covered the mouthpiece with her hand. "It's Greg Hanson from the Blue Ridge Airstrip."

Campbell shrugged. "I don't know any Greg Hanson."

"Yes, you do."

"Okay, I do. But I'm indisposed at the moment."

She put the phone back to her mouth. "Greg? Campbell said…" She paused and then lowered the phone so the earpiece rested on a particular ripe grape he'd been fantasizing about. "He heard what you said, and he wants me to tell you that you should stop acting like a horse's behind and take the phone."

"Tell him I'll call him back tomorrow."

She relayed the message and covered the

speaker grid again. "He says you're lying. You won't call him back tomorrow."

Campbell frowned. "I guess that does prove he knows me pretty well."

Kitty's toe tapped against his maple floor. "This is ridiculous. You told me to answer the phone, so I'll just go ahead and have the conversation you should be having." She walked into the kitchen and carried on a five-minute chat with the man Campbell could probably call his best friend in Sorrel Gap, since he managed the Blue Ridge Airstrip and could handle aerial camera shots with acceptable proficiency. When she came back, she settled the phone onto the cradle and gave Campbell a look that could freeze Gilley's Creek in midsummer.

Campbell picked up the *TV Guide* and pretended to check the day's listings. "So, what did you think of Greg?" he asked with all the disinterest he could muster. She sat on the arm of the sofa apparently abandoning her plan to stay as far away from him as possible and glared down at him. He shifted, putting a few necessary inches between them.

"Why won't you go to the airstrip and talk to Greg about fixing your plane?"

"I don't want to." He sounded like a petulant child. "I'm not ready to." Now he sounded like a prima donna, although that statement was true. He wasn't ready to talk about his leg or the plane or the possibility that he'd ever make a success of his business. Not with Greg, and especially not with this woman who seemed determined to pull the truth out of him.

Lately he'd begun to believe that the crashing of his Cessna was a test of some sort, one that he'd failed miserably. His last image of the plane was a picture taken by a highway patrolman of the Cessna being hauled away on the back of a tow truck. The photo, now in his desk drawer, was burned into the backs of his eyelids, reminding him every day of big plans that now lay twisted among the crumpled right wing and smashed landing gear.

Still, he supposed he owed her a response, even if it wasn't an honest one. "Look," he began, "I was barely making a go of my photography business when the plane crashed into the pasture. Maybe the whole incident was a sign that I should just keep my feet on the ground."

"Oh, really?" She twisted so her knees just brushed his splint. "Considering I'm scared to death of small planes, I can almost agree with you. But you're not afraid of them. Even after this accident, I doubt you're afraid to fly again. And I also doubt that this business venture is a mistake."

The stubborn determination in her eyes

and the set of her lips told him she had him dead to rights—and she knew it. No, he wasn't afraid. Some men were born to fly anything with wings, and Campbell was one of them. But he wasn't about to confess his weakness to her—that he couldn't face the reality of another crushed dream.

"You're wrong," he said, thinking he'd disguise his own inadequacy by placing blame elsewhere. "I'll be broke in less than a year if I depend on the people around here for jobs."

The corners of her lips lifted in a taunting replica of a grin. "And I suppose you've just been an ambassador of goodwill since you came back, using your sparkling personality to drum up business."

He tried to tell himself she was way off base. When that didn't work, he tried not to think about the cold macaroni noodles lying like pebbles in his stomach.

She reached for the phone again and went back to the kitchen.

"Who are you calling?" Campbell asked.

"Greg. I'm letting him know I'm bringing you to the airstrip on Friday."

"Don't push this, Kitty." He remembered the significance of Friday and wondered if the trip to Greg's was part of Kitty's master plan to bring him back to the human race. "Besides, why Friday?"

She smiled. "As if you didn't know. Your first therapy session is that morning. Virgil tells me those ribs should be sufficiently healed so you can start on some upper-body exercises."

Campbell stared at the black TV screen. "Easy for Virgil to say. He's not trying to breathe through my lungs."

"So you did know that your therapy begins in three days?"

Of course he knew. He'd been dreading the inevitable phone call from Wanda telling him she'd pick him up for the session. At least having Kitty chauffeur him around had certain perks Wanda couldn't provide. "I knew," he admitted. "I just didn't think my uncle would rat me out."

"You might as well get started. It'll be good for you. If nothing else, you need to get out of this motel for a while, and afterward we'll go to the airstrip. I want to see what kind of shape this plane is in."

As if she could make a determination about what it would take to get the Cardinal airborne again. He locked gazes with the most determined set of blue eyes he'd ever seen. "You're being a bit too bossy," he said.

"Get used to it." She turned her back to him and punched numbers into the phone keypad.

Campbell groaned. This was the thanks he got for agreeing to let the woman drive his car?

A few minutes later, Kitty returned to the sofa with his medications and a glass of water. She was smiling as if she hadn't just conspired against him with his uncle and his best friend. In fact, she looked so darn pleased with herself that Campbell grudgingly admitted that there was something appealing about her newfound confidence.

"Lighten up, Campbell," she said. "Greg's looking forward to seeing you. And like he says, you can't leave the plane sidelined in his hangar forever."

She set down the glass and pressed his pills into his palm. Her touch was firm but gentle. He grasped her hand. She made a slight protest but soon relaxed, letting him hold her hand close to his chest. "Now what are you trying to do?" she said.

"The way I see it, my deal-making skills are nothing to brag about. I figure I'm going to regret agreeing to anything with you Watleys. First of all, I'm going to hate having Adam in my kitchen. And second, I can tell you're going to nag me unmercifully."

She withdrew her hand and gave him the glass of water. "Makes you think twice about tangling with a pair of desperadoes like us, doesn't it?"

Kitty had as many contradictions in her personality as Ginny Lowe had herb recipes. She was as needy as she was independent. As confident as she was incompetent. As bossy as she was compliant. But he couldn't manage to work up a good head of steam, because it was those contradictions that intrigued him and kept him awake at night. And made him want to know her better. Much better.

He stared into her round blue eyes. "I'll tell you what it does make me think—that when I make my next deal with you, I'm going to come out of it with something *I* want."

She waited while he took his pills. "Do you need anything else tonight?"

He grinned at her. "Do you really want me to answer that?"

She smiled back, and he chose to believe they were having the same thought. She headed to the kitchen. "When I come over in the morning," she said, "I'd appreciate it if you'd have the keys to the Jeep ready for me. And your list for the supermarket. Besides the things you want, I'm going to buy the makings for a picnic."

"Who's going on a picnic?"

"You are. Or rather we are." She stopped in front of the sofa on her way to the door. "After the trip to the airstrip, we'll pick up Adam at Value-Rite and find a nice spot between the store and the motel for lunch."

"I don't like picnics," Campbell said. He wasn't being strictly contrary this time. He really didn't care for eating on blankets and sharing his food with ants. To Campbell, eating was a necessity he'd learned in the military, best accomplished in a minimum of time with a minimum of fuss.

She shrugged and turned toward the door. "I'm sorry to hear that, especially since you're not the one who'll be driving the car."

She went out, and he listened to her footsteps recede through the lobby. Like it or not, even with a bum leg to contend with, he was obviously going on a picnic.

CHAPTER ELEVEN

CAMPBELL SEEMED ALMOST cheerful the next morning when Kitty went to his room to get the keys to the Jeep. She fixed his coffee, brought him a bowl of cereal and some toast and endured his detailed instructions on how to operate his vehicle. "You're absolutely certain you know how to handle a stick shift?" he asked her.

"Yes, I told you I can. I once had a..." She almost blew her cover by admitting that Owen had indulged her on her sixteenth birthday by buying her a sleek four-on-the-floor sports car. Instead she told him she'd once owned a 1975 Volkswagen Beetle, a car that only existed in her imagination.

"Okay, then. We have hills here, though. It can be a little tricky..."

She held out her hand and wiggled her fingers. "Campbell..."

"Fine. I was just trying to give you a word of advice." He placed the keys in her palm along with a shopping list and a one-hundred-dollar bill. "Get whatever you and the outlaw want," he said. As she headed for the door, he asked her if she had the phone number to his apartment. When she assured him she did, he reminded her to call on her cell phone if she ran into any trouble.

"Great idea," she said, "if I had a cell phone—which I don't. And what would you do if I did call? Run to my rescue?"

"No. But I'd call your knight in shining armor, Deputy Tommy Do-right." He then picked up his own cell phone from the coffee table and tossed it to her. "Take this. I can't have you out on the highway without a means to communicate. Besides, I may decide I want chunky peanut butter instead of creamy."

She slipped the device into the pocket of her sweatpants. "I wouldn't want to be unaware of such crucial decisions."

She smiled as she returned to her room because she knew that peanut butter had nothing to do with Campbell's decision to lend her the phone. He'd never admit it, but she believed he was concerned about her going into town on her own for the first time. At least it was possible.

Since her own clothes needed a wash, she dressed in one of the newly altered outfits from the nightstand drawer. When she came out of the bathroom, Adam gave her a quizzical look. "What are you wearing that old stuff for?"

She checked her appearance in the mirror and was pleased with the work she'd done on the skirt and blouse. She reached for her hair gel and immediately set the bottle back on the counter. The simple, draped lines of the clothing called for a more natural look.

"I kind of like these clothes," she said, gently fluffing her hair with her fingers.

"They're okay, I guess," Adam said. "Let's get going. I want to see Campbell's car."

She followed him out the door. "Wow, this is a first. You're actually anxious to go to Value-Rite."

He looked over his shoulder. "Did you hear me say anything about Value-Rite?"

She laughed. "A mother can hope."

Five minutes later they were breezing down Old Sorrel Gap Road. Adam had insisted they put the top down, and he stuck his hand in the air, capturing the wind in his palm. "Wow, Mom, this Jeep is way boss." He fiddled with the knobs on the dashboard before adding, "I wish I had a CD to play in here. I should have figured the beast would have a rad sound system in his car."

Kitty absolutely agreed about the way boss part. Maybe this vehicle wasn't as flashy as her BMW, but driving it was perhaps the coolest thing she'd done in two weeks.

The fresh mountain breeze whipped her un-processed hair about her face. The light gauzy fabric of Patsy Avery's handmade blouse tick-led the hair on her arms. And Kitty felt free, excited and happy, emotions that had less to do with the crisp hundred-dollar bill in her purse and more to do with Campbell's trust that led to her escape from the Saddle Top on this glori-ous morning. She pulled up to the main entrance of Value-Rite and leaned over to give Adam a peck on his cheek.

He flinched. "Mom, I know people here. And I have a rep. I'm considered kind of a bad dude by the rest of the guys."

Kitty frowned. "You're supposed to be liv-ing down your brush with the law, not turning it into folk-hero status."

He grinned with cocky pride. "Don't worry. I'm not going to steal anything else. But what I did has become a sort of legend in these parts."

These parts?

He opened the door and got out. "See you at one, right?"

"Absolutely." Then, deciding she might be taking too much for granted, she amended, "Ei-ther me or Sheriff Oakes."

He rested his elbows on the door frame. "Try not to do anything to tick him off, okay? I don't want Sheriff Smokey to take away our driving privileges."

She bit back a smile. "I'll do my best."

Kitty pulled out of the parking lot to travel the two miles to town. She selected a station on the radio, one of many that blasted country music from the sophisticated speakers. Following Campbell's specific instructions, she made two turns and ended up at Ingles Supermarket. She parked, took her shopping list from her purse and grabbed the nearest cart. Soon she was navigating the spacious aisles of the market and having a great time.

Granted she was only here to buy groceries, but Kitty made the most of her experience. Shopping, in any of its forms, was her thing, and since this was the first time in two weeks she'd been able to pursue her habit, she took it seriously. In the produce department she chose a bag of potatoes as carefully as if she were buying a new dress.

"Isn't that adorable?" a woman behind her said.

"I've never seen anything like it," another responded. "It's got to be an original."

"Should we ask her where she got it?"

"Why not? She looks nice enough."

Kitty ignored the potatoes and faced the two women, both about her age. She pegged them as tourists right away. One had on a crisp new T-shirt from Harrah's Casino in Cherokee. The other carried a canvas bag advertising the Smoky Mountain Railroad. Kitty smiled but didn't speak.

"I'm sorry," one woman said. "But we were admiring your clothes."

Kitty ran her hands down the delicate fabric of the skirt, showing the lines to their best advantage. The women didn't seem to notice the slight fading. And under the lights of the produce department, Kitty didn't, either. "Oh, well, thank you," she said.

The woman held out her hand. "I'm Sherry and this is Gloria."

Kitty shook their hands.

"That fabric is just beautiful," Sherry said. "The way it flows. It would look good on anyone."

Kitty had to agree.

"Did you get those things in town here?" Sherry asked.

"Sort of," Kitty said. "A few miles out of town, to be exact."

"Would you mind telling us where?" Gloria asked.

"I wouldn't mind at all, but this outfit didn't come from a store. It's handmade."

Sherry groaned. "You mean I can't buy anything like this?"

"I'm sorry, but…" She was about to explain that the woman who made these pieces was no longer around. But she never finished her sentence because another thought—crazy maybe, perhaps just a little dishonest—popped into her head. Campbell had told her she could keep the clothing, so technically they were hers to do with as she pleased. Recently it had pleased her to update them with her own modifications. And right now it pleased her to sell them. "You could buy *this* outfit," she said.

"I could?" Sherry said. "How much?"

"Well, I've never sold any of the creations before." Kitty smiled to herself. The garments she'd found in the nightstands had suddenly become *creations*.

"I'd pay you a hundred and fifty for what you're wearing," Sherry said. "Assuming it is truly an original."

"Oh, it is," Kitty said.

"Do you have others?" Gloria asked.

"Yes, one more outfit similar to this."

"Where can we see it?"

Kitty's hand trembled. Three hundred dollars! She wrapped her fingers around the handle of the shopping cart. "Have you got a car?"

"A rental." Gloria grinned as if she were anticipating a great adventure. "If you give us directions, we can come out to your place."

Wait till you see it, Kitty thought. But then she dismissed any hint of embarrassment she might have felt at directing these ladies to the Saddle Top Motel. If she'd been in their places, focused on the find of the century, as she had been many times in her other life, she'd have been tickled to discover it at any out-of-the-way place.

"I guess that would be okay," she said. "Have you got paper and a pen?"

She scribbled directions to the motel. "You'll pass a couple of abandoned buildings, but keep going. Once you go over a hill, you'll see a sign for the Saddle Top Motel. That's me."

"You live in a motel?" Gloria asked.

"I work there," Kitty explained. "Charity work, just temporarily. I'm actually a fashion designer."

Okay, not exactly true, but that explanation lent credibility to Kitty's living quarters.

"We'll meet you there in a couple of hours," Sherry said.

Kitty hurried through the rest of her shopping. She couldn't stop thinking about the pending sales. When she'd loaded the Jeep and was heading back to the Saddle Top, she was buzzing with excitement. Did this count as her first sale in the fashion industry?

The transaction wasn't going to happen as she'd always thought it would, with deals being made next to a New York City runway. But so what? A sale was a sale, and she could imagine herself experimenting with designs similar to Patsy's skirts and blouses. She would add her own touches and include camp shirts and flood pants and crops and sundresses…

WHEN HE HEARD the rumble of his Jeep in the parking lot, Campbell hobbled to the motel lobby. He'd just reached the entrance and looked out when the door to Kitty's room slammed. A few minutes later she emerged wearing her sweatpants from this morning and an old T-shirt. She carried a load of clothes and scurried down the sidewalk.

"Hey, what's going on?" he hollered to her as she disappeared into the breezeway.

"I'll be right back," she said. "I just have to get these things into the washing machine.

He heard the grind of a twisting dial and the rush of water through the old motel pipes. A moment later, she ran back to the Jeep and opened the cargo door. She approached his doorway with a bag of groceries tucked into each elbow. "Coming through," she said.

He got out of the way.

She went back for another load. "What's going on?" he asked again when she passed him a second time.

"I've got people coming out."

He barked his surprise. "What?"

"I met some ladies at the grocery. They said they were going to be here in a while."

"Here? Meaning the motel?" He hardly recognized the pitch of his own voice.

She disappeared into his apartment. "Of course here at the motel."

He hopped toward his room, making irritatingly slow progress. "Why?"

She skirted around him. "Two more sacks."

"Kitty…"

She didn't even slow down. "Go. Sit. I'll fix you a sandwich as soon as I put these groceries away."

"It's only ten o'clock," he shouted to her back. He didn't think she heard him. When she came back, she set to work unloading the food from the bags and shoving it with no apparent order into his cupboards. He sat on the couch and stared, unable to pull his attention from the haphazard task and the tempting tug of her T-shirt when she reached for a high shelf.

"I'll never be able to find anything," he said, feeling inexplicably left out.

"You never *look* for anything, do you?"

Well, no, he didn't. If she wasn't around to bug him three times a day, he'd probably forget to eat.

She flattened the empty sacks without paying any attention to the prefolds built in by the manufacturer. The result was a jumbled stack of crinkled paper that she stuffed into the cleaning closet. He cringed. Less than a minute later, she plunked a plate on the coffee table. It held two slabs of bread with something mysterious between them and half a pickle. She laid a jumbo bag of corn chips next to the plate. "I'll get you a drink in a minute," she said. "I'm going to check the washing machine."

He grabbed her shirt. "No, you're not. First tell me about this company you're expecting."

"I will, but I'm working against the clock." She yanked her shirt free and smoothed it over her waist. "I need to get my clothes in the dryer. I hope I didn't put too much bleach in." She patted his shoulder. "You'll be fine. I'll be right back."

"Obviously I'll be fine," he said, resenting the insinuation that without her slapdash way of doing things, he wouldn't be. "I just want to know…"

"Two minutes." She was gone again, and Campbell, who had no experience with the status of married man, felt like a beleaguered husband who suddenly didn't recognize his own wife. Only Campbell didn't have the fringe benefits that might have made a husband's suffering worthwhile.

She returned in the time promised, glanced down at the untouched plate and grumbled, "Eat."

He picked up the sandwich and took a bite. Seemed easier than arguing about having lunch at ten-thirty.

She brought him a soda in a plastic glass, placed it on the end table and sat in his recliner. Folding her hands on her lap, she sighed heavily. "Campbell, I have to make certain we're clear about something."

It was about time. He hadn't been clear about anything for the past half hour. "What?"

"You remember the other day when I told you about the clothes I found in room six?"

"The ones left by Patsy Avery?"

She nodded.

"What about them?"

"You said I could keep them, isn't that right?"

"Yeah, so?" He couldn't imagine why she'd bring up something as insignificant as those old clothes.

"Well, I made some adjustments to the clothes

and wore one of the outfits to the grocery this morning."

He waited. So far, nothing she'd said seemed particularly noteworthy.

"Two lady tourists commented on how much they liked it," she said.

"Swell."

"And I agreed to sell them the clothes."

He dropped the sandwich. "What? You went to the supermarket for the first time and ended up selling the clothes off your back?" He was hit with an overwhelming sense of guilt. "Kitty, do you need money that badly? I had no idea. You should have said…"

She held up her hand. "No, it's not like that." Her eyes widened as if she couldn't fathom that he'd offer to help her. What kind of monster did she think he was?

"It's no secret I'm not floating in cash right now," she said. "But Adam and I are doing okay. I just saw the selling of the clothes as an opportunity."

"An opportunity for what?"

"Well, to get ahead for when my truck is fixed and we can get back on the road, but also to experiment and make some pieces similar to the ones Patsy sewed."

She waited for a reaction. He didn't have one, so she filled in the awkward silence. "Remem-

ber, I told you I know something about clothing. Fashion design interests me, and since these
things caused such a positive reaction in the
grocery—"

He interrupted. "So selling this stuff is a career decision?"

"Maybe. I'm going to use some of the money…
if these ladies even show up…" She checked her
wristwatch. "To shop for fabric and play around
with some designs. So you're okay with my decision about selling the clothing?"

"No problem," he said.

She stood up. "Okay, but I need Ginny Lowe's
phone number. Do you have it?"

He opened the end-table drawer and withdrew a slim phone book. "You think Ginny's
going to buy your clothes?"

"No, but she knows a girl in the hills who
has sewing skills. Toby Crum's aunt, I think she
said. I'd like to call her and maybe meet with
her for advice."

Campbell flipped pages. "That must be Lyssa,
Lucas's sister." He found Ginny's number and
jotted it on a piece of paper. "Here you go."

She took the paper and folded it into the pocket
of her pants. "Thanks. If you don't need anything more now, I'll go check on the clothes in
the dryer."

He stopped her as she headed for the exit. "Kitty? One more thing."

She turned around and frowned. "You want to know how much I got for the clothes?"

He was a little insulted. "That's your business. I just wondered what you did to your hair today. It looks different."

She raked her fingers through the silky blond strands around her face. "Actually nothing. I just decided to wear it differently."

"It's kind of nice that way."

She flashed him a skeptical gaze before her lips slowly turned up in a smile. Then she smoothed her hand over the hair at her nape and said, "Really? You like it?"

He nodded.

She was still smiling when she closed his door. And he realized he was, too.

THE LADIES FROM the grocery store showed up at the motel as promised. Sherry and Gloria each bought an outfit, and when they left, Kitty folded three hundred dollars and slipped the bills in the pocket of her purse. Her confidence building to what was no doubt an unwarranted level based on only two sales, she gave each woman a makeshift business card with her name, the phone number to room six and the label she thought up on the spot for her new enterprise, Saddle Top Apparel.

On Thursday, with nothing to do until the next day and Campbell's first therapy appointment, Kitty once again borrowed Campbell's Jeep, called Virgil to say she was running errands and spent the morning with Toby Crum's aunt, Lyssa MacDonald. Lyssa turned out to be helpful, forthright and extremely knowledgeable about the area where she'd grown up. After listening to girl talk about her mountain community, Kitty felt almost as if she herself were part of the fabric of the hills.

They dropped Adam at Value-Rite and browsed through bolts of material in the store's craft section. Following Lyssa's advice, Kitty bought five yards of eight different fabrics including natural linen and unbleached cotton and loaded everything into Campbell's Jeep. Kitty also stocked up on elastic and trims, and secured Lyssa's pledge to embroider some of the pieces for a 20 percent cut of the sale price.

Kitty and Lyssa bought take-out lunches in Sorrel Gap and ate them on the town square in front of the sheriff's office. They'd just finished when Tommy Gibbs pulled into his parking spot. He immediately came over, spoke to Lyssa and initiated a conversation with Kitty.

"I see Camp's Jeep over there," he said. "Is he driving these days?"

Kitty explained about Virgil's suggestion. "Mostly I'll be taking Campbell to his rehab appointments," she said.

Tommy feigned a sympathetic expression. "Poor ol' Camp, having to let someone take him where he needs to go. It'll be a while before he'll be able to do even the simplest things."

"He's not all that helpless," Kitty said. "And he's feeling much better."

"That's good, but if you need any help around there…"

Kitty smiled at the young man. "You're sweet to offer, Tommy, but we're fine, really."

Kitty was grateful when Virgil appeared at his office door and called Tommy.

"What was that all about?" Lyssa asked when Tommy had gone inside.

"Nothing," Kitty said. "Tommy is just being friendly."

Lyssa chuckled. "Looked to me like he wanted you to need him out at the Saddle Top."

Kitty shook her head, not wanting to admit to Lyssa that she believed it might be possible. "He's just being friendly. That's it, really."

"I don't know why you'd say that. You're pretty and sophisticated. I'll bet Camp has noticed, too."

Trying not to think of the kiss, Kitty said, "I doubt Campbell notices much beyond his TV remote."

Lyssa responded with one of her very feminine smiles.

They picked up Adam at one o'clock. Kitty dropped Lyssa off at her house up the hill road and returned to the motel. She rushed into Campbell's apartment at one-thirty uttering a hasty apology. "I'm sorry. I know it's late and you haven't had your lunch."

She pulled a can from the pantry and dishware from the cupboards. "What would you like?" she asked him. "I'll make you a hot meal if you want."

He hadn't stopped staring at her since she'd entered his room. She figured he was probably irritated, but she'd had such a good day, she couldn't make herself feel too bad about neglecting him for a couple of hours. Besides, she'd told him where she was going and had even used his cell phone to check in once.

"Anything's fine," he said. "I'm not helpless, you know. I even made it to the kitchen for a trail-mix bar earlier."

She glanced over at him. "Oh, well, good."

"You've been all this time shopping for fabric?" he asked.

She emptied a can of tuna into a bowl and got

celery and onion from the refrigerator. While chopping vegetables, she chatted at warp speed.

"Campbell, you won't believe the buys I got. Lyssa is an expert at choosing just the right material for the designs I have in mind. And she's agreed to help me. With her handiwork on the pieces, I know I can sell…"

She paused when she heard the soft thump of crutch tips on the wooden floor. Turning from the counter, she said, "What are you doing sneaking up on me like that?"

"Sorry, but are you trying to kill me?" He looked down at the cutting board. "There's enough onion there for twenty sandwiches, and I don't even eat onion. Each of those pieces would be like dropping firecrackers into my stomach."

She looked down at the result of her indiscriminate slaughter of veggies. "I'm so sorry!" She scraped the onion bits into the disposal and flipped the switch. "I forgot," she said over the grind of the machine.

"It's okay. I'm glad you're enthusiastic about this whole sewing thing." He supported himself on his crutch and placed his hand in the middle of her back. His knuckles rode a few inches of her spine. She dropped the paring knife and turned off the disposal. When she realized her hands had begun to shake, she grabbed the edge of the counter.

He leaned in, speaking close to her ear. "You all right?"

She stared into the sink. "Of course."

"Good."

He moved back but no more than a foot or so. "What did you think of Lyssa?" he asked. "I remember her as a cute kid."

Kitty removed a jar of mayonnaise from the refrigerator. "She is. And she seems very perceptive...about some things."

He reached around her, picked up a stalk of celery and chomped off the end. "Oh yeah? Like what?"

What had made her say that? She wasn't going to tell him that Lyssa thought Campbell might actually be attracted to her. She spooned a mound of mayo from the jar and plopped it into the bowl of tuna. "Nothing." She glanced over her shoulder. "We were just talking about clothes and things. Girl stuff. You wouldn't be interested."

He gave her a smile that suggested he might be a slight bit perceptive himself. "So, where's the outlaw?" he asked.

"Watching TV in our room." She stirred the concoction in the bowl. "Thanks for arranging that cable, by the way."

"No problem." He squeezed her elbow before heading back to the sofa. "Every guy has to have one hundred channels."

She closed her eyes and breathed deeply. Why was he touching her like this? A press of his hand, a brush of his fingers, so cozy and warm, almost intimate. She liked the feel of him way too much. She'd best remember that just as an impulsive kiss didn't mean anything, neither did these fleeting gestures.

CHAPTER TWELVE

CAMPBELL HATED BEING pushed in a wheelchair. But the administrators of the Spooner County Rehabilitation Center insisted that he be escorted from the facility by an assistant. As they approached the exit, he rotated his neck to relieve tension. The double entry doors opened with an automatic hiss.

Every bone in his upper body ached. He'd been prodded and twisted, flexed and stretched, twice being left alone in an antiseptic room to squeeze rubber balls while the therapist went on to his next victim. "Do that two hundred times with each hand," the cheerful but demanding white-coated young man had said. "I'll be back."

"Is your ride here?" the assistant asked him when they had progressed to the covered drive-through area.

At that precise moment the Jeep shot around the circular pavement and a long, slim arm waved from the driver's window. The Cherokee lunged to a stop in front of them and shuddered once while Kitty clutched, jammed the gear-shift into the idle position and yanked on the hand brake. "That's my ride, all right," Campbell said.

Refusing help from the therapist, he positioned his crutches under his arms and hoisted himself from the chair. Kitty was at his side before he'd taken one step toward the Jeep. "How did everything go?" she asked. "How do you feel? Do you hurt anywhere?"

"Okay, I guess. Lousy. Everywhere. Now, how about cutting the chatter until I get into the car?"

She smiled! Her good humor seemed especially inappropriate, considering that she was wearing that T-shirt with the cartoon eyes again, the one that kept his attention glued where it shouldn't be and seemed to have captured the therapist's attention, as well. Campbell decided to buy her some new things to wear, tops with buttons that climbed all the way to her chin. Nice idea, but he shook his head. She'd never wear them. Once he was settled in the front seat, she asked directions to the location of his airplane. "What do you think it's going to look like?" she asked when they were speeding along the country road to the airstrip.

"I don't have to think. I saw it, remember?"

He stared out the side window. "It's a crumpled pile of metal."

"But you can fix it."

Maybe, he thought but shrugged a response. No point passing his gloomy demeanor on to Kitty.

They pulled into the parking lot adjacent to a galvanized building with a door labeled *Office*. A man came outside before Campbell had gotten out of the Jeep.

"That's Greg," Campbell said.

The airstrip owner waited until Campbell was standing on the gravel surface before slapping him on the back. "'Bout time you got your butt out here," he said.

Greg Hanson's features didn't reflect any animosity, even though Campbell had been putting him off for quite a while. He smiled broadly, his upper teeth white against his dark beard. He'd just started the growth when he visited Campbell in the hospital. Now his jaw and cheek were covered with an admirable patch of peppered whiskers. "Beard's coming in nice," Campbell said.

"Kathy likes it," Greg responded. He patted his slightly rounded stomach. "Says it diverts attention from the results of her cooking." He grinned at Kitty and stuck out his hand. "I bet I know who this is."

Campbell made quick introductions.

Greg pointed to a Quonset hangar about a hundred yards away. "You think we can get this one-legged flyboy over there?" he asked Kitty.

"I think so." They each got on a side of Campbell and proceeded slowly but steadily to the building.

Campbell had expected the worst, but even so, he wasn't prepared for the sight of the Cardinal when they entered. Four other small aircraft occupied the limited space—dependable machines ready to take off at a moment's notice. In the middle of the concrete, sticking out like a three-legged dog, sat his Cessna, surrounded by bent and scratched metal, all of which belonged somewhere on her diminished body. Some of the parts had survived the crash pretty much intact, but mostly he viewed the junkyard remains of his once prized possession.

He took a deep breath and stared, unable to pull his gaze from the wreckage, as if he were staring at a multicar accident by the side of the road. A shudder rippled through him. This was exactly why he hadn't wanted to come here, and yet here he was. He started to turn away and leave the hangar, but a slim hand slipped into his and squeezed. He looked down at Kitty. Her eyes were bright, her smile fleeting but genuine.

"I've seen worse," she said.

Campbell continued to stare at her a moment and then burst out laughing. "I'll bet."

Nearly two hours later Kitty had to remind him that it was time to pick up Adam from Value-Rite. She pulled the Jeep close to the hangar door and waited for him to get in. Greg leaned into the window. "It's a start, buddy," he said.

Campbell nodded. He still wasn't convinced he'd ever make the plane fly again, but he'd forced himself to turn a few screws and tighten a few bolts. But, now that he thought about it, two hours had passed pretty quickly. Maybe Kitty's presence had helped.

"I guess I might have put a couple of wing nuts back in the right places," he said, frowning down at the busted leg, which he'd just lifted into the Jeep. "Problem is, I can't maneuver as well as I'd like to. Stupid splint makes it hard to get in the tight places."

"You're going to need some help," Greg agreed. "I'll be here for you as much as I can, but I'd really suggest you find a decent mechanic who can do the tough stuff for a while."

"I'd have to hire one with an A and P license or the rep from the FAA will never give me clearance even if I do fix her up."

"Don't worry about that," Greg said. "I have the license and I'll supervise the entire project.

As long as you find a guy with some mechanic sense, you'll pass inspection." He drummed his fingers on the window frame. "Tell you what. I'll run an ad in the weekly newspaper, see if I can find somebody who'd lend a hand until you're on your feet again. You can pay him when he's on the clock for you, and I can always use an extra guy around here when he's not working on the Cardinal."

Campbell thought about that. Greg's suggestion could work at least until he got his own parts in working order. He needed someone who knew one end of a screwdriver from another and who could manage the heavy lifting and welding. And now that he'd seen the plane, he was allowing a ray of hope to encourage him to get her airborne again. "Put the ad in," he said. "Sooner the better."

"You got it." Greg stuck his head in the Jeep. "Nice meeting you, Kitty. I figure we'll be seeing a lot of each other now that you've got Camp to take the first step."

She waited for him to back away before grinding the gearshift into first, clutching and accelerating, spitting gravel with the back tires. Campbell lurched forward in his seat. "Didn't you tell me you used to own a stick-shift Volkswagen?"

She kept her eyes on the road. "You know I did. Why?"

"I was just wondering how long you had it before you stripped out the clutch."

"It got me where I wanted to go. More than I can say for that plane we just left behind."

"Don't you worry about the plane," he said, enjoying her teasing grin. "I'll have her flying again before the outlaw has his debt paid."

She continued to smile at him. "In that hangar, I saw the look of determination in your eyes, Campbell. And I wouldn't bet against you. Now, you ready to pick up Adam and go on a picnic?"

He wasn't, but she sure was.

KITTY SPREAD OUT the blanket, and seeing her enthusiasm for everything outdoorsy, Campbell was suddenly determined that this would be the best picnic she'd ever had. He resigned himself to eating with insects, putting rocks on the corners of the blankets to fight the wind and, worst of all, trying to find a comfortable position for his overtaxed leg and sore muscles.

Adam chattered on about Value-Rite to the point that Campbell actually thought the kid might be enjoying his penance. Of course, to reach that conclusion, Campbell had to read between the lines and interpret every negative comment Adam said into a twelve-year-old's enchantment with a world that was new to him. Since the Watleys had come to the Saddle Top, Campbell had become more in tune with an adolescent's way of saying exactly what he didn't mean. Oddly, Adam reminded him of the boy he had once been himself.

So the picnic stretched into a two-hour event that included dry ham sandwiches, weak lemonade, and slightly stale store-bought cake. Yet Kitty's delight in every detail seemed to put both males on their best behavior.

But his favorite part of the afternoon was when the kid saw a rabbit scurry over the crest of a hill and took off after it, saying that if he caught the little guy, he might want to keep it. Campbell just wanted him to keep looking.

As soon as he and Kitty were alone, Campbell helped her pack utensils and leftovers into the basket she'd brought. When they were finished, she sat cross-legged on one side of the blanket while he squirmed around uttering unintelligible squawks of pain.

"Is your leg bothering you?" she asked. "You've been sitting a long time. Maybe I should call Adam and we can leave."

Truthfully his leg wasn't bothering him at all, but he wasn't about to turn down some genuine sympathy, especially since Kitty looked so fresh and appealing in the warm sunshine. And happy.

The strangest thing was, he had to admit that her happiness did matter to him.

He'd been thinking about that kiss every night since it happened. Unfortunately he hadn't come up with a way to make it happen again. Maybe now would be a good time to try. After all, he had to prove to himself that the feelings he'd experienced that day weren't just a fluke.

"Yeah, it's giving me some trouble," he said to answer her question. "Maybe if you could just massage the muscle above the splint."

She gave him a look that said she wasn't buying his plan.

"Come on, Kitty. Aren't we past this cat-and-mouse game of not trusting each other?"

She scooted next to him and rubbed his leg through his shorts. "Better?"

"Thanks," he said. "That helped." He twisted so that his back rested against a tree and gently pulled her into his side. She didn't try to fight him. In fact, a small sigh escaped her lips, all the incentive he needed to put his arm around her shoulders.

"I've been wondering something, Ms. Watley."

"What's that?"

"Have you thought about that kiss?"

He felt her body stiffen a little bit. "No, it was just a combination of things that day. I doubt we should read too much into one kiss."

He nodded. "I suppose you're right. One kiss is a mere fleeting moment, more or less. But two kisses, or even three—now, that's a real test. Don't you agree?"

She looked up at him. "Are you suggesting that we…?"

He slipped his hand under her chin and raised her lips to his. "Nope. I'm through suggesting. I'm acting on pure impulse." He covered her soft mouth, which tasted vaguely of lemons and chocolate icing. When her arm crossed his chest, he held her close to him. So close that he'd never forget how it felt to have her in his arms. When he ended the kiss, his mind tumbled with the realization of what he'd experienced. That first kiss hadn't been a fluke.

Just two weeks ago he'd met a desperate, incompetent woman whom he had accepted into his life because she was the lesser of two evils. Now she'd turned his life around in ways he hadn't thought possible.

He also had to accept that Kitty Watley and her outlaw son had pulled him out of the deepest, darkest funk of his life. He owed her for feeding him, encouraging him, giving him purpose. Granted, he'd have probably survived without her. He eventually would have made his peace with Wanda. He could have called the medi-van to take him for therapy. And Greg might have eventually talked him into coming out to the airstrip in a taxicab. But none of it would have been as fun as tangling with Kitty. And kissing Kitty.

He stretched out his leg and smiled to himself. Funny. He'd started out thinking he'd have to endure Kitty. Now he was dangerously close to wondering what he'd do without her. And the life in the gap that had seemed so hopeless and desolate when he left Diana now seemed about to burst with new beginnings.

He focused on Kitty, her eyes closed, her breathing soft, her hair blowing about her face, and he wondered just exactly what his feelings for her were. And what in the world would he do about them if he ever figured them out? Heck, he was half a man right now.

His mind wandered for a few brief seconds to Diana Matheson. He'd never been on a picnic with her. To Diana, eating outdoors meant planning for the third Sunday of every May when the Mathesons hosted a lavish party in the south gardens to celebrate Leland's birthday. Politicians, country gentlemen, millionaires and even a few regular guys came to celebrate the yearly event. And Diana, in a spectacular dress and wide-brimmed hat, was the perfect Southern hostess.

He studied Kitty's profile again. Her features lacked the haughtiness of Diana's strong chin and patrician nose. For Kitty and her son, who'd traveled into his life in a broken-down truck, eating out of paper sacks by the side of the road was probably a fact of life. And yet today a picnic with him had made her happy. He wished he could fix what was wrong in Kitty's life every bit as much, and maybe even more, than he wished he could fix his airplane.

BY EIGHT O'CLOCK Friday evening, only die-hard golfers remained in the Eagles' Nest Lounge at the Richland Country Club. The married members had gone home to wives and families after sharing a couple of beers. Most of the bachelors had left, as well, probably with plans to keep. But Owen Galloway—whose match had ended three hours earlier—and his five companions remained at the one poker table in the center of the room.

He thought of Billie, who was spending the evening with a gushing cousin he couldn't stomach. Billie had finally agreed to let him back into her life and court her in her fashion. He was taking her out to a five-star restaurant to-morrow night. But, for now, he'd stick with his

poker game, a temporary and inadequate salve
to his pride.

He checked his stack of chips. He'd lost a
few hundred, but he'd brought enough cash to
go on for a few more hands. Maybe his luck
would change. He signaled to the bartender, a
man whose hair had turned white in the thirty-
some years he'd stood behind that bar. "Another Scotch, Wendell," Owen said. Within
seconds the drink was sitting on a cork coaster
that protected the felt playing surface. Wendell
was good and Owen rewarded him with a five-
dollar tip.

"You're the big blind, Galloway," his friend
said, and Owen tossed a ten-dollar chip to the
center of the table.

Before the first card was dealt, Terry Spenser
entered the lounge and walked over to the table.
Owen raised his hand, indicating the dealer
should hold up. "What is it?" he said over his
shoulder.

"There's somebody in the parking lot you've
got to meet," Terry said.

"Now?"

"Yeah, now. He made a special trip. Besides,
you'll want to see him."

"Deal me out this hand," Owen instructed the
dealer. "I'll be back as soon as I can." He scraped

his ante back to his stash, got up and followed Terry outside.

They walked to a black Crown Victoria, at least ten years old but shiny as polished ebony. A car that said *Don't mess with me.* Terry opened the back door and he and Owen got in. The driver rested his elbow on the back of the front seat and waited until the door shut.

"This is Mr. Galloway," Terry said. "Owen, Matt Stark, the PI I hired."

Owen reached over the seat and they shook hands. The PI wore an expensive black silk shirt. His dark hair was neat and styled, his nails manicured. Why not? He made seven hundred a day plus expenses. "What have you got for me?" Owen asked.

Stark handed a piece of paper into the backseat. "Your daughter bought a truck in Clermont more than two weeks ago," he said. "An older-model pickup."

Owen snorted. "A truck? Not my daughter. Never."

The PI shrugged. "See for yourself. Is that her signature?"

Owen recognized the handwriting and Kitty's former name.

"She paid cash," Stark said.

Owen didn't argue. So that was where the

sudden withdrawal from Kitty's bank account had landed—at a Buy Now lot in Clermont.

"The salesman said another woman was with her, so I double-checked with her friend Trixie," Terry said. "Seems her memory has improved in the last twenty-four hours. She now recalls taking Kitty to the lot. And the new license plates for the truck are being sent to Trixie's address. She claims she doesn't know where Kitty is, though," Terry added. "She's waiting for instructions on where to send the permanent plates. For what it's worth, I believe her."

Owen handed the bill of sale back to Stark. "Where do you go from here?"

"The truck was a clunker," he said. "If it broke down anywhere, I'll find it. I've sent a description and the vehicle identification number to mechanics and police departments all over north Georgia and North Carolina. It'll show up on my radar before too long, and when it does, I figure I'll find your daughter nearby."

Owen stared at him. "North Carolina and Georgia? Why there?"

Stark passed a wallet over the backseat. "Have you seen this before?"

Owen's breath caught as he studied the wallet. He wasn't certain it was Kitty's, but he knew the designer label was a favorite of hers. If Stark had her wallet, what had happened to the money? To his daughter? "It could be Kitty's," he said. "Where'd you get it?"

"I have connections with websites that deal in special lost-and-found details. For a price. This wallet was found along the side of a road in a remote area in northern Georgia. There was nothing in it but one of those standard ID cards that come with new billfolds. It had Katherine Galloway's contact info on it."

Owen turned the wallet over in hands that had suddenly begun to tremble violently and looked at Terry. "Was she robbed?"

Terry laid his hand on Owen's arm. "You've been getting the postcards, boss. We know she and the boy are okay."

"That's right. The postcards have been in both hers and Adam's handwriting. But the wallet was empty. What if she doesn't have any money?"

"Maybe she got a job, sir. She wouldn't let anything happen to Adam. You know that."

Owen took a normal breath. Yes, he did know that about his daughter. She was no prize as a mother, but she loved her son. He raised his eyes to Stark. "You're good."

Stark answered with an all-in-a-day's-work shrug. "I'll find her."

"I believe you will," Owen said. "But remember what I told you. When you do, watch her and let me know her location. Don't approach her yourself."

"I remember."

Owen got out of the car. Terry followed, and the Crown Vic took off. "I guess you can see now that Stark is worth his fat paycheck," Terry said. "If anybody can locate Kitty, he can."

Owen headed back to the clubhouse. He clenched his jaw so tight, pain shot into his neck and shoulders. His eyes burned for the second time in years, since his wife died. "I never could control her," he said. "And it got worse after her mother was gone. It broke my heart when she ran off with that degenerate, Watley."

Terry only nodded with sympathy.

"What did I do to turn her against me, Terry? I gave her everything to make her stay so she'd keep Adam close. I thought it was enough. She never said it wasn't."

"Women are hard to figure, sir. She should have been grateful."

"Every decent thing that's come into my life has been taken away. I had two sons stillborn for reasons the doctors couldn't fathom. My wife died. My daughter ran off not once, but twice. And now my grandson, the one shining light I had in my existence, is gone."

Terry didn't speak, just walked solidly by Owen's side. He'd heard this story before, though Owen only rarely expressed emotion about it.

"I've got to bring him home," Owen said. "If Katherine wants to keep the ties broken, so be it. I'll let her go." He blinked hard, for the first time in his life wondering if he was lying to himself. "But I want Adam back," he said. "I'm not going to quit until I find him."

"I know that, Owen. Just let Stark do what you hired him for."

CHAPTER THIRTEEN

CAMPBELL BEGAN HEARING cars pull into the motel lot a little after ten on Sunday morning, which, as he recalled, was when services ended at the small United Methodist Church a mile farther down Old Sorrel Gap Road. During his youth, Sundays in the hills had been designated as the time for visiting neighbors. But only Ginny and Cliff Lowe, and Lucas Crum once, had come to the motel since Campbell had returned. Albeit he hadn't issued any invitations.

Wondering about the activity today, he grabbed his crutches and went to the front entrance. Four vehicles were parked on the gravel, all of them near unit six.

Ginny climbed down from her old Ford truck and walked to Kitty's door. She waved at Cliff who backed away and headed out of the parking lot. Four other ladies got out of two passenger cars and followed her. A kid who looked a lot like Lucas Crum had at a young age jumped out of the back of a Chevy pickup. Two women stepped from the cab and also went into Kitty's room. Each woman carried some sort of container, a box or basket.

Campbell caught a glimpse of the man at the wheel of the truck. "That's Lucas," he said to himself, and couldn't help wondering why his old friend didn't swing by the lobby to say hello. Maybe because he hadn't asked him to.

He turned from the door and began the journey through the lobby to his apartment, easier now that he'd mastered the art of walking with crutches. A half hour later, he gave in to his building curiosity and returned to the front door. Snatches of conversation drifted from unit six, so Campbell ventured down the walkway toward Kitty's room.

He stopped next to her open window and listened to women's chatter—expectant, excited and punctuated with *ooh*s and *aah*s and giggles. The curtains were open, so he leaned in and took a peek. Lace and ruffles and bolts of material lay everywhere, on the beds and spilling onto the floor. On the table, a sewing machine hummed with well-tuned precision under the command of Ginny Lowe. In the center of all this womanly madness stood Kitty with several pairs of hands fluttering around her. She was draped in something white and thin that hinted at the shadowy contours underneath. One of the women fluffed the fabric until all the participants stood back and admired. "I like it," Kitty said.

So did Campbell. He liked it a lot.

"You can stitch this up in an afternoon," one of the women said.

Kitty stole a look over her shoulder at her reflection in the mirror. "I could. That's why I designed it so simply. I have enough material to make at least a half dozen dresses." She smiled. "If I make them short enough."

"Short is in right now," a girl Campbell recognized as Luke's sister, Lyssa, said.

He continued to stare. Kitty's blond hair swept her forehead and fell in soft, shining ringlets to her chin. Amazing to think this was the same hair that had spiked with untouchable defiance just a few weeks ago. "Any woman would feel beautiful in this dress," she said.

Campbell couldn't argue. And he couldn't stop looking. Which explained why his reflexes failed to work when the door burst open in advance of a shooting pain in his lower back. He grabbed one crutch for support, dropped the other and pressed his palm to the base of his spine. He slowly turned around. "What the...?"

Adam and Lucas Crum's boy stood looking up at him, both with shocked expressions on their faces. "Jeez, sorry," Adam said. "I didn't know you were hiding there."

Campbell stooped to pick up his crutch. "I wasn't hiding."

"Why are you standing out here, then?" Adam said. "You never come out of your cave unless Mom makes you."

"Taking a stroll, that's all," Campbell lied.

"You're looking in the window," Adam said. "Why do you care what those girls are doing?"

"I don't." Actually he sort of did but would never admit that to other males. Thankful when he saw a way to change the subject, he pointed to a jar in Toby's hand. "What's in there?"

The kid screwed off the cap, poked his finger in rich, dark earth and pulled out a worm. "Night crawlers."

"You fishing?" Campbell asked.

"Yep."

"Where's your gear?"

Toby nodded down the sidewalk to where Campbell now noticed a couple of rods leaning against the railing. "I left my stuff down there. We're just going to Gilley's Creek out back."

Suddenly Campbell was transported back more than twenty years when two other boys had stood on this same sidewalk with cane poles and worms and high hopes. "Your dad and I used to fish out there," he said. "Bet the brown trout is running pretty good this time of year."

"Yes, sir. Should be."

Campbell squeezed the cushioned handgrips of his crutches and took a step or two. He felt pretty good today. He just might be able to make it across the dirt and weeds to the bank of the creek. But could he wrangle an invitation? "So, Adam," he said. "Do you know how to fish?"

Adam shrugged. "You drop in a worm and haul up a fish. Big deal."

Campbell smiled. "You have enough night crawlers for an extra fisherman, Toby?"

"Sure. Only got two rods, though."

"I just happen to have an old one in my place," Campbell said. "Would you guys mind if I tagged along?"

The two boys looked at each other a minute, gauging reactions. "Be all right with me," Toby said.

Adam shrugged. "Yeah, you can come."

"Great. I'll get my rod and meet you out back." He started toward his room, only managing a couple of energized steps before Kitty's voice stopped him.

"Hold it right there," she said.

Campbell hopped around to face her. In the past minutes she had changed into shorts and a T-shirt. And she still looked good.

"Did you say you're going down to the creek with them?"

"I did."

"Can you make it that far?"

He expelled a quick, impatient breath intended to suggest that Kitty's question was ridiculous. "Of course. It's just through the backyard."

She seemed to think for a minute before she waggled a finger in Adam's direction. "You're responsible for Campbell," she said. "Don't let him fall in the water. He can't get his splint wet."

Campbell figured he ought to be insulted, but he wasn't. He just grinned at Kitty and said, "You're putting the outlaw in charge of me? Isn't that like putting the fox in charge of the henhouse?"

She responded with an unladylike snort. "Honestly I don't know which one of you can get in more trouble. I'm just glad Toby's going along to make sure both of you come back in one piece."

Campbell waved off her concern and, using the three-legged shuffle, hustled to his room. When he came out a moment later with his fishing rod tucked alongside his right crutch, Kitty was still on the sidewalk.

"Have fun," she called to him. "And if you catch anything, I hope you don't expect me to clean it."

"Hey, wait a minute," Adam called from the

back of the breezeway. "I'm not gonna have to learn to cook trout now, am I?"

"Only if we're lucky and the fishing's good," Campbell said, and winked at Kitty.

He ambled off, grinning like a kid on a snow day. He was feeling lucky for the first time since he'd woken up in a cow pasture surrounded by plane wreckage. That day he'd consoled himself by at least realizing he wasn't dead. But today he was going fishing on a Sunday afternoon, and a pretty woman was waiting for him when he got back. All things considered, a good day for any guy from the Blue Ridge Mountains.

OVER THE NEXT few days, Kitty decided that she liked having friends. Sure, she'd had them before. Trixie had been her best friend since they each got their ears pierced at the Richland Mall when they were twelve years old. Trixie had been there during the grief stage when Kitty lost her mother, and the welcome-home episode when Kitty left Bobby, and the pink-tipped hair stage when Kitty had rebelled. She'd listened to Kitty complain about her father's dominance over everyone in his life and her own lack of ambition to do anything about it.

In the past three weeks, since declaring her independence, Kitty had experienced a slowly evolving sense of self-discovery. She'd come to know herself as a person who could do things on her own—care for someone, guide her son, work toward a goal and even make a sad old motel room livable. And she had friends now who fit comfortably into the pattern of her current life, a pattern she'd never known she would even find comfortable.

But where did Campbell fit into this newly established patchwork quilt of her life? He was part of the pattern of her time in the mountains. He was her reason for being at the motel and staying there all these weeks, but his contribution could definitely not be described as friendship.

She, Adam and Campbell had come a long way since the day she'd stood on the sidewalk of the Saddle Top and quaked with fear that the injured war veteran would turn her away. He and Adam had reached a truce after realizing they could share a bond that included a couple of fishing rods, some worms and an hour's conversation by the side of a creek each afternoon. And she and Campbell, well, that relationship remained a mystery, one fueled by her imagination, her admiration and one incredible kiss.

Early one Thursday afternoon, at the beginning of a July that promised warm days and cool nights, Kitty picked Adam up at Value-Rite and then drove to collect Campbell from the airstrip, a duty that was beginning to feel routine. As they were driving back to the motel, she asked him what progress he'd made on his plane.

"Some," he said. "I still need another pair of hands, though. Greg can only devote so much time to my project."

"Has he had a response to the ad he put in the newspaper for a man to help you?" she asked.

"I'll do it," Adam said from the backseat. "Making a plane fly again might be kind of cool."

Campbell looked over his headrest. "Good to know, outlaw. You can certainly help." He focused on Kitty's profile. "Not yet, but I expect he'll get some calls. Folks around here need work."

"I'll drive you out to the airstrip anytime so you can interview applicants."

"No need. I trust Greg to hire the right person."

They reached the motel and Campbell headed for his apartment. Leaving Adam digging for worms in the backyard, Kitty followed him inside. "I made lemonade," she said. "Can I get you some?"

He settled on the sofa. "Sounds okay."

She brought him a glass with lots of ice. He liked his drinks cold. She stood in front of the sofa, and said nothing while he stared up at her expectantly. "You waiting for my taste test?" he said.

"No. You won't have any complaints. It's store-bought."

He smiled.

"I need to talk to you," she said.

He took a sip. "No time like the present."

She started to sit beside him on the couch but decided against it and took the recliner. "I hope you have an open mind today."

He gave her a funny grin. "I'll try. My whole world has opened up in the last weeks, so why not my mind? You've got me going to therapy, the airstrip, on picnics. The outlaw's got me fishing every day. I hardly recognize my own isolated, brooding existence anymore."

"Are you complaining?"

"Has it ever done me any good?"

He slid over to the edge of the sofa, close enough to touch her. "And I hardly recognize my caretaker anymore, the one who still manages to keep a safe, respectable distance between us."

She made a quick appraisal of the dozen inches that separated them. "So I'll ask again. Are you complaining?"

"About that distance, well, yes, maybe."

She stared at her hands clasped in her lap and listened to the cheerful clink of the ice in his glass as he lifted it to his mouth. When he laid a finger on her knee, she looked up.

"I like all the stuff you've done...or stopped doing...with your hair and your makeup," he said. "And you look good with some North Carolina suntan on your face." He moved his finger slowly along her cheek. "There's just one thing..."

She felt the heat of his touch in a warm quiver in the pit of her stomach. "What's that?"

"It's this inverted scale I keep struggling with. The prettier you are to me, the more frustrated I get with having you way over there when I'm sitting here on a sofa with room to spare."

She didn't know what to say. She'd been trying to convince herself she was handling her attraction to Campbell. But if he didn't kiss her right now, she was afraid she'd combust. She licked her dry lips, made an effort to smile as if she didn't take him seriously and said the first thing that popped into her mind. "You need a haircut."

He chuckled, removed his hand. "Probably. Put it on my list, the one you keep of things for me to do. But you should know, I have a separate list of my own."

She swallowed, stood, paced a few steps and forced her mind back to the topic that had brought her here. Pausing in front of him, she said, "I really need—"

"To talk to me. I remember."

She threaded her hands at her waist and breathed deeply. "As you know, I've been spending a lot of time with the women from up the hill road."

"I'm aware of that. I hear your sewing machine humming at all hours. Everything going okay?"

"Better than okay. I've designed some basic patterns for my company, Saddle Top Apparel, and a few of the women and I have sewn some samples. I sent out pictures to the ladies who came to the motel a couple of weeks ago. I'm hoping I'll get some orders."

"That'd be great."

"It would be, yes. But while we've been working, the girls and I...you know Lyssa, Ginny, some others..."

"Yeah?"

"We came up with this idea, and it involves you."

"Me? What would that bunch want with a one-legged pilot?"

She sat on the edge of the coffee table and locked her gaze intently with his. "It's not you exactly that we want. We want part of the motel."

He snorted. "*This* motel?"

"Yes."

"Haven't your new pals seen the spots on the roof where shingles used to be? Haven't they noticed the dry rot on the porch eaves?"

"We want to fix up a couple of units."

"Great. Go ahead." He glanced around the four corners of his room. "Just leave me these five hundred square feet of solitude."

"Okay. Thanks." That was easy. All she had to do now was tell him what she wanted to do with the place. She stood, turned toward the kitchen. Maybe she'd wait until after he'd eaten.

As if reading her mind he said, "I suppose I should ask what you women intend to do with the Saddle Top."

She returned and sat back down. "So, you do care about what happens to this building?"

"Only because it's my home. The only one I've got."

She leaned forward, hoping to fire his imagination with her eagerness. "We want to turn two of the rooms into a cooperative."

"A what?"

"You know, a place where the craftsmen from the hills can sell their handiwork. I figure we can share the expense and offer a good variety of Blue Ridge crafts. Ginny could sell her herbs. Cliff would offer his birdhouses. There's a guy who makes wind chimes, another who carves walking sticks. Lyssa can sell her embroidery. And there's me. I can have racks of my original clothing designs…"

His eyes narrowed. "You? I thought you were headed to Charlotte as soon as the outlaw's time at Value-Rite ends."

"I am, of course. But I can continue sewing things from there and ship them to the co-op."

"What do you know about how a cooperative works?"

"I've been doing research. All the participants agree to share the expenses, which would include rent to you, of course…"

"Glad to hear it."

"And we'd also share the profits, over and above what each artist's materials cost. It requires each of us to be honest about our expenses."

"And naturally you all are," he said.

"Absolutely. I trust all the folks I've met."

He frowned, obviously reminded that he hadn't done much to reacquaint himself with the neighbors Kitty seemed to know so well. "And you think this sad old building can be fixed up enough to draw tourists from Sorrel Gap all the way out here?"

"I know it can. We'll patch and paint, throw out the old furniture and carpet…" She paused before adding, "Assuming you give us the go-ahead, I think we could have the two rooms looking fine after a couple of long weekends."

She could see the wheels turning in Campbell's head. "I assume you're a man who knows when opportunity is knocking."

"Actually I'm feeling more like the guy who knows when disaster is pending."

She smirked at him.

"You're talking about a lot of work."

"Some of the men have agreed to help."

"Lucas Crum?"

"Yes."

Campbell nodded. "Okay. He's got skills. But who's going to run this place? A cooperative business needs a manager."

This question had been brought up, and the ladies had unanimously chosen Kitty to organize the co-op and get it running. She had hesitated to accept, but couldn't help being flattered by their confidence. "I am, until…"

"Until you take off."

She only stared at him. There was no point denying what was true.

"You talk about *me* avoiding my responsibilities. What about you getting these folks all stirred up about something and then hightailing it out of town?"

She frowned. "My situation is different. You live here."

He didn't say anything for several moments, and Kitty feared her plan was doomed. Finally she said, "Look, if you don't want to do this, just say so."

He shrugged. "I'm still thinking." The shrug was punctuated by a grin.

"What's that look for?" she said, though it sounded more like an accusation. Campbell's expression seemed to be saying that he was enjoying this. Was she missing something here?

He settled his leg on the coffee table and asked, "Who are you really, Kitty Watley?"

"What do you mean?"

"All I knew for the longest time is that you're a hard-luck-story woman with a chip-on-the-shoulder kid and you love clothes. And now I've figured out that you're creative, determined and just a so-so disciplinarian. *And* that you're driving me crazy."

She met his heated gaze straight on. "I can't help what drives you crazy."

"Maybe, but you're the only one who can help me figure it out."

Oh.

She went to him then; she couldn't help it. She sat next to him on the sofa, her shoulder touching his. She turned to face him. "Just so you know, this isn't part of the deal."

He smiled at her warmly. Without breaking the connection, he slipped his arms around her and claimed a deep kiss that seemed to last forever. His fingertip lazily stroked the hollow of her throat. She leaned into the kiss, her hands resting on his strong shoulders.

She gasped, needing air, but not wanting the moment to end. "What are you...?"

The words caught in her throat. She'd thought about this many times since their last kiss, the one that had happened on the picnic. She closed her eyes and reveled in the...

"Mom!"

"That's Adam," she breathed.

Campbell's head rolled back against the sofa. "Who?"

Kitty shot up from where she was sitting just as her son came bolting into the room. He held up a plastic bowl. "Worms. Lots of them," he said proudly. He stared at Campbell. "What's wrong with you?"

Campbell raised his head. "Just all aflutter over you having worms," he said.

Adam gawked, looked from his mother to Campbell. "Aflutter? What kind of a word is that?"

Campbell exhaled a long breath. "You'll know when you're older."

"You ready to fish?"

"Can't wait." He looked at Kitty. "Any idea where my crutches are?"

She found them on the floor and handed the pair to him.

He stood up. "Bring your worms, outlaw, and let's catch us some dinner."

Walking back to room six, Kitty didn't even try to wipe a silly grin off her face. Her relationship with Campbell was changing every day. He was fishing, bringing the catch home for supper and getting along with her son. She was driving Adam's friend home in the afternoons and coming back to the Saddle Top to take care of the responsibilities that had seemed so overwhelming just weeks ago. They were almost like a family, and, if she stopped to really think about that incredible kiss, she could almost imagine that she and Campbell were almost like a couple…

"Stop it, Kitty," she said aloud. "What do you really know about this man? And he certainly doesn't know anything about you. The two of you are like a pair of leaves caught for an instant in a Sorrel Gap breeze, touching once and

doomed to separate and follow your own paths."
Her smile faded. The thought of her future away
from Sorrel Gap had suddenly made her sad.

CHAPTER FOURTEEN

OWEN TOOK THE TUMBLER Terry handed him and gave his assistant an approving nod. "You were right about this one," he admitted.

"And I'm glad I was," Terry said, settling into an easy chair in Owen's study.

Owen picked up the photo Terry had just handed him and stared at the two people pictured. Kitty and Adam, walking along a sidewalk outside a run-down motel. "No doubt about it," he said. "Stark did his job."

Terry smiled with satisfaction.

"Let's go over the details of our next step," Owen said. "Billie's due here in a few minutes, and I don't want her having any input in a decision regarding Katherine."

"How are things between you and Billie?" Terry asked.

"We're finally settling back into an even keel. But I'm sure she still believes I'm guilty of being too controlling. If she finds out I've paid a private eye to spy on Kitty, I'll never hear the end of it."

"She just doesn't understand the circumstances, sir," Terry said.

"No. Billie's never had kids. She doesn't know how they can break your heart." Owen took a sip of bourbon, let it mellow on his tongue as he contemplated the unacceptable prospect of living without Billie. No matter how the woman raised his blood pressure, she kept his blood pumping. "We keep this between ourselves, Terry."

"Understood."

"So, what's Stark doing now?"

"He's got a guy keeping an eye on Kitty and Adam for now. Just the way you ordered."

Owen took another look at the picture. "Imagine those two living in a place like this."

"You'll have Adam home before long," Terry said.

"Did you find that phone number I asked you about?"

"I did. Bobby's still on the fringes of the golfing world, playing minor tournaments."

"With any success?" Owen asked, though he suspected a negative response.

"My sources say no." Terry handed him a piece of paper with a phone number on it along with a small newspaper clipping. "And here's a copy of the classified ad Stark got from the local paper in Sorrel Gap. Are you going to make that call tonight?"

Owen reached for his portable phone. "I hate having to call this bum. It cost me plenty to get Watley out of Kitty's life eleven years ago, and it's going to cost me plenty now. But I want this call over by the time Billie arrives."

Owen had only punched in one number when Billie breezed into his office. She spoke to Terry and walked to the desk. After planting a warm, lipsticky kiss on Owen's cheek, she said, "What are you up to, Owen? What call don't you want me to know about?"

Owen chuckled, and hoped Billie wouldn't notice the sudden flush to his face. Maybe she'd think it was the bourbon. "What did I tell you, Terry? It's darn near impossible to surprise this woman."

"A surprise for me?"

Owen returned the phone to the cradle. "We'll conclude this first thing in the morning, Terry."

"Indeed we will, sir." Terry said good-night to Billie and left the room.

AT TEN O'CLOCK Friday morning Campbell ably swing-stepped to the passenger door of the Jeep. He opened it, smiled at Kitty as Adam got out of the front seat. "Outlaw," Campbell said, happy to be leaving the rehab facility.

"Beast." Adam got into the back and Campbell settled next to Kitty, who was wearing a pink T-shirt from Disney World. Campbell looked over his shoulder at Adam. "What are you doing here? Quint give you the day off from the chain gang?"

"Yep."

"No kidding?"

"I was surprised, too," Kitty admitted. "But it's true. I double-checked with Quint to make sure Adam wasn't conning me."

Adam leaned his elbows on the back of Campbell's seat and spoke with the indignation of the truly injured. "Is it so hard for the two of you to believe that somebody might actually be nice to me?"

Campbell shot an amused glance at Kitty. At the same time they both said, "Yes."

Adam leaned back in his seat. "Quint's a dork, but once you get past that, he's okay. I told him I wanted to work with Campbell on the plane today and he said okay."

"Good for Quint," Campbell said. "I've said it before. He's a stand-up guy."

"And that's not all," Adam added.

"Oh?"

"He's coming to the motel tomorrow to help out with painting. So is Deputy Gibbs."

Campbell smiled at the exchange. "Great

news, eh, Kitty? The town's most eligible bachelor is coming out to help you."

"One eligible bachelor isn't."

"Who's that?"

"You. I haven't heard you say you'll help."

He snorted and pointed down at his splint. "A lot of help I can be."

"That broken leg won't keep you from sitting in a chair and sanding a door."

Adam hooted from the backseat. "Busted, dude."

"Yeah? What are you doing tomorrow?"

"Same as you," Adam said. "I got my work orders this morning."

Campbell started to respond, but a mechanical rendition of "Take Me Out to the Ball Game" interrupted him. He glanced down between the seats for his cell phone. Kitty snatched it up before he had a chance and read the caller ID. "It's for me," she said.

"You?"

"Yeah. When you said I could use the phone, I gave a couple of people the number." She pressed the answer button. "Hi, Bette. It's me."

Campbell looked over the headrest. "Who's Bette?" he asked Adam.

"Some relative I hardly remember."

"We're fine," Kitty said. "How about you?"

Campbell stared out the windshield, his attention focused on Kitty's end of the conversation. So Kitty Watley wasn't without family. Campbell had just sort of imagined her homeless and orphaned. So where had this so-called relative been when she and Adam needed help?

"Yes, I'm sure," Kitty said. There was a pause before she responded, "I'm so glad you got the application. No, our plans haven't changed. We're still coming." She listened to her caller, stealing a glance at Campbell. "He's been a perfect gentleman," she said.

Campbell chuckled, appreciating the blush that crept into Kitty's cheeks because he knew she was remembering the kisses.

"Yes, of course," Kitty said. "I'll call if I need anything, but we're fine, really. Don't worry. And, Bette…you know I'm grateful to you for keeping your promise. Under the circumstances it couldn't have been easy."

She ended the call. Setting the phone back on the console between the seats, she said, "I hope you don't mind, Campbell. I gave instructions to anyone who has the number to only call in the mornings while you're at therapy or at the airstrip. You won't be bothered by anyone trying to reach me."

Realizing the number of the last caller was stored in the phone, he thought about the opportunity to find out more about Kitty. What promise had she been talking about? And what circumstances? It was his phone after all. Who would blame him for calling the mysterious Bette and doing a little investigating? Oh, right. Kitty would blame him—big-time.

"It's okay," he said.

They'd reached the drive into the airstrip and Kitty skidded to a stop within view of the hangar. Two men stood outside talking. One was Greg, who strode toward the Jeep. The other one ducked inside the building. Greg reached the Jeep before Campbell got out. He leaned into the window and said, "I've got good news."

Campbell opened the door. "What's that?"

"I hired a guy just this morning. He's got some mechanics skills and claims he's a quick learner. Seemed interested in the Cardinal and willing to do whatever you tell him." He looked back toward the hangar and squinted. "Where'd he go?"

"The guy you were talking to?"

"Yeah."

"He went inside."

Greg scratched his chin and shrugged. "Well, never mind. He's probably looking over the plane. You'll like him."

"I'm sure I will." He lifted his leg out of the Jeep and let Adam push the seat forward to get out. "That makes two helpers today. This is Kitty's son, Adam."

"Nice to meet you," Greg said.

"Same here." Adam headed for the hangar, a bounce in his step. A person might actually think the kid was anxious to work. "How will I know which plane is yours?" he asked.

"It's the one that doesn't look much like a plane anymore," Campbell said. "You can't miss it."

Greg stood aside waiting for Campbell to get out, and Campbell suddenly wished his friend had followed Adam and left him alone with Kitty for a moment. Her lips were tinged a pale pink. Her eyes sparkled under lids shadowed with the merest hint of lavender. A feeling of calm settled over him and he had the strangest urge to tell her to drive carefully, to have a nice day. He wanted to lean over and press a quick kiss to those full lips like a man would do if he were saying goodbye to the woman he parted from every morning. The woman he looked forward to coming home to every night.

Ridiculous. He was thinking like a sap. Still...he reached over, gave a lock of her hair a tug and picked up his crutches. "See you in a few hours," he said, standing up. "Don't wreck the Jeep."

CAMPBELL STOPPED SANDING when he heard the inviting snap of a pop top and the hiss of released carbonation. "That had better be a beer, and it had better be for me," he said to whoever had come up behind him.

He recognized the deep-throated chuckle. Lucas Crum pulled a paint bucket next to Campbell's lawn chair, upended it and sat. He passed an ice-cold can into Campbell's hand.

Campbell took a long swig. "Thanks."

"You're welcome."

The two sat in companionable silence a minute or so until Lucas said, "These women are determined to get these two rooms ready for retail, aren't they?"

Campbell nodded and stared over the parking lot, which was much improved thanks to three truckloads of gravel delivered a couple of days before. He couldn't argue with Lucas. A new paint job, replaced shingles, removal of the old road sign—all had spruced up the motel. Maybe someday he'd even think about redoing the whole building.

Lucas drank his beer. He was a big man and should have looked ridiculous on a plastic pail, but he'd always had the ability to appear comfortable in any situation, a trait Campbell had envied. Lucas raised his can in a sort of toast. "You know, Camp, sharing a beer with you reminds me of the Saturday afternoons you and I spent together in the past. Although back then we weren't sanding and painting."

Campbell focused down the walkway where Kitty, Lucas's wife, Suzie, and his sister Lyssa were washing windows. "Yeah, but even in those days, like now, there were some good-looking girls around. As I recall, we didn't think a Saturday was complete without the ladies."

"True, but now that we're not hormone-driven youth anymore, maybe you can explain how this particular bunch of females roped us into these chores."

"Can't speak for you," Campbell said. "But I'm stuck here and dependent on that blonde down there for every meal. She's not much of a cook, but starvation is still a good motivator."

Lucas took a swallow and wiped his hand across his mouth. "Gibbs hasn't stopped staring at her all day."

Campbell didn't need to be reminded of the deputy's presence. He turned his attention to Toby and Adam, who were squirting each other with garden hoses, getting soaking wet and accomplishing nothing. "Now, those two remind me of us back in the day," he said.

Lucas laughed. "That's the truth. My boy and your boy…" He paused a moment and cleared his throat. "Whoa, I don't know where that came from."

Campbell smiled to himself. "Don't worry about it. A few weeks ago if anyone had dared hint that Adam was in any way connected to me, I would have denied it with my last breath. Since then, I don't know, the kid has grown on me."

"I hear ya," Lucas said. "At first I was worried that he might be a bad influence on Toby. Everybody knows how he came to stay here at the Saddle Top. But he's a good kid."

"I think Toby's the one who's been the influence," Campbell said. "Toby and a guy who's been working at the airstrip."

Lucas continued watching the boys. "Yeah? What guy? Somebody new in town?"

"Greg hired him to help around the strip and I'm paying him extra to give me a hand with the Cardinal."

"Where's he from?"

Campbell tried to remember exactly what Greg had told him, but the truth was, he didn't have much information about the mysterious Rick. "Some place out West, I think."

"Is he a mechanic?"

"I'm not sure what he is," Campbell said. "He follows directions well and knows his way around a toolbox. And since he doesn't have a broken leg, he's more productive than I am."

Lucas laughed at his son, who'd just taken a direct hit from Adam's water blast. "What did you mean that this guy has been an influence on Adam?"

Campbell considered avoiding what had become a touchy topic for him but decided to open up to Lucas. "His name's Rick Simmons and he's taken Adam under his wing. The guy has a certain charm, I guess, as well as the latest video games and a monster ATV that Adam can't resist."

Lucas smiled. "Do I detect a bit of jealousy on your part?"

Campbell shrugged. "I don't know. I was just beginning to get along with the kid, and that hasn't changed really, but Rick is the current cool guy du jour."

Lucas tapped Campbell's shoulder with his beer can. "Heck, Camp, you were always the coolest guy around. I know one thing. Toby's gonna be sorry to see Adam leave when his penance is over."

Ah…another topic Campbell didn't allow himself to think about—more than ten or twelve hours a day.

"And the women will hate to say goodbye to Kitty," Lucas added. "She's got this whole project humming like a bee's wings."

It was definitely so. In the past week Kitty had moved symbolic mountains to get the Sorrel Gap Cooperative off the ground. She'd spoken to county officials about licenses, applied for sales tax numbers for her dealers, even rented a truck to haul away the old carpet and junk from the rooms. Kitty had become a sight to behold as she attended to her chores around the apartment with her clipboard of notes and the portable phone to her ear. Of course, she was a sight to behold almost all the time.

"Just wondering out loud, Camp," Lucas said. "What brought you back to the gap anyway? Was it strictly a job change, or was a woman involved?"

Years had passed, but two old friends never lost that special kind of radar. "Is it that obvious?" he said.

"To someone who used to know you like a brother, it is." Lucas took a swallow of beer. "You wanna talk about it?"

The cool, sophisticated, auburn-haired perfection that was Diana took shape in Campbell's mind. He quickly banished the image, discovering that wasn't nearly as difficult as it once had been. Diana wasn't perfect. Nobody was.

Kitty waved at him from the end of the sidewalk and he returned a two-finger salute. She bore her ever-emerging attributes with more dignity than Diana had her inbred ones. Had it only been a month since he pegged Kitty as a kooky eccentric he'd have to endure to avoid

Wanda? Suddenly he was struck with an undeniable reality. Kitty was pure, honest, fundamentally decent. And, kooky or not, she stirred his blood in a way that made his days seem short and his nights endless. "Maybe someday," he said to Lucas. "But for now I'm doing okay."

Lucas glanced down the sidewalk and grinned. "I can see that," he said. "Maybe you should figure out a way to make her stay."

Campbell rolled the cool can between his palms. Could this old friend be right? Did he want Kitty to stay? But under what conditions? And what could he promise her to make her give up her plans to go to Charlotte? Considering the truth had just hit him squarely between the eyes, he began to wonder if the way to accomplish that goal lay on this deserted scrap of land in the valley—and in a couple of renovated rooms soon to be called the Sorrel Gap Cooperative—the last place he ever thought he'd care about.

CHAPTER FIFTEEN

EVERY OTHER WEDNESDAY Kitty drove Campbell to the orthopedic surgeon's office, where he had X-rays and sat through consultations ending with the surgeon telling him to keep up his regimen of therapy and exercise. But on this particular Wednesday morning, Campbell was hopeful that he would finally get the news he'd been waiting for. He spoke to the X-ray tech as he stepped down to the floor in the radiology room. "How's everything look to you?"

"I'll pass these on to Dr. Powell," the efficient middle-aged woman said.

Campbell tried not to appear irked at the typical withholding of information.

"You can go to his office now," she said.

Campbell entered the dark-paneled room lined with shelves of medical books and was surprised to see Kitty occupying a chair on the other side of the doctor's desk. Usually she waited in the reception area until he was finished. Campbell sat next to her and anticipated bad news. "This can't be good," he said to her, "if you think I need moral support."

Kitty patted his hand. "I know this is a big day, and I wanted to be here, good news or bad."

Campbell watched the doctor slide his films into the viewer mounted to the wall. "So, Doc, will I ever fly again?"

Dr. Powell switched on the background light. He cupped his fingers under his chin and studied the X-rays. "After what you've been through, are you sure you want to?"

"Once a fool..." Campbell said, trying to sound cheerful.

Kitty seemed to be holding her breath.

"From these pictures," the doctor began, "I'd say you'll be able to fly and even dance an Irish jig."

Kitty exhaled as Campbell let his shoulders sag. "Great. I never could dance an Irish jig before."

Obviously missing the old joke, the doctor said, "Your bones have knitted beautifully, Camp. Better than I'd hoped."

"So what's the next step? Can I get the splint off and the rods removed?"

The doctor switched off the viewing screen and sat behind his desk. "How does Friday sound?"

"Like forty-eight hours too far away."

The doctor smiled. "Nevertheless, that's when we'll do it. Won't hurt to give these fractures another couple of days of protection and besides, I need to order some equipment for you."

"Equipment?" Was this a black cloud on his horizon? Campbell sat forward. "What kind of equipment?"

"You can't start jogging on that leg just yet. We discussed this. You'll still need a Velcro walking boot. But you can take it off for showers and sleeping at night. For any extensive walking, though, wear the thing until I tell you it's okay to stop."

"And when will that be?"

Dr. Powell wrote something on a prescription pad and handed the paper to Campbell. "This is for a mild pain medication. Only take it as needed. You should be cleared to walk without the boot in another couple of weeks. And of course you'll have to continue the therapy after that."

Campbell glanced at Kitty who was offering a smile of encouragement. "Will I be able to drive on Friday?" he asked the doctor.

"Sure. You can drive. In fact, you can resume almost all your normal activities. But I'm expecting you to use common sense. If you experience any pain, stop whatever you're doing and rest."

Campbell should have been ecstatic to hear the doctor's prognosis. He was. But foremost in his mind was the realization that this good news would alter his relationship with Kitty. Would she immediately call Virgil and talk to him about leaving the gap? And if she did, could he stop her? Should he?

"You must be so relieved," Kitty said a few minutes later when they were in the Jeep. "You'll be able to fly, drive—" she grinned "—cook for yourself."

He stared at her as she sped toward the Value-Rite to pick up Adam. A strand of her hair stuck to whatever pale pink gloss she'd used on her lips. She brushed it away, glanced sideways at him and smiled.

He clasped his hands between his knees and focused on the rubber mat under his feet. "Yeah, I will. But part of me will miss the novelty of the outlaw's cooking."

"I'll bet."

Campbell sat back, tried to concentrate on the positive aspects of his future. The Cardinal was being repaired. Maybe he could restart his fledgling photography business before too long. He could drive the Jeep out of the gap whenever he wanted to. *Normal activities*, the doctor had said. There hadn't been anything normal about

Campbell's life in weeks. He stared at Kitty now. Did she know he was thinking about her?

Her hand curled over his lower arm, and he jerked forward.

"What's wrong?" she said.

"Nothing." His voice was hoarse. He coughed.

"Well, good. Because everything's going your way." She pulled into the Value-Rite parking lot. "You'll probably even have Adam and me out of your hair soon. Now that you can take care of yourself…"

"Can we please not talk about that?"

He didn't look at her, but he imagined her eyes rolling at what she would call another typically brooding reaction from him. "Whatever you say."

He turned slowly in his seat to study her profile. "You've turned my life upside down, you know."

"What exactly do you mean?"

He couldn't start a conversation now. Adam would be at the car anytime, so he said, "This whole…cooperative thing. If it actually works out, there will be people coming out, milling around. Noise, confusion…I don't know. It's not what I came back to the gap for."

She smiled indulgently. "Maybe it's what you need."

He snorted. If she only knew what he needed.

KITTY DROVE DOWN the center aisle of parked cars to the entrance of Value-Rite. When she noticed Sheriff Oakes and Adam standing to the side of the doorway, she hit the brakes. "Do you see that, Campbell? Every time your uncle's with my son I get this sick feeling."

Campbell squinted into the sun. "I think it's all right. Virgil's got his arm around the kid's shoulders—and I don't see any handcuffs."

Kitty slumped back in her seat. "Thank goodness. I thought he had him collared again."

Campbell chuckled. "You don't think Adam is rehabilitated after all this time?"

Kitty thought about her answer. "Yeah, I think he is. But I've learned never to take anything about a twelve-year-old for granted."

"Relax, Mom. His life of crime seems to have stalled out in Sorrel Gap."

She pulled up to the door and a smiling Adam ran to the driver's window. "Hi, Mom. Sheriff Oakes has news for you."

Virgil stepped up behind Adam and leaned toward the window. "I just got an accounting from Quint. Your boy will have finished his sentence by the end of next week. All paid up."

"Really?" Kitty grinned at her son. "Congratulations. I'm proud of you for sticking with this."

Adam shrugged. "Like I had a choice. But

if I have to stack another tower of toilet paper packages in the next two days, I'm turning in my staff vest early."

"Way to go, kid," Campbell said. "Looks like this is a big day for both of us." Campbell told Virgil about the doctor's visit as Adam scrambled into the back of the Jeep.

Virgil settled his hat low on his brow and said, "Congrats to you, too, Kitty. I'll be in touch before next Friday so we can go over some details. You'll be free to leave our fair village, all debts paid."

This should have been good news. They'd completed their end of the bargain. Just six weeks ago she'd thought this day would never come, and now that it was actually happening, she felt only a strange void in the pit of her stomach and a longing that didn't make any more sense than a whole lot of other emotions she'd been struggling with lately.

"How do you feel about all this, Adam? We'll be leaving Sorrel Gap," she said.

"Not yet. We have a whole week."

Kitty glanced at Campbell, whose eyes had grown round with surprise. "You almost sound like you want to stay," she added.

"Well…not forever," Adam said. "This is still a Podunk town and all, but it's better than dumb Charlotte where I'll have to visit a relative

I don't even know and probably have to have good manners all the time." He stuck his head between the seats. "Mom, when the week is up, are we going to leave right away?"

She stole a glance at Campbell. His expression was unreadable. "I imagine so, Adam. We had plans when we left Florida. Those haven't changed."

But had they? Being in Sorrel Gap, living with Campbell, had caused her to rethink those plans over the past couple of weeks. Campbell had just said she'd turned his life upside down. Well, he'd done a bang-up job of upsetting the balance of her life, too. She'd had goals when she left Richland—to get away from her father's influence, to become a better mother, to make a responsible citizen out of her son and herself. But hadn't she done all those things right here in Sorrel Gap? And what about her plans to go to design school? But hadn't she started designing clothes right here in Sorrel Gap?

Campbell's attention remained focused out the front window. He hadn't spoken in moments. What was he thinking? He'd been the most difficult man. Obstinate, gloomy, judgmental. Yet she was missing him already.

"If we did stick around for a while," Adam said, "would that be okay with you, beast?"

"As long as you like, kid. No rush as far as I'm

concerned." Campbell exhaled a deep breath. "In fact, I think your mom should follow through on this cooperative project she's got going on."

"Yeah, Mom, how about that? You've been saying all this stuff about responsibility. That applies to you, too."

"Adam, I don't know…"

"Well, doesn't it?"

"It's complicated, honey…"

"I'm just saying, Toby and I have things to do while it's still summer, and it'd be okay if I hung around the airstrip with Rick and the beast for a while longer."

A muscle worked along Campbell's jawline. Kitty had noticed that reaction before when Adam mentioned the extra hand Greg had hired. She hadn't met the ultracool Rick yet. He always seemed to be missing in action whenever she was at the airstrip. Only now she suddenly realized that Campbell was jealous of him. She smiled to herself. Campbell, jealous of someone her son, the outlaw, admired. She had witnessed many changes since she came to Sorrel Gap, not the least of which was Campbell's attitude toward Adam.

Campbell remained silent during the rest of the drive to the Saddle Top. When Kitty drove into the lot, he laid his hand on her arm. She turned to look at him, but he spoke to Adam.

"Call Toby, Adam," he said. "Ask if you can have dinner at his house this Friday."

"What for?"

"If you must know," Campbell said, "I'd like to take your mom out to a restaurant."

Kitty stared at Campbell. Adam stared at both of them. A few moments passed before he said, "You're taking her out?"

Campbell nodded once but didn't shift his gaze from Kitty's face. She didn't blink. She couldn't swallow. Part of her brain seemed to be shutting down while another part had reached maximum alert status. "That's right," he said. "So, can you go to Toby's as long as it's okay with your mother?"

Kitty pursed her lips, waited, for what, she didn't know. And then nodded. "It's okay."

"I'll call him, but don't think I'm stupid. I know you're going to hit on her."

"I never thought you were stupid," Campbell said. He and Adam got out of the Jeep.

Kitty sat behind the wheel for a while longer. A brisk breeze coming in the window cooled her skin. Campbell came around and leaned on the door frame. "What's for lunch?" he said.

She didn't answer. She couldn't have told him what was for lunch if she'd already prepared it and it was sitting on the kitchen counter.

"Are you mad?" he asked her.

"Yes."

"He's not a baby, you know."

"But he might be upset…"

"Did he seem upset to you?"

"No. I guess not."

"You're not going to be my nursemaid any longer, and when this splint comes off, I'd like to see some changes around here."

He was suddenly so full of that macho obstinacy she'd once hated but now found exciting. And then he gave her a grin so boyish, she trapped a sigh in her throat. This was a different Campbell—teasing, fun, and irresistible.

"What if you're not ready for changes?" she said.

"Oh, honey, I'm ready. You and I have plans for Friday."

He readjusted the crutches under his arms, headed for his room and didn't look back. When he'd gone inside, Kitty stared at her hands clasped in her lap and said, "Holy cow."

CHAPTER SIXTEEN

KITTY CAME OUT of the bathroom and smoothed the pencil-straight skirt of the black designer dress Owen had bought her for her birthday last year. She then adjusted a simple circular medallion on its black cord so it lay perfectly centered above the scooped neckline. Turning her back to the mirror, she checked her fanny. The acetate-spandex fabric was snug, but not too bad considering she hadn't pursued her low-fat diet since coming to Sorrel Gap.

From the bed, Adam appraised her with a narrowed gaze. "That's what you're wearing?"

Kitty hopped on one foot as she adjusted the strap on the rhinestone-studded sandals she hadn't worn since leaving Richland. She immediately turned back to the mirror. Getting dressed in a small motel room with her twelve-year-old son a few feet away hadn't been easy, and now his comment made her question her choices.

"What's wrong?" she asked. "It's basic black. You can never go wrong with basic black."

Adam shook his head. "I dunno. Looks to me like plenty can go wrong if you wear that dress."

What? Her son was judging her? Was the dress too revealing? "Isn't that the dress Grandpa bought you?"

"It is."

"You wore it to the fancy restaurant in Orlando on your birthday."

Back in Richland, she'd thrown the designer piece into her suitcase at the last moment, thinking she might need it in Charlotte. Maybe she'd eventually go to another five-star gourmet restaurant sometime, even if her father wasn't picking up the tab. And, after all, it was basic black.

"You wore that dress for Terry," Adam said.

"No. I wore it because it's a great dress. And, for your information, I didn't even invite Terry to go along that night."

"I know. Grandpa did."

She reexamined the cut of the dress. "I would never have worn this for Terry Spenser."

Adam smiled. "But you're wearing it for the beast."

And then it struck her. Adam wasn't judging her. He was teasing her, and she wasn't sure she was comfortable about it.

"It's a nice dress," he said. "Grandpa was happy that he got it for you. Billie helped him pick it out."

And Kitty had been thrilled and surprised when she opened the distinctive gift box. She never would have splurged so much.

Adam sat against the headboard. "I've been thinking about Grandpa," he said. "I know we've been sending him those postcards, but I think we should call him."

She sat down close to her son and considered his request. Was she ready to do that? She'd kept her father apart from Adam for all these weeks. Her purpose hadn't been to make Owen miserable, though she was sure he was. Maybe enough time had passed for him to accept that she'd established herself as Adam's mother, and he needed to back off.

"We might do that," she said, trying to come up with a way to contact Owen while still protecting their whereabouts. "If we do call him, that doesn't mean we're going back to Richland anytime soon."

"I know. But Grandpa might be okay with us staying here for a while. I mean, we could probably even tell him about the beast and Quint and Toby. After all, except for somebody stealing our money, nothing bad really happened to us."

Was this the same boy who'd threatened to sue Sheriff Oakes? The same one who complained every day about working off his debt? The one who'd thought everything about the mountains was lame? This child of hers had come a long way, and she allowed herself to think she was partially responsible. She leaned over, brushed his hair back from his face and kissed his temple, expecting him to pull away. He didn't, so she held tight to him for a couple of precious seconds. "No, nothing bad happened," she said. "I'll think about calling him."

Headlights speared through the crack in the drapes and Adam jumped up from the bed. He went to the window and peeked out. "Toby and his dad are here," he said. "I gotta go."

"Have fun. I'll wait up for you."

He grinned at her again. "Look who's telling who to have fun." He grabbed his ball cap and called from the door, "Don't stay out too late."

She stood up and said, "Have you got Campbell's cell phone number?"

"Yeah." Just before the door slammed, he hollered, "Quit being a mother for one night, can't you?"

Lucas Crum's pickup had barely backed out of the parking lot before a bout of intense nerves made Kitty sink to the bed again. Adam was gone. She was alone in their room waiting for her date with Campbell Oakes. She clenched her hands and took several deep breaths, and then another pair of headlights showed through the drapes. He'd actually driven the Jeep down to her room.

"This is it," she said, picking up her purse and clutching it to her chest. Her stomach felt queasy. Her palms were damp. Her legs, which she'd shaved and lotioned so they'd look smooth and feminine, felt as if they were made of clay. She hoped she'd pass inspection on the outside, because inside she was a mess.

She hadn't seen Campbell since ten this morning when he'd driven back to the motel after his doctor's appointment. He'd been like a kid with a new toy, or an old favorite one, shifting gears, applying the gas with a contented smile on his face.

He'd dropped her at her room and, with a grin that held a dare and a promise, told her he'd see her at seven-thirty. Since then he'd taken care of himself. He'd fixed his own meals and driven the Jeep away from the motel to mysterious destinations. Maybe she'd discover that he'd even cleaned his apartment—something a guy would do if he had plans for later, and Campbell's way to reacquaint himself with his former meticulous life. A life that no longer needed her in it—for housekeeping anyway.

When a knock sounded on her door, Kitty jumped up from the bed and opened it. Campbell stood there, tall, straight and gorgeous, minus the splint, in dark slacks, a cream-colored shirt and a black leather sports coat. She now knew one place he'd gone when he left earlier in the day. Somewhere in the vicinity there existed a hairstylist who knew exactly how to tame that rich coppery-brown hair into a tangle of thick waves.

"You look nice," she said, nearly choking on the words. Nice didn't begin to describe him.

He smiled, uttered an appreciative "Wow," before tilting her face up and kissing her with featherlight precision. "You took the words right out of my mouth."

She ran her tongue over her damp upper lip. "Thanks." She'd watched him put the walking boot from the doctor in the back of the Jeep this morning. He wasn't wearing it now. "Where's the boot?" she asked.

"The doctor said I could leave it off for short periods."

She smiled. "Do you consider this a speed date?"

He chucked her under her chin. "Not if I have anything to say about it." He stepped away from the door. "Ready?"

"You bet." She walked around him and headed toward the Jeep. Every inch of her skin tingled. She was as ready as any woman ever had been.

He followed her to the passenger door, opened it and waited until she'd settled in. Then he closed the door and got in the driver's side. He'd left the air conditioner running, and she was grateful for the cool blast of air that hit her face and the fresh scent of evergreen coming from the vents.

He curled his hand over the knob of the gearshift but didn't engage it into Reverse. Instead he stared at her, his eyes bright in the fading sunlight.

She cleared her throat, an effort to release the breaths that seemed trapped in her lungs. This was a totally new experience for both of them. He was healed and driving, completely and masterfully in charge of the vehicle and the situation. The concept made her weak with anticipation.

His lip curled into a tight grin. She fidgeted with a curl that fell loose over her cheek. "Is something wrong?" she said.

He stilled her hand by covering it with his own. Then he ran his palm down the side of her face, slowly, deliberately, stopping at her bare collarbone. "Everything's fine." His voice was almost a growl. "We should probably go."

"I guess we should." Her voice trembled.

He backed out of the spot and headed across the parking lot toward the road. When he hit the edge of the pavement he stopped, scanned both ways down the highway and looked back at her. When their eyes met, something happened. Something unexpected, electric, supercharged with sensations that felt so good they made her shudder with their intensity.

"Did I mention that you look fantastic?" he asked.

"You did, yes. But it's nice to hear a second time."

He swallowed, glanced over his shoulder to the motel. "I'm really glad we don't have any guests in this run-down dump."

"Why?"

"Because tonight is strictly about us."

Yikes. He leaned in and kissed her cheek. Her thoughts tumbled. Was this man, with all his flaws, the man she'd needed all her life? Brooding? Yes. Difficult at times? No doubt. Perfect? Not nearly. Neither was she. But she'd made him care again. He'd made her want to do better. His heart had touched hers, and she now understood with startling clarity that she'd been waiting, hoping for this moment perhaps since the first time she saw him.

With a soft chuckle, he kissed her lips. She kept her eyes closed, relishing the way he made her feel.

Slowly she allowed the waning daylight to

filter under her lids. When she looked at him, she found his smile warm and intense, as if it were purely for her.

"What now?" she said.

"Now we go to dinner," he said. "Although we may be a few minutes late for our reservation." He put the Jeep in gear and slowly moved out of the parking lot.

What now? she'd said. He'd taken the question literally. She'd meant so much more.

CHAPTER SEVENTEEN

TERRY SPENSER WALKED into Owen's office at Galloway Groves, shut the door and took the seat across the desk from Owen.

Something was up. The smirk of triumph on Terry's face indicated it was something good. Owen leaned back in his chair. "So? What brings you here?"

"Just talked to Watley," Terry said. "Now's a good time for you to get involved. He and Adam just got back from trail-riding on the ATV. They're in the hangar where Oakes's plane is, but for once Oakes isn't there."

During the two weeks that Starks's man had been watching the hangar, he'd reported that Oakes had rarely let Adam out of his sight. The apparent protectiveness the fly guy felt over Adam had made Bobby's job more difficult, but not impossible.

Owen didn't know much about Oakes, other than the few details his sources had provided. The guy was considered a war hero, a skilled pilot who, after serving his country, had wrecked his private wings and ended up in the hospital. Owen knew, too, that for some reason Kitty had taken up lodging at Oakes's remote, dilapidated motel. Probably a desperate attempt to keep Owen's feelers from finding her. Plus, money had to be a motive, because Owen had made certain Kitty couldn't get into her usual accounts. Well, once Owen made this next phone call, the pilot would soon be free of her—or she could stay. Owen didn't care.

"Get me Watley's number," Owen said to Terry, and a few seconds later he was dialing.

The voice that answered was crisp and confident. "Yes, sir."

"You with the boy?"

"Sure am," Bobby said. "Oakes is over at the strip manager's office. It's just me and Adam."

"And you're getting along with him?"

Bobby chuckled. "The kid loves me like a father."

Owen flinched. He still hated the creep. Nothing would change that. He took a deep breath, and let the sweet smell of victory erase the stench of Bobby Watley. "Put him on the phone."

Bobby yelled, "Hey, Adam! Phone's for you."

Adam's response seemed to come from across the room. "Me? On your phone?"

"Yeah. Get your butt over here."

Owen heard footsteps coming closer, then a

soft rustle. Maybe Adam was wiping the phone against his pants leg. "Hello?"

Owen's chest constricted with welcome pain. The kid sounded so good. He cleared his throat. "Adam? You know who this is?"

"Grandpa, is that you?"

At the excitement in Adam's voice, Owen grinned over the desk at Terry. "You betcha, son."

"Did Mom call you?"

"No. I found you on my own."

"How'd you do that?"

"Don't worry about it. Just know that I've never stopped looking."

"We've been in this Podunk town all along, Grandpa. Me and Mom have been living in a motel."

"I know all about the place, Adam. You can give me the details later, but for now, I just want to know how you are."

"I'm okay. At first I thought I'd go crazy living here, but then I kinda got used to it. You got our postcards, right?"

"I got them."

"I wanted to call you, but Mom said I should wait…"

"Forget about that, Adam. I wish you had called. I would have come and taken you away from there, brought you home where you belong."

"I couldn't, Grandpa. I promised Mom."

"Some promises are meant to be broken, Adam. You'll learn that as you grow older." Owen leaned forward, resting his elbows on the desktop. "But we can talk about all this another time. I've got something to tell you."

"Are you coming here?"

"I'll be there before you know it. But until you see me, you've got to keep this phone call a secret between us."

"A secret? I don't know, Grandpa. I think Mom will be okay with it. She always said she wasn't mad at you or anything."

"You want to come home, don't you, son?"

"Well, sure."

"Then don't give your mother any reason to run from the place you are right now. I need you to stay put." Owen took a fortifying breath. Now was the time to deliver his ace in the hole. Owen had given his grandson a lot in his short life, but he'd never given him the one thing he'd always wanted—his father.

Bobby had done his part in the past two weeks. He'd established a relationship with Adam, one that would ensure that Adam would want to come back to Richland. Now Owen was banking on the fact that the boy wouldn't want to be separated from Bobby ever again. Of course, that meant Owen had to put up with Bobby's presence in their lives, but he could do it—for Adam.

"I want you to know something, Adam," he began. "You're not alone."

"I know that. There's Mom and Campbell, and this kid…"

"No, I mean, I've got your back, even from here. We both have."

"Both? Who are you talking about?"

"Where's that fella who's been at the airstrip helping out, the one who takes you trail riding?"

"You mean Rick?"

"Yeah, him."

"He's right here."

"Son, I've got news. It's big."

"What kind of news?" Skepticism clouded Adam's voice. For a moment Owen experienced the first twinge of uncertainty that maybe this plan wouldn't work after all. But too much depended on the truth, so Owen looked at Terry, who nodded his encouragement. "That man, Rick," Owen said. "That's not his name."

"What do you mean?"

Owen forced the words out on a trembling rush of air. "He's your father, son. I found him for you. You've been with Bobby all this time."

"What?" His voice seemed to raise an octave.

"I know it's a shock, but isn't this what you've always wanted? After all these years…"

Owen nearly dropped the phone when Adam spoke. "You—you've been lying to me all this time!"

The accusation wasn't aimed at Owen. Bobby's placating tone responded. "Now, kid, calm down…"

"All these years when you could've called, or written me a freakin' letter! Now you come here and lie about who you really are!"

Sensing his plan escalating out of control, Owen intervened. He shouted into the phone, "Adam, listen to me. You've got this all wrong."

Adam hollered back, releasing years of frustration. "What'd you do, Grandpa, pay him to come be nice to me?"

Ouch. "He wanted to come, Adam," Owen said, struggling to calm the situation. It wasn't really a lie. Yes, money had been involved, enough to finally make Bobby step up to his responsibilities.

"I don't believe you," Adam said.

Owen could picture his grandson's scowl aimed at Bobby's face. The kid had spunk. "Look, Adam," Owen said, ready to bend the truth if he needed to. "There's a lot you don't know, and now you should. Your mother took you from Bobby. He didn't send you away. Your mom didn't want anything to do with him. She didn't want him to be a father to you." *And neither did I, until now.*

There was a long sigh followed by a stretch of silence. Owen wished he could see his grandson's face, put his arm around him. When Adam spoke next, his voice was calmer. "He didn't try very hard."

"No, I didn't," Bobby said. "And I'm sorry about that. I've always been sorry. But I knew it wouldn't do any good. Once your mother makes up her mind, there's no changing it."

"You know that's true, son," Owen said. "When you were a baby, your mom didn't stay and fight for you to have a father, and a few weeks ago she didn't stick around so you could be here in Richland."

More silence, but Owen sensed Adam was listening, taking it all in and maybe deciding to give Bobby the benefit of the doubt.

"Adam, you know I've always wanted what's best for you," Owen said. "And I've always seen that you had the best. Do you really believe your mom wants what's best for you? Does a mother pull her kid away from his home and everyone who loves him and dump him in some rattrap motel?"

"I already told you it wasn't so bad once I got used to it," Adam said.

"Sure, you made it work, because that's the kind of kid you are. Resourceful. And I know you care about your mother. But ask yourself why she put you in that situation."

"She said I had to learn responsibility."

"Okay, and I bet you have. But now it's time to come home. I'm heading to North Carolina to meet up with you and your father, to bring you both back here."

Another long pause before Adam said, "What about Mom?"

"Your mom can come, too. I want her to come home. I want these miserable weeks behind us."

"Is this what you want—to come live in Richland?"

Owen kept quiet, knowing this question was directed at Bobby. And the lowlife better not blow it.

"It is," Bobby said. "Look, kid, I hated pretending with you, but I had to prove to you that you could trust me, that we could be pals, like we should have been your whole life."

"And you're not going to cut and run?"

"I'm not the one who ran the first time, Adam. I'm going to look for a golf pro position right where you live. I'm staying for the long haul."

Owen gripped the phone. *As long as you don't screw up the position I arranged for you.*

"Grandpa?"

"Yeah?"

"What if Mom won't come?"

"She'll come."

"I think she kind of likes it here."

Owen shook his head. No way. His spoiled daughter couldn't be happy in a ratty motel in the middle of nowhere. She'd made this move out of spite, and Owen would wager his last dollar that she'd take the first avenue he opened up to get back to her life. In a few days she'd even thank him.

"She likes you more, kid," he said. "She'll come home with us."

"When are you coming?" Adam asked.

"Tomorrow. Terry and I are chartering a plane. I want you to find some excuse to stay at that motel all day and not come to the airstrip. Then just sit tight and wait. And, Adam?"

"Yeah?"

"Don't tell your mother. If you do, she might take off again, dragging you with her. And who knows where you'll end up next time? Maybe someplace even worse."

No response.

"Adam? Son, you hear me?"

"Yeah, I hear ya."

"If you need anything, just call your father. He's there for you until I get there."

"Okay."

"I can't wait to get you home. I'll make sure Esmeralda has all your favorite foods."

"That'll be good."

"It's all good, son. I'll see you tomorrow."

They disconnected and Owen stared over the desk at Terry. "Is that true, Owen?" Terry asked. "All good?"

"Soon will be. By this time tomorrow, Adam will be home. You make the arrangements to get us to Asheville in the morning."

"Are you going to tell Billie?" Terry asked.

A ticklish question. After a moment he said, "Sure. I don't like to keep anything from Billie. I'll tell her…just as soon as we get back."

Terry smiled. "Good plan."

CAMPBELL CAME OUT of the breezeway with a can of crickets and two fishing rods, his own and the one he'd bought Adam at the sporting goods store on Friday after he finished with his date night preparations. He'd figured the kid had borrowed Toby's gear enough. Today was Monday, and the rod hadn't cooled off much since Adam had taken possession.

He stopped on the sidewalk and stared down at the mostly reformed outlaw who sat on the recently painted steps of the soon-to-be craft shop. His elbows rested on his bent knees, while his chin sat in his hands. Adam had been in a funk since they'd returned from the airstrip a couple of hours ago. Odd, since there was a lot to celebrate lately. Campbell had his own private reasons for thinking life was pretty darn good right now. Orders were coming in for his photography business, and of course there had been that dinner with Kitty, a real date, but so much more than a first step. Besides all that, the improved section of the motel was a sign of hope and prosperity in the gap.

So, Campbell had to wonder, what was eating Adam this afternoon? Was the kid ticked off about him taking his mother out the other night? Campbell didn't think so. Saturday and Sunday had been great days, filled with work and fishing and culminating with a barbecue on the old grill last night to thank everyone for working on the common cause. But just in case the date could have caused a problem, Campbell had tried to be sensitive about Adam's feelings today. So, here he was, fishing poles in hand. He sat down beside Adam on the steps. The kid hit a control on his music player and looked at him. "What?"

Thinking his intent should be obvious, Campbell tapped the poles against the bottom step. "You game?"

"I don't feel much like fishing."

"Really? You mad about something?"

"No, just thinking."

"Okay. Thinking's good, but your mother's all busy with her sewing stuff, I've got these two good legs I'd like to use, and nobody to play with."

Adam sort of smirked. "You'll manage."

"Sure I'll *manage*," Campbell said. "But like I told you a couple of weeks ago, I've been finding you a lot less irritating than when you first got here. I'd rather fish with you than by myself." He smiled. "Can't believe I just said that."

Ordinarily Adam would have come back with a typically smart-aleck remark. This time he pulled a leaf off a plant Kitty had brought back to life, tore it to bits and sailed the pieces into the air.

Campbell set the rods on the ground beside them. "All right, I get it. You're ticked off about something. You want to tell me what it is?"

"I'm not mad exactly."

"Then what are you?"

"I told you. I'm thinking."

"And you can't think down at Gilley's Creek?"

No answer. Just a subtle shake of his head.

"You can't be mad at me," Campbell said. "I haven't even given you any grief lately...have I?"

"No. You've been pretty decent."

"That's a relief." He sat quietly for a few moments contemplating whether he should ask the big question. "Are you upset with me because I took your mother on a date?"

Adam turned to stare at him. "What? No. I woulda been if she hadn't had a good time, but she didn't have any complaints."

Campbell smiled to himself. "Well, good, because I didn't, either. But I want you to know something. If you have any problems with me, you can talk to me about them. I don't know as I'm going to change a lot to make your life easier. I'm pretty set in my ways, but I'll listen to you and if I can do anything to help you, I will."

Adam pinched off another leaf. This one he just twirled in his hand.

"Talking to me is better than killing that bush, isn't it?" Campbell said.

Adam smiled before tossing the leaf to the ground. "Sun's beginning to set," he said after a few minutes.

"Yeah. That happens nearly every day."

He stood. "I'm just saying because the fish tend to bite when the sun's going down. We'd better head on down to the creek."

Campbell handed Adam's rod to him and stepped toward the breezeway. "Let's go, then. We're wasting valuable time."

As they walked across the backyard, Adam told a couple of stories about his latest escapades with Toby. Campbell laughed and decided that the past few minutes hadn't been wasted at all. In fact, he felt almost the same as he had over twenty-five years ago when he and his own father had carried cane poles down to Gilley's Creek.

He looked down at Adam and felt a burst of pride in the kid that he'd never expected to feel. And he decided that as soon as they were done fishing, he'd call Travis Oakes and tell him all about Adam and his mother, and how Kitty Watley had healed him in ways that went far beyond his busted leg. He knew his dad would be happy for him.

And then he wondered how Adam would react when he found out that he intended to ask Kitty to stay on at the Saddle Top indefinitely. His feelings were growing stronger every day, every time he kissed her. Didn't they deserve to know if this was the real thing? She had to stay on, and Campbell had to convince her.

CHAPTER EIGHTEEN

CAMPBELL TOOK A SIP of coffee and said, "So, what are your plans for today?"

Kitty turned off the stove burner, set a plate of eggs and toast in front of him on the counter and smiled with satisfaction. The eggs were just the way he liked them, over easy. The toast wasn't burned. She was getting good at this homemaking stuff. And liking it way too much. "Lyssa's coming down. She's going to do some embroidery on a few pieces I made, and I'm trying out a new pattern I designed."

He picked up his fork and dove into the eggs. "This afternoon when I get back from the airstrip I'll work on putting together those clothes racks you ordered."

"Thanks."

"Will you need the car?"

Kitty reminded herself not to get too comfortable with the easy familiarity of these recent exchanges with Campbell. She'd become as comfortable with him as if she'd known him for a long time, not just a few weeks. As if they were… She halted the thoughts before they led her to conclusions she shouldn't be making. Along with her nearly constant urges to be alone with Campbell, she had to keep her fantasies from ending with any idea of forever. "No," she said. "You go ahead and take it."

Campbell glanced over at Adam, who was sitting on the floor having breakfast on the coffee table. His cereal bowl was still full and his glass of milk hadn't been touched. The TV blared away, but Adam didn't seem to be watching it.

"Hey, outlaw," Campbell said. "Eat up. The guy from the FAA board is supposed to be in today to examine the Cardinal. We need to tighten a few bolts before he gets there."

Adam looked over his shoulder. "I don't think I'm going in with you today."

Campbell stopped eating, a corner of toast still in his hand. "What? Why not?"

"Are you feeling okay?" Kitty asked.

"I've kind of got a stomachache."

She walked over and laid her palm against his forehead. "You don't have a fever. When did this start?"

Adam shrugged away from her touch. "I don't know. This morning some time."

"Do you feel sick?"

"I think I ought to lie down."

Giving in to motherly skepticism, Kitty frowned.

"You know, Adam, this ailment seems remarkably similar to the I-have-a-math-test-today attacks you have during the school year."

"Is not. I really don't feel good."

"But you promised Campbell…"

"It's all right," Campbell said. "Adam doesn't have to go with me."

"Yeah," Adam said. "You've got Rick to help you today. You don't need me."

"Sure. We'll be fine."

Kitty grasped Adam's elbow. "Come on, then. I'll walk you back to our room." She looked at the dirty dishes scattered around the apartment. "After I make sure he's settled, I'll come back and pick up the mess."

"I still remember how to wash dishes," Campbell said. He smiled at her. "But if the outlaw's okay, I'd like to talk to you about something before I leave."

She agreed to come back and walked through the lobby with Adam. "What's going on with you?" she asked when they were on the sidewalk heading to their room.

He frowned. "Jeez, Mom, can't a guy be sick?"

"Yes, a guy can, but you're not. I predict that in a half hour you'll be munching on a bag of chips in our room and asking me for a soda."

He mumbled something, his gaze plastered on the walkway.

Once in the room, he toed off his sneakers and crawled between the sheets of his bed. "Can I have the remote?" he asked.

She handed it to him but kept her palm over the buttons so he couldn't turn the set on. "Something's up," she said. "Did you have an argument with Toby?"

Adam crossed his arms over his chest. "No."

"Are you mad about anything?"

"No. Why do people keep asking me that?"

"Did somebody do something..."

"Let it go, Mom! I've just got an upset stomach. Go back to Campbell's and leave me alone a few minutes."

She released the remote. "All right, I will. You call over there if you need anything. I'll be back in a few minutes."

The sound from the TV drowned out his last comment, and Kitty left the room. When she entered Campbell's apartment he was stacking the last of the dishes in the drainer. "How's he doing?" he asked.

"Something's going on with him. I can always tell." She grabbed a dish towel. "Not that he always tells me what it is, unfortunately."

Campbell took the towel from her, set it on the counter and led her to the sofa. "Maybe he just needs some alone time," he said.

"That's what he told me."

"Then I wouldn't worry too much about it."

Campbell sat beside her and took her hands. "Speaking of needing alone time…"

She smiled. "I know what you mean." Aware that they weren't going to have much time now, she sighed and said, "You want to talk to me about something?"

He buried his face in the crook of her neck. His breath whispered over her ear. "Did I say that?"

He was making it impossible to ignore the tempting shivers running up her spine. "Yes, I'm quite sure you did."

He kissed her gently, and she wrapped her arms around his neck and kissed him back.

"I suppose it's possible that Adam could come in at any time."

She leaned back on the sofa. "Kids. They are nothing if not unpredictable."

Campbell chuckled and leaned over to press a more urgent kiss to her mouth. She longed to stay in his arms indefinitely, but the phone rang. Campbell dropped his forehead to the sofa cushion and groaned. "Let's ignore it," he said.

"Could be Greg."

"Yeah, and?"

"The FAA inspector, remember?"

He hoisted himself over the arm of the sofa, read the caller ID and said, "It's only Virgil."

Kitty grabbed the phone, pressed the connect button and handed it to him. "We can't ignore the law, Campbell."

He sat up, frowned at her and scrubbed his palm down his face. "Hello, Virgil. What's up?" After a pause he said, "Yeah, she's here. Just a minute." He handed Kitty the phone. "He wants to talk to you. Adam told him you were over here."

Virgil Oakes had never called her before. She'd called him several times as he'd instructed when he gave her permission to drive Campbell's Jeep, but he'd only communicated with her through Adam or in person at the motel. Even after all this time of successfully avoiding her father's reach, she experienced a moment of panic. Her hand shook when she placed the receiver to her ear. "Hi, Sheriff."

CAMPBELL GOT UP and paced the room. He walked to the window and back to the door while Kitty talked to his uncle using short, nondescript responses. Each time he passed her he watched her expression. At first she seemed dazed, then satisfied.

"I'll take care of getting my driver's license replaced as soon as I can."

Her hand tightened on the phone. "That's not necessary. No, thank *you*. I'm pleased with how everything worked out. This has been a good experience for Adam from the start."

She finally looked up and met Campbell's gaze. Her eyes were large and luminous. "I expect we will," she said. "Thank you again." She returned the phone to the cradle but remained silent.

"Well?" Campbell prompted.

She bit her bottom lip before saying, "My truck is fixed. Virgil handled the repair cost and said it's running great now."

His breath caught. "That's good news, isn't it?" A pain in his chest alerted him that it might not be.

"Sure. Virgil even got an extension on the temporary tag I had on the truck." She tried to smile, but her lips trembled with the effort. "I'm legal, and, Campbell..."

"What?"

"Tommy Gibbs and one of the other deputies are bringing the truck out here this afternoon. Adam and I will soon be free to go."

Six weeks ago he'd never have imagined that those words would affect him so deeply, so physically. His lungs seemed incapable of drawing a breath. "Is that what you want?" he said, his voice a hollow croak. "You want to go?"

She walked to the kitchen and placed her palms flat on the counter on each side of the sink. How many times he'd watched her standing there, the sunlight through the window turning her hair the color of corn silk. Her incompetence back then had made him shudder even as it had made him smile.

When he thought he couldn't stand her silence a moment longer, she turned to him and said, "I had plans to go to the design school in Charlotte. You know that. Adam and I need to establish a life for ourselves. Otherwise what has all this been for?"

He crossed the room, wrapped his hands around her arms. A hundred answers to that question filled his mind, yet suddenly he was uncertain about expressing them. Had he been wrong about her feelings for him? "You don't know?" he said.

"I thought I did. My goal when I accepted Virgil's offer was to keep Adam out of detention. And to be a good mother, a good person…"

"You are those things."

"I'm better, yes, but I've a long way to go yet."

Her eyes glistened with tears, and he pulled her to him, unable to resist her welcoming softness and warmth against his chest. She drew in a long, shuddering breath. He wasn't wrong about her. She cared deeply about her son and, he had to believe, about him. But how much did she really care about those plans? He could make her change her mind. "I wanted to talk to you, remember?" he said. Her head moved under his chin, a barely perceptible nod. "Sit with me. There are things I need to say."

She walked with him to the sofa. He sat beside her and took her hands as he'd done so many times. The familiarity of the act made his heart ache with the pure satisfaction her nearness instilled in him. He rubbed the pads of his thumbs over the backs of her hands. "There's something going on between us," he said. "You know it."

"Yes."

"We've only known each other a few weeks, but don't you think we owe it to each other to see where this leads?"

She looked up at him, her expression guarded.

"Look," he said, "I have to admit that you aren't anything like the woman I thought I'd eventually settle down with." He smiled. "Heck, for a few months before you got here, I'd pretty much sworn off women altogether."

Her lips turned up just a little. "What a surprise. You were so jolly, I never would have known."

He chuckled. "I realize I wasn't an easy patient." When her eyes widened, he said, "Or even decent a lot of the time. I basically wallowed in a mountain of self-pity. I was angry over the accident and my business going up in smoke. I'd recently come out of a longtime relationship..."

She put her hand up as if to stop him. "You don't have to tell me about—"

"Yes, I do because it's the only way I can explain my attitude, my initial reaction to you."

She exhaled. "Okay, then."

"Diana and I were together for most of four years. She was nothing like you. Your backgrounds are obviously different. She was rich, spoiled..."

Kitty's spine stiffened and he increased his gentle massage of her hands, an attempt to put her at ease.

"I worked for her father, who was a successful man in Raleigh. Now that time has passed, I can look back on my relationship with Diana and recognize that our time together was destructive for both of us.

"I think Diana cared for me in her way, the most she was capable of. At least she kept coming back to me." He squeezed Kitty's hand because what he was about to say was the most difficult part. "But I have to be honest with you, Kitty. I adored her. She sparkled with a brilliance that could blind a man. Her laughter was infectious. She was like a drug to me, one that

I couldn't shake no matter how often she left, or how convincingly she lied. I couldn't get it through my thick head that she was the entirely wrong woman for me."

Tears glistened in Kitty's eyes. Campbell wasn't surprised that she would be feeling his private pain so deeply. That was just the way she was. Honest and direct. Guileless where Diana was manipulative.

"Wh-where is Diana now?" she asked.

"With her father, I assume. She always returned to him no matter how far she traveled. And he indulged her. I guess that was her biggest flaw as I think about her now, her inability to exist on her own. Her father gave her whatever she wanted to make her happy and keep her close. He accepted her the way she was, knowing he'd helped mold her into the woman she ultimately became."

Campbell blinked away the memories that hurt him still and increased his resolve to tell Kitty everything. "When I left her, the ache was deep down and raw. Coming back to these mountains, I made this run-down old motel my penance. I left Diana's light and plunged myself into the darkness of reshaping my life without her." He paused, took a breath. "And for a long time it really stank."

Kitty drew her hands from under his and

stood. "Why are you telling me about Diana now?"

"So you'll know what you've come to mean to me." He rose. "You are the total opposite of Diana in almost every way."

A sound like a sob came from Kitty's throat. She turned away, and he hoped she understood that by comparing her to Diana, he was telling her how much the differences mattered. How much he valued the woman she was. He prayed she would look at him again. She stared at the door.

"Ultimately," he continued, "you are everything Diana isn't. You arrived in a broken-down truck with a desperate kid and no money. You were bossy and blunt, and you tried so darn hard all the time. You just wanted to please me and make me better. I was used to a woman who wanted to make me different, not better."

He closed the distance she'd put between them and wrapped his arms around her from behind. She didn't yield to his embrace as he'd hoped she would. "At first I resented you for being nothing like Diana. Stupid, I know. It's like not wanting the medicine that will make you forget the pain. But now..."

He tightened his arms around her. "Now I'm grateful every minute for all the ways, the big ways, the small ways that you are who you are.

Truly, painstakingly, with determination that I've only begun to admire, you are a complete person. And believe me..." He lowered his head and spoke into her ear. "Your light is nothing like Diana's, but it is every bit as dazzling."

She took in a quick, deep breath as her hands came up to clench his arms. "I don't know what to say..."

"Then let me continue, because I actually do have a point to all this." He turned her in his arms. The sadness in her eyes was nearly his undoing. He hadn't intended to make her sad. "What's wrong?"

"I need to check on Adam."

"Okay, but I've got to finish what I've started here." He drew in a deep breath. "Kitty...I don't want you to go. I want you to stay and finish what you've started...with your clothing designs, the craft shop, but mostly with me."

"I don't know if I can."

Panic squeezed his chest. He hadn't expected this reaction. He'd expected her to need him as much as he needed her. "Through the rest of the summer at least, honey. Let's see where this leads." Maybe he sounded desperate. Suddenly he was. "I've just told you a lot, maybe too much, about my past. But I know very little of yours. I want to know it all, every detail. I want to know you, to see if what's happening here is what my heart tells me might be what I've always wanted."

She pressed her hands against his arms, forcing him to release her. "I've got to go."

"But you haven't said…"

"I can't. Not now." She opened the door and practically ran across the lobby.

He started after her but stopped when he saw her hand cover her mouth and her shoulders quake. What had he done? He'd handled this all wrong by talking about Diana. He should have just told her what she meant to him, how she'd healed him, made him better, stronger. When the front door slammed, he turned and went back into his apartment. She needed to sort all this out. As difficult as it would be to leave her alone now, he'd give her the space to think about what he'd said.

Picking up his keys, he headed out. He still had to face the inspection of his plane. He'd try again later with Kitty. He'd get her to stay.

KITTY WAS GLAD Adam was sleeping when she entered their room. She went into the bathroom, sat on the cold toilet lid and let the tears flow. Campbell hadn't said he loved her, and it had been all she could do not to shout those words at him. But she hadn't. Because if he knew the truth, how she'd lied all these weeks, how she and Diana were more alike than different, love would be the last thing he'd feel.

GREG OPENED THE FRIDGE in his office and took out three beers. He handed one to Campbell, one to Rick and twisted the cap off the third for himself. "I have a soda in there for the kid," he said. "Can't believe he's missing this celebration."

"Yeah, kind of surprised me, too," Campbell said. "But I'll give him the good news about passing the safety inspection."

Campbell clinked his bottle with Rick's. "Couldn't have done this without you," he said. "You made a big difference with the detail work."

Rick took a swig. "It's been a while since I've used any of the skills you needed from me, and I've never worked on a plane, but I'm glad I could be of some help."

Campbell had let go of his resentment of the ultracool Rick. He'd told himself many times that it was stupid and juvenile to be jealous of Rick's association with Adam. Besides, now that the Cardinal was ready for a test flight, Rick would probably be moving on. Greg didn't have enough work to keep him employed full-time. And he'd take his ATV with him.

Greg nodded toward the garage door opening of his office, which afforded a view to the tarmac where the Cardinal sat in the sun. "So, when are you going to take her up?"

"Not today," Campbell said. He couldn't tell Greg that all he cared about now was getting back to Kitty, making things right. "Maybe tomorrow. You going with me?"

Greg smiled and took another swig. "I don't know. You sure that when you guys did all that work you fixed the fuel line?"

Campbell chuckled. "I'm sure."

"All right, then. I'll go up with you. You'll need an experienced pilot on that glued-together wreck."

All three men laughed. "Not to mention I need a camera guy," Campbell said. "I've heard back from several of the customers I'd lined up before the crash. Some of them are still willing to give Oakes Aerial Photographs a try."

Greg raised his bottle in a toast. "Told you."

A few minutes later, when the beer bottles were empty, a minivan pulled up at the open door. Rick stood. "There's my ride."

"You taking off early?" Greg asked.

"Taking off for good," Rick said, picking up a duffel bag that Campbell had just noticed was next to a bank of lockers. "My work here is done."

Greg's eyes widened in obvious surprise. "You don't give notice?"

"No time," Rick answered. "I turned my rental car in this morning and packed up. You guys don't need me anymore, and I've got an opportunity out of town." He draped the strap of the duffel over his chest. "Travel light and never look back, that's my motto."

Campbell looked at Greg who'd suddenly become speechless. To cover the awkward moment, Campbell rose and held out his hand to Rick. "Good luck to you."

He followed Rick to the exit. Rick got in the back of the van, which was driven by a young guy in a polo shirt. An older man sat in the passenger seat.

"What about your ATV out back?" Greg called before Rick shut the van door.

"Keep it. I don't need it anymore."

The driver executed a tight circle in front of the office and sped away. After a moment, Greg rubbed his thumb over his beard and said, "That's about as quick a getaway as I've ever seen."

Campbell watched the dust settle over the parking lot. "Downright weird," he said. "You'd think Rick was a hired gun, and he just heard there was a new sheriff in town."

CHAPTER NINETEEN

IN THE AFTERNOON, Kitty and Lyssa added the garments they'd just finished to the ever-increasing stacks of clothing and embroidered pieces in every corner of the room.

"Everything is working out so well," Lyssa said, stretching her back. "I should be able to buy what I need for the new baby."

"I hope so," Kitty agreed. "Babies are expensive." She recalled the dismal way she'd lived with Bobby Watley when Adam was born, and was grateful Lyssa would have more opportunities. "Only three weeks until we're ready to put a sign out."

"I'm so thankful you came to Sorrel Gap, Kitty. This never would have happened without you."

Kitty looked away, knowing she didn't deserve all the credit. Fate, both good and bad, had played a bigger hand than Kitty herself had. There was a plane crash and a broken-down truck and a theft. But Kitty's resolve to finally do the right thing for Adam had also played an important part. Kitty Galloway was a better person for having come to this magical valley in the Blue Ridge Mountains.

Lyssa stood up and retrieved her sewing basket from the floor. "I'll see you tomorrow?"

"Sure." As Kitty walked Lyssa to her car, they passed Adam, who sat reading a comic on the porch.

After Lyssa left, Kitty sat beside Adam on the steps. She ruffled his hair. "You know, honey, you've spent about seven hours moping. I think that's enough."

"I'm not moping," he said.

"Good to hear." She took the comic out of his hands. "Then you won't object to taking a walk with me. I've been cooped up inside all day, and—"

"I can't go anywhere."

"Why not?"

"I'm supposed to stay—"

When he clamped his mouth shut, she leaned over to better see into his eyes. "You're supposed to what?"

"Nothing."

"Do you have instructions for today that I don't know about?"

"No."

He reached for the comic. She held it over her head. "Did Campbell tell you to stay here?"

"You know he didn't. He wanted me to go with him to the airstrip."

"And you didn't want to go. And Toby wanted to come down here when Lyssa came. And you told him you were too sick." She set the comic on the step out of reach and put her arm around Adam's shoulders. "You're not sick. I know that. What you are is lying, and I want to know why."

He tried to shrug away from her, but she only held on tighter. "I'm not a kid anymore, Mom," he said. "You don't have to know every little thing about me all the time."

"Maybe not. But this little thing has me worried. So fess up."

He stared over the parking lot, his face resolute. But her determination was just as strong, so they sat that way for interminably long seconds before he said, "Okay, I'll tell you. You'll find out soon enough anyway."

"I'll find out what?"

He opened his mouth to speak as a minivan crested the hill and headed toward the motel. When the directional indicator signaled a turn into the parking lot, Adam pressed his lips together again. The van pulled in and stopped a few feet from them.

"This conversation isn't over," Kitty said to Adam.

Her next words became trapped in her throat.

She gripped the stair railing and stood up slowly, the simple movement suddenly painful. The front doors of the van opened, revealing the occupants she'd only glimpsed through the windows. It couldn't be. Terry Spenser stepped onto the gravel from the driver's seat. Her father got out the other side. The doors slammed shut, explosive sounds that echoed in her brain. Her body jerked in reaction.

"Hello, Katherine," Owen Galloway said.

"Daddy…"

Terry, cool and collected, leaned a hip against the hood of the van and grinned at her. "What have you done to yourself, Kitty? You look different."

The urge to run fought with a paralyzing shock that had taken possession of her limbs. She could only stare at the two men.

Owen took a step away from the van and opened his arms. "Come here, son."

Adam looked up at Kitty with eyes that held both stubbornness and pain. "I was going to tell you just now, Mom."

"You knew they were coming?"

He didn't say anything, just walked over to his grandfather. Owen nestled him close to his side.

Contradictory emotions whirled in the haze of Kitty's mind. The anguish of betrayal that her son had obviously conspired against her. Anger at herself because she didn't know her son better, hadn't recognized his signs of stress. And pity for what Adam had been going through today. Suddenly his behavior made a devastating sense.

Though only a few feet away, Adam stared at her from what seemed a chasm the size of the Grand Canyon. "I'm sorry, Mom," he said. "But I want to go home."

"You hear that, Katherine?" Owen said. "He's had enough."

She wanted to ask Owen how he found them but realized the details didn't really matter. Maybe she'd made a mistake in covering their tracks. Or maybe Adam had called him. She placed her hand on her throat to stop a sob that would reveal the gut-wrenching hurt she would feel if Adam had summoned his grandfather. She took a step toward them, hoping to bridge the gap between her and Adam that seemed only worse now for all her efforts in the past weeks to eliminate it.

She heard her voice as if through a fog. "Adam, why didn't you say anything to me? I thought you were happy, or at least that you'd accepted—"

"He's telling you now, Kit," Owen said. "His words are loud and clear."

Was this it? Was this moment truly the end? She reached out to Adam. "Honey, can't we talk about this...?" But the words stopped and her arm dropped as the back door of the van opened up and another man got out. Kitty's blood chilled as if she'd suddenly been plunged into an icy lake. No. Not this.

She stared long and hard at the man whose once-familiar brown eyes were now hidden behind heavy sunglasses. Despite his heavier build and thinning blond hair, she knew beyond a doubt that she was looking at the darkest part of her past, face-to-face with the man she'd left in a dusty, forsaken campground eleven years ago. The man who'd become an old newspaper clipping to a boy who'd longed for so much more.

A single word rasped from her throat. "Bobby?"

He pulled down his glasses and gave her an intense scrutiny that made her wish she and Adam could simply be swept away on the next breeze out of the gap. "Hello, Kit. You are looking good, honey."

"What are you doing here?"

"I'm seeing my son."

And suddenly her father's masterful manipulation of their lives became crushingly clear. He'd used the one link that would bind Adam to him forever. How could Kitty compete with the fantasy of that newspaper clipping? Her hands fisted until her nails dug into the soft flesh of her palms. She had to try. "Now? Now?" Her voice rose in a crescendo of desperation. "Now you come into his life?"

Adam approached her, put his hand on her arm. "He's been here awhile, Mom. This is Rick, the guy who helped out at the airstrip."

She understood with Adam's simple but devastating confession that there were no limits Owen wouldn't go to, no devices he wouldn't use to get Adam back. As if already celebrating his victory, Owen met her determined stare head-on, his gaze steady, challenging as always.

She grabbed her son's shoulders and held him tight in an effort to shield him from the emotional blackmail personified by the man a few feet away. "Adam, you know, don't you? This isn't Rick. This is Bobby Watley, your father."

"I know. He told me yesterday." Adam scowled up at Bobby. "It was a rotten thing to do and I told him so. But he's coming back with us to Florida. He's going to stay in Richland."

A long agonizing breath filled her lungs. She glared at Bobby. "You're lying to him."

"Katherine." Owen's voice was low and threatening. A warning.

"I'm not," Bobby said. "I've got a job at a golf club down there. I'm going to be around for Adam for the long haul. You'll see."

She looked from Bobby to her father. Her mind raced to come up with a plan for escape, revenge, any way to protect her son. When neither man spoke, she loosened her grip on Adam and pointed to the motel. "Go to our room," she said. "Stay there until I come in."

When he glanced up at Owen to get his permission, tears of humiliation filled her eyes. "Go ahead, son," he said.

The instant Adam was inside, she turned on her father. "How could you do this? How could you bring Bobby back into our lives?"

His eyes were cold as he said, "How could you have taken Adam from mine? You did this, Katherine. You brought it on yourself."

"But Bobby is toxic. You know that."

"Hey, I'm right here," he said, mocking her.

She continued. "At best he'll stick around a few weeks and then leave. At worst, he'll stay longer, doing damage that you and I will never be able to undo."

"I had to pull out all the stops, Katherine," Owen said. "You left me no choice."

"In case you forgot, I'm Adam's mother. I decide what's best for him, not you. I'm the one who should protect him, guide him—"

Owen stopped her with a derisive snort. His arm swept out to encompass the motel. "This is what you guide him to, Kit? This godforsaken place in the middle of nowhere? What if Adam had gotten sick? Where is he supposed to go to school if you let this fantasy of yours continue into the fall? How have you been making a living? By living off of someone else's pity?"

She could have answered him. She could have told him that Adam's welfare had always been her top concern. That she'd planned for him to go to school in Charlotte. That he'd been around wonderful people who cared for her, who didn't pity her. That she'd been making a living the way she'd always wanted to with her designs. That until ten minutes ago, her future had been brighter than it had ever been. That she'd learned to love...

She stopped the litany of responses playing in her mind. As always, this wasn't about her. Owen wouldn't care about her dreams, her future.

His voice became a hum in her mind as she struggled to accept that everything she'd done— for Adam, and for herself, was crashing down around her. "For all I knew," Owen said, "you could have been poisoning the boy against me, telling him things that weren't true but fit your cockamamy scheme to cut me out of his life."

"I never did," she said. "I never said a word against you." Her voice was pleading. She hated herself at that moment.

"I hope that's true," Owen said. "Just like I hope you come back to Florida with us."

She could only stare at him. He didn't want her back. He didn't care about her.

"It's true, darlin'," he said. "You can have your old job back. I can try to forgive you for what you did, but I can't do that if you don't come home."

But can I ever forgive you? Or myself?

"Adam needs you. I would never cut him out of your life like you cut me out of his."

She looked down at the parking lot as tears flooded her eyes. She prayed they wouldn't fall and reveal even more weakness.

"You go on and pack your things," Owen said. "We've got a plane at the Asheville airport, and we'll all go back together." His voice took on a familiar edge of steel. "Or don't. It's up to you, Katherine. Adam has made his desires known. I've made mine clear. Now it's up to you."

SHE STOPPED OUTSIDE their room to compose herself. No good would come from letting Adam see her like this—defeated, hurt, desperately grasping for strength she didn't possess. But even after she'd taken a couple of deep breaths and scrubbed the moisture from her eyes with the heels of her hands, her fingers shook when she twisted the doorknob.

Adam was sitting on the bed, his hands clasped in his lap. When she came in, he jumped up. His expression was guarded as if he didn't know what to expect from her. "I know what you're thinking, Mom," he said. "You think I called Grandpa, but I didn't. I swear. I kept my promise to you."

She shook her head. "It's okay, Adam. I don't think that."

"And I didn't know Rick was my dad until yesterday."

"I believe you." She took his hands in hers. If only she'd checked out the mysterious Rick, she might have prevented him from gaining such a dangerous foothold in Adam's life. She almost laughed at the foolish thought. She'd never have prevented Owen from getting what he wanted and using any means to succeed. Owen would never have stopped looking, and eventually, if not today, he would have found them.

And the true irony of that admission was that, despite his methods, Owen deserved to be there. When she'd taken Adam from Richland, Kitty never intended to sever the ties with her father forever. She'd only hoped to... She stopped, looked at Adam and saw the uncertainty in his wide brown eyes. All at once her goal, which had been so clear just a few weeks ago, now blurred in her mind's eye just as the furnishings of this old room swam in her unshed tears. Deep down she'd always known she would never have gotten away with this plan for very long. *But not today*, she thought. *I'm not ready today.*

Settling next to him on the bed, she said, "What do you want? Do you really want to go back to Florida?"

"Well, sure. Mom, you always said this was just like a vacation, that we would go back." His gaze wandered to some indistinct point in the room. "I know you meant to go to Charlotte, but being here in Sorrel Gap…it's enough, right? I learned the stuff you wanted me to."

Her lips twitched. Adam turned to look at her, and she hoped he would think she was smiling. "Yes, I think you did."

"And I did kind of like it here," he said.

"I kind of did, too."

He drew a long breath and his eyes widened. "Mom, you're not thinking of staying here without me, are you? You're coming home with me and Grandpa, right? Grandpa wants you to. He told me so."

Just the thought of turning any aspect of Adam's care over to Bobby made Kitty sick to her stomach. She remained silent for a moment, caught between what she wanted and what her son needed. She would do anything for Adam. But to go back to Owen's house? Could she do it, after the journey they'd made, even for her son? Finally she stroked her hand down the side of his face and summed up all her feelings. "What kind of mother would I be if, after all we've been through, I let you go back to Richland without me?"

His shoulders slumped with relief. "Right. You wouldn't do that." He gave her the impish grin she'd fallen in love with when he was only a few days old. "I suppose I'm old enough to take care of myself, but I'd miss you."

She smiled, though her stomach cramped with an old familiar ache. "You would, huh?"

"Of course."

She envisioned their future, one that looked bleak right now, and she came to a conclusion. She'd find their own place in Richland, an apartment where she and Adam could be together, just the two of them, and she'd do whatever was necessary to protect him from Bobby. At least she could do that.

He went to the dresser and opened one of the drawers. "Grandpa wants to go soon. I should start packing this stuff."

She didn't say anything, just dragged the trunk she'd brought from Richland to the dresser and flipped open the top. Adam began stacking his clothes inside. Unable to face the inevitable conclusion of packing her own things just yet, Kitty stood aside and watched.

"You know, Mom," Adam said when his drawers had been emptied, "if you're sad about leaving, if you like the beast, you can come back anytime. Heck, I'll even come with you and see Toby. Grandpa won't care. You can buy plane tickets and rent a real car…" He smiled at her. "You'll have money again, Mom. You can do anything you want."

Yes, it's always about money. With total recklessness, she began tossing her clothes on top of Adam's. If her son only knew. Once Campbell found out who she really was, how she'd tricked him and everyone in this valley, he would never want to see her again. The woman who'd taken credit for healing their war hero, for inspiring the artisans, was a fraud.

When the trunk was full, she pulled a suitcase from under the bed and put her sewing supplies inside. Even as she packed the life she'd built for herself in this gap between the mountains, her mind wouldn't let her give up completely. Even when she moved to the bathroom vanity and scooped her things into a bag, she had to keep reminding herself that there was no other option.

Her hair gels, wild shades of eye shadow— items she didn't use anymore—she threw in the waste can. She wasn't the same person who once believed she needed all these trappings to define herself. When she'd completed the task, she stared into the vanity mirror. "Was it all worth it?" she asked the image looking back at her with dull, sad eyes. She shook her head. Only time could answer that.

Finished, she said, "Guess I'm ready, Adam."

He looked around, as Lyssa had done only a short time ago, at the piles of clothes that waited for the racks Campbell had promised to assemble. "What are you going to do with all the stuff you made?"

"I'll leave them," she said. "Lyssa can sell the things I made and keep the money."

"That's nice of you, Mom," Adam said. "Heck, you won't need the money anyway. You'll be working for Grandpa again."

She jumped when a loud knock sounded on the door. "Let's go in there," Owen called. "Time's wasting."

She clasped the top on her sewing machine. "Go ahead, Adam. I'm going to the bathroom and then I'll meet you outside."

She waited in the bathroom until the men had removed their belongings. Then she came out, sat at the worn Formica desk where for weeks her sewing machine had hummed over unbleached muslin and soft cotton in tune to the new, gentler flow of her life. Taking a piece of yellowed Saddle Top stationery from the drawer, she began to write. *Dear Campbell...*

CHAPTER TWENTY

DRIVING BACK TO the motel on the rarely used Old Sorrel Gap Road, Campbell thought about Kitty's craft store. He'd invested almost as much determination and optimism as she had. Kitty's enterprise would be good for the craftsmen and for the gap. Now all he had to do was convince her to stay. He had a plan. He'd be simple and direct, say what was in his heart—not always an easy task for a guy like Campbell, but he could do it because the life he wanted depended on it.

When he pulled into the parking lot he was glad Lyssa's car wasn't there. Maybe Toby had come to the motel with his aunt, and he and Adam were down at Gilley's Creek. If so, Campbell would have the opportunity to be alone with Kitty. He got out of his Jeep and went directly to her room. He wiped his palms along his jeans. For the first time he worried if he should have planned his words. No. He'd let them come naturally until the right ones convinced her to stay.

He wasn't alarmed when Kitty didn't respond

to the knock on the door. He went to his own apartment and looked for her. Then he skirted around the back of the motel and headed to the creek. Nobody there. "She and Adam must have gone for a walk," he said, figuring he'd leave a note in her room. He knocked once again, and still receiving no answer, went inside.

The blood drained from his face as he crossed the threshold into a vacant room, empty except for Kitty's projects still stacked in pretty pastel piles of women's things and fancy needlework. Two envelopes leaned against the dresser lamp, one addressed to Lyssa and one to him. He picked up his with a trembling hand. A Dear John letter? As if the paper burned his fingers, he tossed the envelope onto the bed, refusing to give the notion credence.

Two empty dresser drawers gaped open. A quick examination confirmed Campbell's worst fear. The other drawers had been stripped of their contents. Kitty's sewing machine no longer sat on the desk amid spools of thread and fabric trimmings. The trunk Tommy Gibbs had brought to the motel the day Kitty arrived wasn't at the end of Adam's bed. Campbell opened the closet door and discovered more saleable items but none of Kitty's own clothes hanging there.

He went to the window and tore open the drapes, hoping this was all a mistake and he would see her coming across the parking lot. Maybe she'd made a room change, that's all. But, except for his Jeep, the lot was empty. So he forced himself to look at the envelope he'd sailed onto the bed.

He picked it up and sat on the edge of the mattress. A delicate scent wafted up from the linens—Kitty's fragrance, light and floral, reminding him of hopes he'd only begun to allow himself to have for the future. The flap had been sealed at the point, and Campbell lifted it with his index finger. He took out two sheets of paper and, with trepidation, unfolded them.

Dear Campbell,
This is the most difficult letter I have ever written, because I did not know when we talked this morning that I would be writing it just a few short hours later.

Circumstances that I could not have foreseen have forced me to leave the Saddle Top. I am deeply sorry to tell you this in such an impersonal way, but staying to say goodbye would only have made this decision harder for all of us.

Please know that my weeks with you have been the happiest of my life. I will always be grateful for your generosity in taking us in, your kindness, your caring, your guidance with Adam. Neither of us will ever forget you.

Please see that Lyssa gets the letter I wrote her. I wish you and the craftsmen of the gap much success with the new store. I hope they will move forward with the opening.

Kitty

PS Please tell Sheriff Oakes I'm sorry that Adam did not complete his assignment. Your uncle may keep my truck. I left the title in the desk drawer. I hope that will make up the difference.

Disbelief made him read it again, and then a third time, though with each reading the message only became clearer and more devastating. Of all the outcomes he could have imagined for him and Kitty, this was the one he hadn't even considered. She'd come here needing a home, a job. And because she'd become vital to his existence, he'd been prepared to fight for her today, to convince her to stay. He hadn't been prepared to lose her before she'd given him the chance. He hadn't been prepared to have his heart broken.

He resisted the urge to tear the letter into shreds. The anger and hurt inside him had no place to go, and he drew upon the military resources that commanded him to remain calm, to think. So he stared at the yellowed stationery, with no direction for the rest of his day, the rest of his life. How could he have been so wrong about a woman again? He believed Kitty loved him, and yet all she expressed in this note was gratitude. Had she been planning this all along?

He recalled the phone call from his uncle this morning. Had Kitty just been biding her time waiting for her truck to be fixed so she could leave the gap? Leave him? If so, if she was leaving the truck to Virgil, how had she left the motel? And how could her kisses have been so sweet, so eager, so loving?

He walked to the door and turned one last time to witness the eerie quiet of a room that had so recently buzzed with hope and plans and dreams. Just as his life had. Though Campbell longed for numbness, adrenaline coursed through his body. He couldn't sit, couldn't stand in one place. Questions tumbled in his brain in a desperate search for answers. Why had she done this? Had she been playing him for a fool from the beginning? How long ago had she left? Where had she gone?

Despite doubts that should have convinced him to forget her, to move on, he couldn't shake the bitter curiosity to find answers. He was, at his core, a logical man, one who needed to make sense of the inexplicable. He picked up his phone and dialed the sheriff's office. His aunt answered and put Virgil on the line.

"Virgil, it's Camp."

"Oh, hi, Camp. What can I do for you?"

"I'm wondering if you've heard from Kitty."

"Not since this morning when I called her. As a matter of fact, I'm waiting for Tommy to come in off patrol and take the truck out to your place."

"Don't bother." Campbell spoke aloud, though the question was more a mental exercise. "How did she and Adam leave?"

"Leave? What are you talking about?" Virgil said. "Kitty and the boy are gone?"

His uncle seemed almost as surprised as Campbell had been. "Yeah. She left me a note, said they had to go away."

"Without that truck? That's a weird one, Camp. I can't see how she'd get away from the motel. We don't have but one taxicab and it went elsewhere today." His voice was muffled as if he had put his hand over the speaker grid. "Wanda? Has anyone asked about Kitty today?" He paused before adding, "That's right. She's taken off, her and Adam. Seems mighty mysterious to me."

A feeling of unease tingled along the back of Campbell's neck. If Kitty hadn't called Virgil and needed a way out of the gap, she would have called Lyssa. Yet the letter with Lyssa's name on it indicated that Kitty hadn't told her friend she was leaving. "I've got to go, Virgil," he said, intending to retrieve the second letter from Kitty's room. "I'm going to call the folks up the mountain to see if Kitty asked any of them to drive her out."

Virgil's voice lowered. "You know, Camp, we can't keep her here if she wants to go."

"But something just doesn't seem right," Campbell said. "I need your help."

"I'll do what I can," Virgil said. "I'll check the bus lines and the planes. Do you think she might be heading back to Florida?"

"I don't know." Hope and dread seemed to be battling for dominance in Campbell's brain in equal measure. "Maybe. But something definitely doesn't add up."

"I agree with you, Camp. I can't see that girl just leaving without telling folks goodbye. She doesn't seem like the type to do that."

No, she doesn't. Campbell hung up and took the county phone book from a drawer. For the next ten minutes he called everyone he knew Kitty had associated with up the hill. No one had helped her leave the motel. Everyone was shocked that she'd gone. He read Lyssa's letter in which Kitty basically told her to sell the garments under Kitty's label and keep the money. And she provided pretty much the same explanation for her bizarre behavior—unforeseen circumstances.

Campbell's apprehension grew. What if Kitty had been forced to write those letters? What if she and Adam were in danger? What if he was out of his mind and making up a movie-script scenario as a salve to his wounded ego? He paced his apartment and pounced on the phone when it rang.

"Camp, it's Virgil. I've got some news."

"What is it?"

"It seems Wanda remembers something that came over the internet about Kitty some weeks ago." Virgil's tone was impatient. "Something she failed to mention to me. Wanda doesn't remember everything, but there were pictures of Kitty and Adam in a missing persons alert. Somebody from Florida was looking for them."

Campbell's heartbeat was barely contained by his rib cage. "Somebody was looking to do them harm?"

"No, Wanda says to the best of her recollection it wasn't anything like that."

"To the best of her recollection? Where's the alert now? Have her bring it up."

Virgil cleared his throat. "Wanda might have mistakenly deleted the file."

Campbell balled his free hand into a fist. "Well, what does she remember?"

"Lucky for us, Camp, she remembers a name. Apparently Kitty has been using an alias."

"An alias? Why would she do that?"

"You'd have to ask her that, but I looked up what Wanda gave me. It's Galloway, and there's a company by that name in a town near Orlando. Galloway Groves."

Campbell scratched the name on a piece of paper. "That's a start. You got anything else?"

"Yeah. I did a quick search. The owner of the company is Owen Galloway. He chartered a private plane in Florida this morning."

Though he already suspected the answer, Campbell said, "Where was that plane headed?"

"Asheville. And it's fixin' to take off in about thirty minutes."

Campbell looked at his watch. At best it was an hour's drive to the Asheville airport. Now at five o'clock, during rush hour, who knew how long it would take? "Can you stop that plane, Virgil?" he asked.

"Not without good cause. The FAA has got its own restrictions about that sort of thing."

Certainly true. A local sheriff couldn't halt air traffic on what seemed a whim. There was no reason to suspect foul play. Campbell snapped his fingers, coaxing his mind into action. "Virgil, do you know which carrier is handling the flight?"

"I can find out."

"Good. Call me on my cell phone with the name. And can you get me clearance to land at the runway designated for its operation?"

"When?"

Campbell checked his watch again. If he broke all land-speed records, he could be at Greg's airstrip in ten minutes. "About thirty minutes from now?"

There was an uncomfortable pause after which Virgil said, "Camp, you're not planning to fly your Cardinal into Asheville, are you? You haven't tested her since the accident."

"Can you do it, Virgil? Can you get me clearance? Say it's top priority?"

Virgil blew out a long breath. "I can probably do it, but—"

"Thanks. I owe you." A man named Owen Galloway. It wasn't much to go on. Kitty's father? Maybe. Her husband? He could only hope not. But so what? Campbell had learned the day he crash-landed into that cow pasture that life was a series of risks. This was another. He tossed the phone onto the sofa and grabbed the keys to his Jeep.

CHAPTER TWENTY-ONE

THE RIDE TO the Asheville airport was the most miserable hour and a half of Kitty's life. Owen had dictated the seating arrangements. He and Terry sat in the front seats, Bobby and Adam in the middle seats, and she sat by herself in the back with her trunk, suitcases and sewing machine. She'd hoped Adam would sit with her, and she would have a chance to question him even more about his desire to return to Florida. Yes, he'd said he wanted to go, but a persistent doubt niggled at the back of Kitty's brain. What if her son was only trying to meet his grandfather's expectations? She watched Adam carefully now, knowing how easy it was to fall under Bobby's on-again, off-again charm, especially when the creep had been her son's lifelong fantasy.

So Kitty sat by herself, twisting her hands in her lap and wishing she and Adam were anywhere but here, that things had turned out any way but how they had. She'd failed everyone. Adam, Campbell, Lyssa and the folks from the hill, herself. Even Sheriff Oakes and Quint from the Value-Rite.

Yet, in these last minutes of her time in North Carolina, all she could do was sit in the back of this van and reexamine the previous six weeks and the choices she'd made. Now that it was too late, she realized she could have done things differently. She should have talked to Adam about going to Charlotte, asked his feelings about staying in Sorrel Gap. She'd intended to do that today before giving Campbell her answer. Maybe it wouldn't have mattered, and Adam would have reacted the same when his grandfather showed up, but now she'd never know.

She tried not to think of Campbell. When her thoughts strayed to him, the motel, the letter she'd left, she forced her mind to focus on her son. She had to think of Adam and redouble her resolve to protect him. She had to be a mother now and bury her feelings about what she was leaving in the gap for another time when she was back in the cold vacuum of the town and the job she'd left behind.

Campbell would be all right, she told herself. He would go on now that his leg was healed and his plane was fixed. He was better off just believing she was the flaky woman she'd appeared to be when she arrived and never knowing how she'd deceived him from that very first day. And, in a way, she was better off ending the relationship in this manner, quickly, without explanations or goodbyes. She couldn't have stood his contempt when the truth came out.

But sadly, as the lush North Carolina countryside rushed by her van window, she knew she loved Campbell Oakes completely. Love. The word alone brought fresh tears to her eyes. Not so long ago Virgil Oakes had taken her to a run-down motel and told her that this might be "the best summer" she and Adam ever had. She bit her bottom lip to keep the tears from falling. How prophetic the sheriff had been.

"ARE YOU OKAY, MOM? You haven't said anything in a long time."

Kitty and Adam were in the passenger waiting area of the hangar, anticipating the all-clear to board the plane for Florida. This was the first time they'd been completely alone. "I'm fine," she said, knowing some lies were important to tell.

He slumped down in his seat. "I'm thinking that you really want to stay here."

"I want to be wherever you are," she said, and decided to risk probing into Adam's mind while they shared their last minutes in North Carolina together. "Is there any part of you that wants to stay here?"

He shrugged. "It hasn't been so bad. I guess if we *had* to stay, if Grandpa hadn't come..." He cut off his answer when Bobby returned from a conversation with Owen and sat beside him.

"So, sport, you looking to get back to your room and your big house?" Bobby asked.

"Sure." Silence stretched between them until Adam said, "Do you fish, Ri...I mean, Bobby?"

Bobby leaned back and gave Adam an odd grin. "Call me Dad, Adam. That's what I'd like."

"Okay. Anyway, do you fish?"

"No. I never saw much point to it. Golf is my game."

"I don't golf," Adam said.

"But you'd be willing to learn, I bet. And I'll teach you." Taking advantage of a topic he could use to connect with his son, Bobby's expression became animated. "Golfing requires skill, kid. Finesse. A lot more talent than fishing does. Anyone can drop a line into some water."

Adam's brow furrowed. "I used to think that, but fishing takes a lot of skill. You have to know which bait to use at each time of day. You gotta choose the right line and bobbers. And you have to be patient and jerk the pole clean at the right time or you'll lose your dinner."

Bobby hunched one shoulder with seeming indifference. "But fishing's a solitary man's thing. I'm going to teach you a sport that will benefit you in the days ahead. Golf is a gentleman's game. You make contacts with important people. You can expand your opportunities on a golf course, something you can't do on the side of a pond somewhere."

"I met some okay people fishing," Adam said.

Bobby patted Adam's knee. "Well, sure, maybe. But trust me, kid. There's nothing like eighteen holes of healthy competition, not to mention the clubhouse afterward. That's where the fun really begins."

"Maybe I can do both—fish and golf," Adam said, staring down between his knees.

Owen interrupted them when he waved from the exit to the tarmac. "Plane's ready to board. Let's go."

Kitty stood. When a chilling rush of panic threatened to overtake her, she forced her feet to move forward. She felt as if she were being led into an operating room for major surgery and her life was suddenly in someone else's hands.

Bobby hurried outside, leaving Adam to walk beside her. In a gesture very unlike her son, he slipped his hand into hers and she calmed. "I can tell that you don't like that Bobby's here," Adam said.

"No, I don't. But I'm here, so I don't want you to worry." Her body had stopped betraying her with uncontrollable trembling, and she smiled. "I'll keep my eye on him."

Adam chewed on the inside of his cheek as they entered the fading sunlight and headed toward the plane. The urge to flee was still strong, but since her hand was locked tight with Adam's, Kitty didn't let her mind dwell on a life that was becoming more impossible with each step over the tarmac.

They'd nearly reached the plane when the hum of an engine drew her attention. A small aircraft was coming in for a landing. Not unusual for an airport, but Kitty released Adam's hand and stopped long enough to let her mind focus on the new activity. She watched the pilot execute a skilled glide to the asphalt. But the plane didn't turn toward the hangar as she'd suspected. It kept on a course toward their aircraft, coming to a stop a few yards away.

Adam halted on the stairs to their jet. His face broke into a grin and he exclaimed, "Holy cow. It's the *Kitty Hawk*."

Kitty shielded her eyes. "The what?"

"Campbell's plane. That's what he renamed the new improved model. Just painted the words on it Saturday and told me not to tell you."

Her heart pounded in her chest as she tried to see into the cockpit of the single-propeller plane. It couldn't be. Her mind raced to catalog certain details she'd only seen a couple times. She recognized the red trim on the doors. She took in the shiny new metal fittings of a recently repaired wing. Even with the evidence mounting before her, she refused to allow herself to hope. How could Campbell have known where she would be?

And then the cockpit door opened and Campbell, still in the jeans and T-shirt he'd had on that morning, approached them across the tarmac. Her knees went weak. And her eyes stung with fresh tears.

"Who is that?" Owen asked Adam.

"That's Campbell." Adam bounded down to the pavement. "Hiya, beast," he said.

His attention on Kitty, Campbell nodded once. "Outlaw. You going someplace?"

"Yeah, we didn't have a chance to tell you, but Mom and me are going…"

Owen stepped between Adam and Campbell. "What's the meaning of this?"

Campbell held out his hand as if they were about to be formally introduced. "Campbell Oakes." He darted a quick glance at Kitty. "A friend of Kitty's and Adam's. And you are?"

Owen's hand remained at his side and he flexed the fingers. "I'm her father. I assume you're that pilot who's been keeping my family at his motel."

"*Hosting* them is more like it," Campbell said. "Nobody keeps Kitty."

Owen walked back to Kitty, put his hand on her back and nudged her toward the plane. "Well, say goodbye, young man, because the party's over."

She sidestepped away. "Not so fast, Daddy. I need to talk to Campbell."

"Better late than never," Campbell said. He raised his sunglasses to his forehead and took a moment to study the other people gathered around the plane. When his gaze settled on Bobby, a smirk curled his lips. "Rick, buddy. What's your role in all this?"

"His name's not Rick," Adam said.

"You don't say."

"I'm just collecting what's mine," Bobby said, though his voice was suddenly flat and tentative.

"And by that you somehow mean Kitty and her son?"

She positioned herself between the two men. "He's my ex-husband, Bobby," she said. "And Adam's father. I haven't seen him in more than eleven years." She glared at Bobby as a spurt of courage flowed through her veins. She spoke to Campbell in a whisper so only the three of them could hear. "I guess some rocks aren't big enough to keep certain snakes from crawling into the daylight."

Campbell rubbed his hand over the nape of his neck and stared intently at Kitty. "Actually, other than the fact that he's a lying no-good jerk, he's not really my concern. But you, on the other hand, Kitty *Galloway*, are."

Any confidence she might have been experiencing evaporated under the heat of raw emotion in Campbell's eyes. She'd been responsible for all of it—the hurt, humiliation, the confusion. And what she had to tell him now would only aggravate the pain he was already feeling. She exhaled a deep breath. "We should go someplace private."

"You're not going anywhere, Katherine," Owen said. He swept his arm toward the plane. "This is your last chance. I want you on this plane now."

"What's your hurry, Mr. Galloway?" Campbell said. "You can't give her a few minutes?"

"I could give her a few hours and it wouldn't change what's going to happen," Owen said. "I don't think you have any idea who you're dealing with, young man."

"I know you grow oranges. And you've got enough money to hire a private jet. Beyond that, why don't you tell me?"

This was it. Kitty squeezed her eyes shut.

She couldn't bear to see the disappointment in Campbell's face when her father told him the truth. But then she sensed Adam beside her, his hand on her arm, and she opened her eyes. Her path to happiness was paved with this moment of truth. She'd known that since she'd first met the man who would end up changing her life and helping her realize who she could be.

Owen squared his shoulders and stared at Kitty. "This woman, who for some reason I have yet to fathom, has been content to remain under your roof for weeks, is a Galloway." He nodded at Adam. "Her son is the heir to Galloway Groves."

Campbell passed a quick glance at Adam. "Wow, outlaw. That's a curveball I didn't expect."

Owen sneered at Campbell. "Now, maybe that's just 'growing oranges' to you, but in central Florida, the name Galloway Groves commands a great deal of respect."

Campbell's face expressed nothing more than a calm acceptance of the facts. "I'm sure it does."

"Katherine and Adam were raised in wealth and comfort," Owen continued. "A few weeks ago, Kit got it into her head that she had to take the reins in this family, and in some cockamamy scheme to prove she could suddenly turn herself into a maternal role model, she snatched her son and took off."

Campbell's lips twitched. "*Snatched* her own son, did she?"

Ignoring the sarcasm, Owen said, "I've been looking for them ever since."

"Because you love your daughter and were worried about her well-being?" Campbell said.

Kitty's stomach knotted.

"Certainly I love her," Owen said. "But she's headstrong, always has been. Without a thought of the consequences, she took the boy from our home and put me through the worst weeks of my life. But it's over. In a few minutes my grandson and I will be on that plane flying to Florida."

He leveled his attention on Kitty, and for the first time, she sensed a weakening of his confidence, as if, just possibly, everything wouldn't turn out exactly as he'd planned.

"I'm not so sure about Katherine anymore," Owen said. "But she can do what she wants. I'm through fighting her. She can come back with us. She can stay."

He narrowed his eyes at Campbell. "But accept a word of advice from someone who knows Kit, Oakes. She won't stay for long. My daughter is a taker, and she doesn't know how to give back. You must have seen that. Spend one day with her, and you know she's never worked an honest day in her life." He looked at Kitty. "Maybe not today, but someday soon, she'll call me. She'll want to come home."

Campbell's jaw clenched in time to the throbbing of his temples. Each word seemed like a physical blow. Kitty stopped breathing as she imagined the memories flooding his mind. She was just like Diana. History was repeating itself. She wanted to scream at her father to stop. She wanted to tell Campbell none of it was true, but she couldn't, because for years she'd been the person her father was describing. Maybe in some deep dark part of her she still was, and Campbell truly would be better off without her.

Her father's voice droned on, each word like a knife to her heart. "…gave her everything… ungrateful…"

And then Campbell's simple question stopped him. "Is this true, Kitty?" he said. "It's all been a lie?"

She prayed for the right words to come, but in the horrible silence of his accusatory glare she could only shake her head and say, "I'm sorry. I should have told you."

"Darn straight you should have. From the first day when you showed up at the Saddle Top, you've lied to me."

"You leave her alone!"

Campbell's eyes rounded as Adam charged

him with clenched fists pumping at his sides. "You can't talk to her that way."

Kitty hurried to stop him, but Campbell put up his hand. "Leave him be." He looked down at Adam. "You've got something you want to say to me?"

"You bet I do." His eyes bright and wide, he looked at Kitty before narrowing in on Campbell. "You can't call my mother a liar. She hasn't lied about anything. Our money was really stolen and our truck really broke down. She wouldn't even lie to get me out of working at Value-Rite. And anything that happened before that doesn't matter because you didn't even know us then."

Campbell pressed his lips together and kept silent.

"And what about all that stuff she had to learn to help you out? And how she got you to go and fix your airplane. Was all that a lie?"

He shook his head. "No."

"And all those skirts and things she made. And all those people she got together to fix up your stupid old motel rooms. Were those things a lie?"

"No."

"And what about me getting on with Toby and Quint and old Cliff Lowe. Lies?"

"Adam—"

"And you and me fishing down at Gilley's Creek? Lie?"

"No."

Adam blinked hard several times. "All right, then. I'll tell you who the liars are." He stared at his grandfather, pain shimmering in his eyes. "My grandpa told me to lie to my own mother."

Owen took a step toward Adam. "I did that for your own good, Adam, to get you out of here."

"Still a lie. And that guy over there..." Adam thrust his finger at Bobby. "He's the worst liar of all because he lied to everybody..." Adam's shoulders began to quake. He sniffed. "He lied to everybody from the very first..."

Kitty reached out to her son. She'd never been more proud of him than she was at this moment. And he was right. For the first time, because she saw herself through Adam's eyes, she could believe in her own honesty, her worth. She had changed. She was a better person, and the proof stood right in front of her, all five feet four inches of stubborn, emerging manhood. She'd set out to accomplish the most important goal of her life, and it had worked.

Campbell stopped her before she made the mistake of smothering Adam in love and gratitude. "This is between us," he said to her. And then he did the strangest thing. He looked down at Adam, gave him a little grin and opened his arms. "C'mere, outlaw."

Adam flew at him, wrapped his arms around Campbell's waist and buried his face in his chest.

Owen called out, "Adam, come here, son. The plane…" But Adam didn't move. He just stood there, wrapped in Campbell's fierce hug with Campbell's cheek pressed on the top of his head and his body quivering with released rage and frustration. And pride.

After a moment Campbell said, "Good grief, outlaw, the other day when I told you to come and talk to me about anything, I didn't expect you to wail on me quite so hard."

Adam stepped back, rubbed a finger under his nose, and said, "She's my mom."

"Yep, she is, and she'd do anything for you." He settled his hands on the tops of Adam's shoulders and spoke in a low, soothing baritone. "I didn't fly over here to this airport to call your mom a liar, Adam." He focused on Kitty's face. "I came to tell her that she can't get away with just up and leaving like she did. Not when I still had an offer on the table."

"An offer?" Adam said.

"Yeah. You never gave me your answer, Katherine Galloway. Do you want to stay?"

In what Kitty saw as a last-ditch effort on her

father's part, Owen blustered, "Yes, Katherine, it's time to make up your mind. The rest of us are leaving."

Her voice was barely a whisper, but it was the most she could manage. "I want to stay." And then in case there might be some confusion about her answer, she spoke more forcefully. "I do!"

She blinked moisture from her eyes so she could clearly focus on her son, but his face blurred anyway. "Adam?"

He stared first at his mother and then Owen, and her heart pounded. What would she do if he started for that plane?

Owen waved his arm. "Let's go, Adam. The plane's leaving now. Your mother will come when she's ready."

Adam blew out a long breath. "Grandpa, I can't go back to Richland with you right now." He shook his head at Kitty. "My mom needs me. I got us into this situation and I can't bail on her."

Through her tears, Kitty watched Campbell's face split into a huge grin. Near-hysterical laughter bubbled up from her chest. "Yeah, this really is all your fault, Adam," she said.

"No doubt," Campbell said.

Adam nodded slowly, a wise old man suddenly taking responsibility.

Owen thrust his hands on his hips and just stared at his grandson. Bobby stared at Owen. "What the heck is going on here? What happens to me now?"

Adam opened his mouth to answer, but a blinking blue light on top of a speeding patrol car drew everyone's attention. "Look who's here," he said. "Sheriff Oakes."

The car jolted to a stop and Virgil got out. "Everything okay?" he asked.

Campbell assured him that everything was just fine. "I think these out-of-towners are getting ready to take off," he said. "But we can sure use the patrol car to get Kitty and Adam's things back to the Saddle Top."

"Glad to be of service."

A crew member hurried to open the cargo door. He and Campbell carried the trunk and suitcases and sewing machine to Virgil's car.

Kitty walked over to her father. She wished she could put her arms around him like she used to when she was a girl, when her mother was alive, before everything changed. "Daddy, I'm sorry. I don't want you out of Adam's life. Or mine. I want you to believe that."

"Yeah, Grandpa," Adam said. "You know where we are now. We're not hiding and we won't go anywhere without telling you, right, Mom?"

"Absolutely."

Owen placed his hand on top of Adam's head. "I hope you know what you're doing, Adam."

Adam nodded once. "I do."

"You can ride with me, Adam," Virgil said. "Maybe your mom wants to take her first flight in the *Kitty Hawk*."

Adam walked toward the patrol car, but stopped halfway there and turned around. He ran back to Owen. "I love you, Grandpa."

With his hands lightly on his grandson's back, as if he'd already accepted that he had to let him go, Owen looked at Kitty over the top of Adam's head. For once his gaze wasn't filled with condemnation. Only sadness. "I love you, too, Adam," he said. "If you change your mind…"

"I know," Adam said.

Owen dropped his arms to his sides. "Take care of him, Kit," he called.

She stopped midway to the *Kitty Hawk* and nodded to her father.

Campbell opened the passenger door of the plane and helped her inside. When he was in the pilot's seat, he reached over and wiped his finger under her eyes. "If you're going to be copilot, you'd better stop that blubbering," he said.

She smiled and tried to do as he told her. "I'm not partial to small planes," she said, staring out the side window at the ground she was about to leave.

"There was a time not too long ago when I would have agreed with you," Campbell said. "But I guarantee you, there isn't a machine in the sky today that's any safer than the *Kitty Hawk*. She'll get us where we need to go, on grit and determination, just like her namesake."

Kitty buckled her seat belt. "I'm not worried," she said. "I happen to believe in the pilot."

EPILOGUE

OWEN STARED AT the gas logs in Billie's parlor fireplace. There was enough of a nip in the air to appreciate the spirit of the flames, if not the actual heat. He rubbed his palms over the soft leather of his wing chair, the one piece of furniture in the fussy room Billie maintained especially for him. For the first time at one of Billie's traditional Thanksgiving meals, he was nervous.

She was hosting the usual relatives, including a couple of her cousins and an elderly uncle. Also this year she'd invited Esmeralda and Hector, and Bette, Owen's deceased wife's cousin. Kitty had wanted her to come.

"We'll have an international flavor," Billie had said, explaining that Esmeralda was bringing a South American dish, and Bette was bringing, of all the insufferable things, some sort of British fruitcake passed down from generations. Owen already anticipated the heartburn he would suffer.

He settled back in the chair and breathed in

the rich, flavorful aroma of roasting turkey. And then a glass of red wine was deposited in his hand. "It's after noon," he said. "I want a whiskey."

Billie swept around the chair and sat in front of him, fluffing her skirt over a plush ottoman. "We're having wine," she said. "I'm determined to civilize you, especially on the major holidays."

He took a sip and grunted. It was good.

She handed him three photos. "Here are the pictures Kitty emailed me the other day of the house they're building behind the motel."

He flipped through them. Since he'd seen the last pictures, the framing had been completed and the windows were in. "Still looks small," he said.

"It's not. It's four bedrooms."

"I'll take your word for it," Owen said. "Kit must be selling lots of blouses and things."

"She's doing very well, I understand," Billie said. "So is Campbell with his photography business."

Owen conceded with a shrug.

"They're due any minute," she said. "Kitty called from the airport to say they'd picked up Bette."

He checked his watch without mentioning

that he'd been doing that every few minutes for two hours.

"I can't wait to go up there for the Christmas wedding," Billie said. "We'll get to meet Campbell's father for the first time."

Owen took another sip of wine. "I wonder if he plays poker."

Billie smiled. "That's certainly important to know." She waited for Owen to comment further, and when he didn't, she said, "I'm going to make a couple of predictions."

"Oh?"

"I predict that by next Thanksgiving, you will be very close to being a grandfather for the second time."

He sat straighter in the chair. "You think so?"

"I do. And I predict that if you continue to behave yourself, you'll have the best seat in the house at your daughter's wedding."

He set his glass on an end table and stared at her. "If you're toying with me, woman, I'm not going to forgive you this time."

She stood up, sat lightly on his lap and put her arm around his neck. "I'm not toying with you, but even if I were, after all the times I've forgiven you…"

"All right, all right." He kissed her. "If you're by my side at that wedding, I will be a happy man, Billie."

A horn sounded from outside. "That's them," she said. "Let's go be the perfect host and hostess."

All at once that didn't seem like such an impossible request. Owen went to the foyer and opened the front door. Adam ran up the sidewalk. "Hi, Grandpa! Hi, Billie!" After administering quick hugs, Adam went inside.

Owen managed a gruff greeting, surprised that his voice had suddenly failed him. He watched his daughter get out of a Jeep and open the back door for a spry-looking Bette. Kitty walked up to the door, arm in arm with the man she'd given up everything for to gain what she most wanted. She wore a simple ankle-length rust-colored skirt and a gold sweater. Her hair was silky and smooth, tied at the back with a gold ribbon. She looked like an angel, like her mother, and for the first time in too many years, Owen Galloway remembered his daughter's face when she was happy.

And when she kissed his cheek, he wished he had a mirror to see his own happiness reflected in the glass.

* * * * *

LARGER-PRINT BOOKS!

GET 2 FREE
LARGER-PRINT NOVELS
PLUS 2 FREE
MYSTERY GIFTS

Love Inspired®

Larger-print novels are now available...

LILP15

LARGER-PRINT BOOKS!

**GET 2 FREE
LARGER-PRINT NOVELS
PLUS 2 FREE
MYSTERY GIFTS**

Love Inspired®

SUSPENSE
RIVETING INSPIRATIONAL ROMANCE

Larger-print novels are now available...

YES! Please send me 2 FREE LARGER-PRINT Love Inspired® Suspense novels and my 2 FREE mystery gifts (gifts are worth about $10). After receiving them, if I don't wish to receive any more books, I can return the shipping statement marked "cancel." If I don't cancel, I will receive 4 brand-new novels every month and be billed just $5.49 per book in the U.S. or $5.99 per book in Canada. That's a savings of at least 19% off the cover price. It's quite a bargain! Shipping and handling is just 50¢ per book in the U.S. and 75¢ per book in Canada.* I understand that accepting the 2 free books and gifts places me under no obligation to buy anything. I can always return a shipment and cancel at any time. Even if I never buy another book, the two free books and gifts are mine to keep forever.

110/310 IDN GH6P

Name	(PLEASE PRINT)	
Address		Apt. #
City	State/Prov.	Zip/Postal Code

Signature (if under 18, a parent or guardian must sign)

Mail to the **Reader Service**:
IN U.S.A.: P.O. Box 1867, Buffalo, NY 14240-1867
IN CANADA: P.O. Box 609, Fort Erie, Ontario L2A 5X3

**Are you a current subscriber to Love Inspired® Suspense books
and want to receive the larger-print edition?
Call 1-800-873-8635 or visit www.ReaderService.com.**

* Terms and prices subject to change without notice. Prices do not include applicable taxes. Sales tax applicable in N.Y. Canadian residents will be charged applicable taxes. Offer not valid in Quebec. This offer is limited to one order per household. Not valid for current subscribers to Love Inspired Suspense larger-print books. All orders subject to credit approval. Credit or debit balances in a customer's account(s) may be offset by any other outstanding balance owed by or to the customer. Please allow 4 to 6 weeks for delivery. Offer available while quantities last.

Your Privacy—The Reader Service is committed to protecting your privacy. Our Privacy Policy is available online at www.ReaderService.com or upon request from the Reader Service.

We make a portion of our mailing list available to reputable third parties that offer products we believe may interest you. If you prefer that we not exchange your name with third parties, or if you wish to clarify or modify your communication preferences, please visit us at www.ReaderService.com/consumerchoice or write to us at Reader Service Preference Service, P.O. Box 9062, Buffalo, NY 14240-9062. Include your complete name and address.

LISLP15